Praise for *Breathe, Annie, Breathe*

★ "In this expertly paced and realistic romance, Kenneally gives Annie's sorrow a palpable weight, but she writes with such ease that Annie and her goals become exceedingly likable and familiar and never overwrought." —*Booklist*, starred review

"*Breathe, Annie, Breathe* is an emotional, heartfelt, and beautiful story about finding yourself after loss and learning to love. Her best book yet." —Jennifer L. Armentrout, *New York Times* bestselling author of *Wait for You*

"Heartfelt, uplifting, and quite possibly enough motivation to make readers reach for their running shoes." —*Publishers Weekly*

Praise for *Things I Can't Forget*

"Kenneally's books have quickly become must-reads." —*VOYA*

"Entertaining and poignant." —*School Library Journal*

"[A] compassionate and nuanced exploration of friendship, love, and maturing religious understanding." —*Publishers Weekly*

Praise for *Catching Jordan*

"Sweetly satisfying." —*VOYA*

"A must-read! Whoever said football and girls don't mix hasn't read *Catching Jordan*. I couldn't put it down!" —Simone Elkeles, *New York Times* bestselling author of the Perfect Chemistry series

"*Catching Jordan* has it all: heart, humor, and a serious set of balls. Kenneally proves once and for all that when it comes to making life's toughest calls—on and off the field—girls rule!" —Sarah Ockler, bestselling author of *Twenty Boy Summer* and *#scandal*

Praise for *Stealing Parker*

"Another engrossing romance from Miranda Kenneally with a hero who will melt your heart." —Jennifer Echols, author of *Endless Summer* and *Playing Dirty*

Jesse's Girl

MIRANDA KENNEALLY

Also by Miranda Kenneally

Catching Jordan

Stealing Parker

Things I Can't Forget

Racing Savannah

Breathe, Annie, Breathe

Jesse's Girl

MIRANDA KENNEALLY

Published by Sourcebooks Fire, an imprint of Sourcebooks, Inc.
P.O. Box 4410, Naperville, Illinois 60567-4410
(630) 961-3900
Fax: (630) 961-2168
www.sourcebooks.com

Library of Congress Cataloging-in-Publication Data

Kenneally, Miranda.
Jesse's girl / Miranda Kenneally.
pages cm
Summary: On Career Shadow Day, Maya gets paired with pop star Jesse Scott who rose to fame at a young age and has no real friends, and although the last thing Maya wants is to be reminded of how music broke her heart, she and Jesse might be just what the other needs, but can they open up enough to become real friends--or even something more?
(alk. paper)
[1. Love--Fiction. 2. Friendship--Fiction. 3. Music--Fiction.] I. Title.
PZ7.K376Je 2015
[Fic]--dc23

2015000025

Printed and bound in the United States of America.
VP 10 9 8 7 6 5 4 3 2 1

For Don and Brady

Side A

The Space Between

Backstage, there's so much security, you'd think it was the White House.

I've been to plenty of concerts, but I've never had a backstage pass, so I follow Dr. Salter's lead and keep flashing my all-access badge over and over. My principal squeezes between two beefy men in security jackets and knocks on a door stamped with a red star.

A man in a tailored black suit and shimmering blue tie opens the door. He's got better skin than any girl I know, and I bet his haircut cost a small fortune. "Oh good. It's you," he says to Dr. Salter, giving him a bright smile. The man takes my hand. "You must be Maya."

"Yes, sir."

"Come on in."

Inside the dark dressing room, I spot a vintage Gibson guitar, three flat-screen TVs all showing the Braves game, and a table piled high with burgers and corn on the cob. I thought nothing could smell more delicious than my mom's cooking, but I was wrong.

"Maya, this is Jesse's manager, Mark Logan," Dr. Salter says.

Mr. Logan pats my back like I'm one of the good ole boys. "Jesse will be out in a minute to meet you. Why don't you get yourself a drink?" He gestures at the bar, which appears to be booze-free. Seems like a good move, considering Jesse got drunk and fell off that yacht a few months ago. The press had a field day with that, because it was totally out of character for *Jesse Scott*. Yeah, he's a famous country star, but everyone thinks of him as this sweet, quiet boy from down on the farm.

"Could I have a word next door in private?" Mr. Logan asks my principal. "Jesse's telling the crowd tonight."

Dr. Salter's face goes from happy to anxious, and they step back into the hallway where the security guys are buzzing around in their yellow jackets.

All alone now, I gaze over at Jesse's guitar. I'm itching to try it out. What I wouldn't give to throw the strap around my neck, charge out of the dressing room onto the stage, and rock out to Queen. But would I do "Somebody to Love"? Or "Another One Bites the Dust"? It's a silly idea—I wouldn't make it three feet before the beefcake security guys tackle me. I'd bite the dust. Literally. And if I sang, it's a one hundred percent possibility my voice would crack. Playing onstage at the Opry…wouldn't it be great, though?

I love playing guitar and performing more than anything. Before I started The Fringe, which was originally an eighties tribute band but has since become heavy metal only, I even went to church on Sundays just to sing with the youth choir. All the crotchety old people would whisper and point their walking canes at my bright red lipstick, but I doubt God cares about that or the diamond stud in my nose. God only cares that I sang "I'll Fly Away" at the top of my lungs.

That was before I gave it up to focus on my band. I also used to be a proud member of my school's show choir, which isn't anything like the cool groups in *Pitch Perfect*. You know, that a cappella movie? We sang songs like "When the Saints Go Marching In" and wore billowing green dresses, like you'd see on the cover of a historical bodice-ripper romance novel. If that doesn't tell you how much I love music, I don't know what will. If the choice had been mine, we would've worn leather pants and tight tanks, but my director said that isn't proper attire for our school's *most distinguished arts program*.

However, as much as I love music, I am generally *not* a fan of country. I don't like banjos. I don't like sappy lyrics about trucks and hauling hay. Dolly Parton is my mortal enemy—my mom plays "Jolene" over and over and over and over, and it makes me want to chop my ears off like van Gogh. Yeah, yeah, I'm from Tennessee, where it's a crime if you don't love country, but I like deep, rumbling beats and singing loud and fast and hard. I do not like closing my eyes and crooning to a cow in the pasture.

Yet here I am at a Jesse Scott concert, getting ready to meet him and to see if he'll let me shadow him next Friday. My school requires every senior to "shadow" a professional for a day. It's their way of helping us figure out what kind of career we want. Like, if you want to be president when you grow up, you might get to shadow the mayor. Want to be a chef? Have fun kneading dough at the Donut Palace.

When I said "I want to be a musician," I figured they'd send me to work in the electronics section at Walmart.

I certainly never expected to shadow the king of country music.

It turns out that Jesse Scott is my principal's nephew. Jesse won TV's *Wannabe Rocker* when he was ten and has gone on to become very successful. In sixth grade, every girl in class—myself included—took the *Teen Beat* quiz: "Would Jesse Scott Like Your Kissing Style?" (Obviously the answer was yes.) In middle school, I had a Jesse Scott poster on my ceiling. It's hard to believe he's only eighteen, because he's already won three Grammys. When he was younger, his songs were about family, fishing, and playing baseball, but lately they're about love and making love and all things sexy.

I wouldn't say I'm a fan anymore, but I would never give up an opportunity to learn from a professional with such a gorgeous, pure voice. I want to learn what it's like to perform day in and day out. Despite what everyone and their mom says—that I'll struggle as a musician—all I want is to play guitar in front of a crowd and hear people cheer for me.

I can't believe I'm backstage at the Grand Ole Opry! I bounce on my toes. *Jesus, is that an archtop Super 4, the model Elvis played?* I've never seen one in real life. It probably cost more than my house.

I'm ogling the guitar when Jesse Scott comes out of the bathroom, drying his hair with a towel. He pads across the room to the couch, wearing nothing but a pair of rugged jeans with more holes than Swiss cheese.

The lighting is dim, and he doesn't seem to notice I'm here, which is good, because I've moved from ogling the guitar to ogling him. Who wouldn't? He was one of *People* magazine's "50 Most Beautiful People," and it is a truth universally acknowledged that you should stare at people who've made that list.

The guy's gorgeous. Like in the boy-next-door way. His wet, wavy, brown hair curls around his ears and nearly hits his shoulders, and while he doesn't have a six-pack or anything, his body is fit. I wish he'd look my way so I can see his famous brown eyes. They always remind me of those caramel chews Poppy gives me when I visit. Jesse has some sort of Celtic symbol tattooed on his left shoulder blade. I want to reach out and trace the design.

God, get ahold of yourself, Maya. Don't be a horndog. Besides, he's so not my type. I don't do pretty boys.

Jesse grabs a black T-shirt from his bag and pulls it on over his head, then heads to his personal buffet. Humming to himself, he piles a bun and a burger onto a plate and scrunches his nose at a plateful of pickles, which is just crazy, because pickles are what make the burger. Instead he grabs a bottle of ketchup, unscrews the lid, and tries to shake some onto his burger. It's not budging. Must be a new bottle.

"Try hitting the little fifty-seven on the side—"

He startles. "What are you doing here?"

"Excuse me?"

"Did the Opry arrange for a ketchup expert to be at my beck and call?" he snaps.

"Clearly you need one." I stride over, grab the bottle out of his hand, and tap the little fifty-seven with the heel of my hand. Ketchup pours out.

"Thanks," he says calmly. Then he yells, "Security! Another girl snuck in," as he strides to the door in his bare feet. Jesse yanks open the door, revealing Dr. Salter and Mr. Logan. "I'm beginning to think you guys are letting them in just to torture me."

The manager claps once. "Oh good. So you've met Maya? Have you discussed the possibility of her shadowing you next—"

"I'm sick of these groupie meet and greets," Jesse says as if I'm not here. "Can't I eat my damned dinner in peace?"

"You can now that you've got your *damned* ketchup," I reply. "If you'll excuse me."

Mr. Logan and Dr. Salter gape at me. Throwing Jesse a look, I squeeze past Beefcake 1 and 2 into the hall.

I can't believe how rude he was! Dr. Salter invited me to the concert so I could meet Jesse, and since I've already had the *pleasure*, I see no point in staying. I don't want to shadow a spoiled pretty boy who sings about making love on tractors anyway. It's still early. If I drive back to Franklin now, maybe I could meet up with Nate, and my Friday night won't be a complete bust.

As I charge down the hall, pulling the all-access badge off from around my neck, a bunch of screaming girls rush my way. What in the world? A hand grabs my elbow. I go to shake it off and find Jesse, still holding the ketchup.

"I'm sorry—can you come back inside?"

Before I can answer, the horde descends on him. It's scarier than a zombie apocalypse.

"Shit," he mutters.

"Oh my God, I love ketchup too!" a girl squeals at the bottle in his hand. "We have so much in common!"

"Want to come to my house, Jesse? My parents are out of town."

A girl screeches and grabs his wrist. Another gets up on tiptoes to kiss his cheek, and he jerks back.

"Jesse, Jesse! Can I sing a song for you?"

"Jesse! I want you!" This one yanks her shirt open.

I snort at her hot pink bra. Jesse smirks at my reaction as security breaks the group apart.

Jesse pulls me through security back into his dressing room, where he drops my arm and scans me. I'm wearing a great outfit—black ankle booties, skinny jeans, the belt I made out of duct tape, bleached blond hair, black tank top, the silly glittery bracelets I wear ironically, and a bronze military star medal from World War I that hangs from my necklace. Kids at school often make fun of my clothes, but I don't care. I feel so Madonna right now.

Jesse shakes his head at me, then goes to give Dr. Salter a side hug. "Hey, Uncle Bob."

Dr. Salter pats Jesse's floppy hair and takes in his freckled face. "I'm looking forward to the show, son."

"Thanks for coming," Jesse says quietly.

"Wouldn't miss it," Dr. Salter says. "Where're your mom and dad? Will they be here soon?"

"They blew me off again. What else is new?"

Until a couple of years ago, my dad was a truck driver and often missed my performances because he was on the road, so I understand how Jesse feels. But my parents have always been supportive. It shocks me that his parents aren't at every show.

While Jesse speaks in a low voice only Dr. Salter can hear, I decide to check my phone. My best guy friend, Dave, texted: I need a play-by-play of how hot Jesse is. Do we think he's bi?

I also received a text from my bandmate, Nate. His reads: Hannah told me where you are. Did you really sell out and go to a Jesse Scott show?

Groan. I love hooking up with Nate, but jeez. Why are guys so dramatic?

"What's the girl doing here?" Jesse asks.

"Remember I told you about shadow day?" his manager asks.

"Remind me," Jesse replies through a big bite of burger.

"You agreed to meet with Maya. She's pretty talented on guitar," Dr. Salter says.

Jesse stares at me, chewing. "So you play, huh?"

I ignore him. When he realizes I'm giving him the cold shoulder, he turns to Dr. Salter. "Seriously? I'm missing the Braves for this?"

My principal gives me the glare he reserves for kids who cut class. "I'd like you to consider letting her shadow you, Jess."

Jesse just shrugs.

I should've known this would be a bust. Shadow day assignments always are. Students never get paired with professionals who can actually teach them something. Last year, Rory Whitfield said he wanted to be a movie director and ended up at the infant portrait area at Sears.

Dr. Salter says, "You should've seen her play guitar in the school talent show last spring. She's amazing."

"Did you win?" Jesse asks me.

I shake my head, cringing at the memory. Why did Dr. Salter have to bring that up? After my band declared the school talent show "lame," I decided to perform on my own, adding a hard edge to one of my favorite songs, "Bohemian Rhapsody," and had a great time rocking out. That is, until I started to sing, and my voice cracked under the pressure. Kids at school called me *the siren* for weeks. People have always said I have a great voice, but when all eyes are on me, something usually goes wrong—like the time I fainted during a solo.

I wish their eyes had somewhere else to focus. That's why I prefer being part of a band.

Jesse takes another bite of his burger and gives me a bored stare, and I feel like the pickle he turned his nose up at. What a letdown. I figured *People* took personality into account when developing their beautiful people list. Apparently not.

You'd think Jesse would be as sweet as his songs.

Okay, okay. I'll admit it—even though my musical tastes have evolved, Jesse wrote this one song, "Second Chance," that I've loved since middle school. When Dave, my first crush and now best friend, wasn't interested in dating me because he was too busy liking other boys (I didn't know that at the time), "Second Chance" helped heal my broken heart.

So it kind of sucks meeting the real Jesse. I've seen more life out of mannequins. Granted, I haven't smiled at him, but he was incredibly rude after I helped with his ketchup. I had really been looking forward to this opportunity, but he's nothing more than a beautiful voice and a hot body with a cool tattoo.

Dr. Salter must sense our meeting is going downhill real fast. "Jess, you really should see Maya on guitar."

"Hmph."

Spoiled ass. Two can play. "My Martin's much cooler than your Gibson," I say, even though it's a total lie.

Instead of taking another bite, Jesse turns his head toward me, wide-eyed. "Shut up. My archtop is the best guitar there is."

I gesture at it. "What year is it? A '67?"

Jesse nods.

I can't help but ask, "A Super 4? Like Elvis had?"

"Right…" A smile forms on his face, but a second later, he winces.

"So is it okay, Jess?" Dr. Salter asks. "Can Maya shadow you?"

Jesse studies me. "Mom and Dad'll *love* that I'm hanging out with a sexy punk girl. So whatever you need, Uncle Bob."

"Jesse!" Dr. Salter and Mr. Logan blurt simultaneously.

What a jerk.

Wait. Did he say sexy?

Mr. Logan claps his hands together again. "Well, I think Maya seems fabulous. I'm okay with her shadowing Jesse next week as long as it's okay with him."

Silence engulfs the dressing room.

Jesse takes a long look at his uncle, then bites into his burger and talks with his mouth full. "Fine, she can shadow me."

"I'll see if I can work it into my schedule," I say, then turn and walk out.

♪♫♩

Against my better judgment, I decide to stick around for the concert, because I've never been to the Grand Ole Opry.

Performing here is every country music singer's dream, and

while I'm not into yodeling, I still respect the Opry. When I looked at Jesse Scott's website, it said he's already done ten concerts here. I guess that means he's really somebody. Which I could've told you, considering his face is on every tweeny bopper magazine down at the Quick Pick and he's at the top of the iTunes charts.

I stand in line for what seems like hours to buy myself a puffy pink cotton candy, then head inside the main concert hall. Heat from the crowd presses against my skin as I squeeze past shrieking girls and make my way down to the stage, which looks like an old red barn.

"Maya!" Dr. Salter calls out. "Over here." He gestures for me to join him in the center of the first row. The best seat in the house.

I edge around another pack of squealing girls to meet my principal. "I was wondering where you went," he says.

I hold up my cotton candy, offering him a piece. He pinches some off and pops it in his mouth. The other reason I didn't leave early is because I've always liked Dr. Salter, and I don't want to let him down. He tells funny jokes during the morning announcements and always takes a turn in the dunking booth during homecoming. It's odd, though, seeing him in a Van Halen leather jacket and not his usual sweater vest and bow tie.

I point at the stage with my cotton candy. "We've got better seats than God, huh? From this close, Jesse oughta be able to see me *not* clapping for him."

Dr. Salter gives me a stern look. "I'm sorry about my nephew… He's not used to… He doesn't meet a lot of new people."

"I figured he meets people all the time."

"There's a difference between meeting people and actually speaking with them."

The banshee convention I met backstage was something else, all right.

"I thought…" Dr. Salter pauses. "I thought that shadow day might be good for both of you. You can get some music advice from Jesse…and he needs a break and needs to spend time with somebody his age… It's hard when everybody scrutinizes every single thing you do."

As the lights go down, the band takes the stage, and the screaming crowd crescendos to just about the loudest noise I've ever heard. A spotlight bathes the stage in blinding white light. Smoke billows in the wings. Dr. Salter puts two fingers in his mouth and whistles.

Then the most beautiful guitar lick rings out, echoing in the concert hall.

The screaming stops, because everyone wants to hear that sound.

Jesse Scott steps into the spotlight with his cedar-colored vintage Gibson strapped around his neck. He plays a riff and brings his mouth to the microphone.

"How you doin', Nashville?" Jesse yells into the microphone in a deep Southern drawl, tipping his beige cowboy hat before starting to play "Campfires," this country pop song about hiking and fishing with his grandfather. "Gimme fireflies, gimme trout, gimme burning logs, hell—gimme a mosquito, but keep your damned electricity."

The bass ripples through the concert hall and makes the floor vibrate, and my heart beats in time with the drums.

During the chorus, Jesse flips the guitar around to his back, grabs the mike with both hands, and gives the audience a full view of his great body. He's wearing the tight black T-shirt that hugs his biceps and chest, bright red cowboy boots, and a belt buckle shaped like a skull. *Hey, it matches the skull pajamas I wore to bed last night!* I feel silly for a beat, because my inner monologue sounds just like that girl backstage: "I like ketchup too!"

I've never seen anyone play guitar like him. Jesse blisters through the solo, and he's so into his music, it's like the crowd isn't even here. Meanwhile, the girl next to me is bawling like her face is a busted fire hydrant.

When the song is over, Jesse grabs the mike with one hand and says, "Thanks for coming out tonight, Nashville. I may travel all over the place, but I want my fans to know this is my one true home."

Everyone screams as Jesse looks down and tips his cowboy hat at Dr. Salter. Jesse's face seems sad as he scans the rest of the front row. He gives me a fleeting look before starting to rock out on guitar again. The next song is "Agape." It's about how he lives for music.

After his third song ("Ain't No City Boy"), Jesse wipes the sweat off his face with his T-shirt sleeve and says into the mike, "Damn, that popcorn smells good. Can I get some up here?" Ten seconds later, a stagehand rushes out with a bucket. Jesse eats a few pieces. "Perfect," he says, licking his fingers. "Y'all want some?" The crowd roars, so he throws the bucket out into the crowd, sprinkling us with popcorn.

About halfway through the concert, Jesse makes everyone sing "Take Me Out to the Ball Game" with him, but instead of singing "Root, root, root for the home team," we sing "Root, root, root for the Braves!" And then with his eyes shut, he does this insane acoustic rendition of "Amazing Grace," set to the tune of the Eagles' "Peaceful Easy Feeling."

Jesse performs all of his hits, but the encore, "Second Chance," is the highlight. He sings, "She may have been Paris, but I needed the soft sun, so I let her fly."

I actually clap when the song's over, and he looks down at me again. The crowd roars. He may not have a great presence offstage, but when he's onstage, he's on.

He yanks off his cowboy hat. "Thanks everybody." A pause. "As many of you probably know, in November, I'll begin a six-week tour of North America and Europe." The crowd roars again. He speaks over the noise. "And after that, in December—" His voice breaks. He takes a deep breath. "I'll be leaving the industry."

What?

Boos and cries—mostly cries—rattle the auditorium.

The king of country music is quitting? Is this the announcement Mr. Logan mentioned to Dr. Salter? I turn to my principal. His eyes are watering.

"I just wanted to say—wanted to make sure y'all know—my fans mean everything to me." His voice cracks again.

And my heart breaks for him, because whatever is going on must be pretty serious. I can't imagine giving up music for any reason whatsoever.

"Thank you, Nashville!" he yells into the mike and jogs off-stage, carrying his guitar.

I find Dr. Salter's eyes. "He's really doing this, huh?"

"I guess so… The thing is, Maya, I don't think he truly wants to."

Where Is the Love?

After my morning shift at Caldwell's, where I work reception and do the occasional oil change, I drive my Suzuki straight to Hannah's garage for band practice. Even though Jesse was an ass and I still can't understand why in blue blazes he wants to retire, his concert last night totally energized me, and I'm ready to rock out.

I speed the entire way, barely stopping at stop signs.

I formed The Fringe last year, handpicking each member. Nate as lead singer. Me on backup vocals and lead guitar. Hannah on synth, Brady on bass, and Reed on drums. I had planned to do covers of Madonna, Michael Jackson, and of course, Queen, but Nate has sort of taken over. I don't mind that he wants to lead, but I wish we'd branch out in terms of musical choices. My throat hurts from scream-singing all the time.

But I want to perform. I *need* to play guitar. The only time I ever truly feel peaceful is when I'm strumming its strings. I don't know how far I can get with my music, but I want to find out.

The Fringe is really good. Nate has an interesting gritty tone, and I've been playing guitar since I picked up my dad's in first grade. Which is why I want The Fringe to try out for *Wannabe Rocker*, the competition Jesse Scott won.

The *Wannabe Rocker* audition videos are due in three weeks, and first prize is a deal with Rêve Records. If I want to be a professional musician, I should take every opportunity I get, and it's high time The Fringe tried out for bigger gigs than playing at the two heavy metal clubs in Nashville.

Wannabe Rocker is going into its twelfth season now, and it's still as popular as ever. The bands and solo artists who win have all become super famous in the recording industry, in movies, and even on Broadway. It's my dream to make a living with my music.

I park my motorcycle on the street outside Hannah's house, pull off my helmet, and walk across the yard, kicking up red and gold leaves. As I get closer, I can see Nate and Hannah through the garage window. They're standing close, talking. Hannah broke up with her boyfriend last week, and it's really sweet that Nate's comforting her.

I smile. I love hooking up with him, though I wish we could be more. He doesn't want to *ruin the dynamic of the band* by starting a relationship. I get that; a bad breakup could mess up everything, and I won't risk the success The Fringe has had so far. Not many kids can say they've played at two clubs in Nashville.

None of the other band members know we fool around.

They think Nate tutors me in geometry, which is true because I suck at it. But our "study sessions" are mostly kissing, and sometimes we go further. I just wish he'd use his *tutoring skills* on me more often.

I'm fixing to open the side door to the garage when I see Hannah dragging her black fingernails up and down Nate's arm. I hold my breath, watching as her fingertips then stroke his face, tracing his eyebrow ring. He hates when I touch it. He always pushes my hand away. He just smiles at her.

So it's okay if Hannah does it?

"Hey guys," I announce. "What's going on?"

They jump apart.

"Hey, Maya," Hannah blurts. She turns on her synth and plays a scale to warm up, avoiding my eyes.

Weird. Hannah always says that we spend too much time "dicking around with unnecessary warm-ups." She doesn't have to spend time tuning a keyboard like I do with my electric Fender Strat.

Nate turns on the mic and plugs his guitar into the amp. I do the same and begin running through licks to warm up my fingers. I glance at the set list Nate prepared for practice. I sigh when I see it's only metal songs. I love music, so I'm willing to try anything that my band likes, but the thing is, metal doesn't make me tingle. Sure, the vibrations shake my body, but they don't touch my soul.

When Reed and Brady arrive and start settling in, I clear my throat and speak loudly over the drums. "Guys, I have something to talk to you about."

"Like how you're BFFs with Jesse Scott?" Nate asks with a laugh, and everybody joins in except me. Nate smirks, almost imperceptibly, but I keep my back straight and proud. *Take that, buddy.* I won't let him see that he hurt my feelings.

"No, but Jesse reminded me of something I want us to consider." I strum my strings slowly. "I think we should audition for *Wannabe Rocker*."

Hannah abruptly stops playing keyboard. Reed's drums go silent.

Nate crosses his arms on top of his guitar. "Why?"

"I figure we have a good chance of making the semifinals." My voice shakes like the cymbals. "We'd get to be on TV. And who knows? We might even make it further! We could get a record deal."

"The people on that show never end up playing the music they want to," Brady says. "You have to perform a different genre every week."

Reed starts nodding. "Like that rapper Ansel Richard. He had to sing that *Titanic* song during Celine Dion week and bombed in front of a billion people. Never would've done that if he'd just stuck to rap."

"We'd be selling out," Nate adds. "We'd be giving up our artistic freedom."

"But it's an opportunity to put ourselves out there and get recognized. Think of what it would be like to record an album!"

"Is money all you care about?" Nate asks.

"Come on. You know I care about the art. I love music…I only wish we played more than just the hard stuff all the time. That'd be another great thing about the TV show—we could really stretch ourselves. We need to experiment with our sound and try new things."

My band looks everywhere but at me. Finally, Nate says, "Maya, can we talk outside?"

"About?"

"The band."

"Shouldn't we all be here if you want to talk about us?"

Nate glances from Reed to Brady. "We feel you don't have the same vision for The Fringe. You keep trying to make us play music that's just not *us*, and it's wasting our practice time."

What in the world is he talking about? "We were supposed to be an eighties tribute band," I say. "You're the one who wants to play heavy metal."

"I'd rather play metal," Reed says, and Brady nods.

Nate nervously adjusts his leather wristbands. "We've been talking to Bryan Moore about taking over as lead guitar."

I carefully place my Fender back on its stand before I'm tempted to smash something, and it's what's in reach. "I'm lead guitar! This is my band. I started it!"

Hannah's eyes grow wide at my outburst.

"Hannah?" I ask, but she looks away silently, confused and upset. I get the feeling she didn't know about this. But why isn't she speaking up?!

Nate sets his guitar down too. "We think Bryan's a better fit for us."

I mouth the name Bryan Moore. "Are you talking about that guy who plays down at Freddie's Oyster Bar on Friday nights? Women only like him because he plays shirtless and has nice biceps. He can't even play a B7."

Nate takes my elbow, gently leading me outside to the driveway, where we stand next to a planter of wilting orange and purple mums.

"I want you to hear this from me and not anybody else." He drags a hand through his hair and focuses on the pavement. "I asked Hannah out."

I shut my eyes. Dig my teeth into my lip. *Is he freaking kidding me?* "But you said you didn't want to ruin the band's dynamic by dating another member. Last I checked, Hannah is the synth player!"

His voice is gentle. "I really like her, My. I have for a long time. I just never had the chance to tell her while she had a boyfriend."

I try to think if I've ever seen him staring at her. I don't think I have… God, this sucks. Obviously he doesn't care about the band's dynamic. He just didn't want to date *me*.

I sniffle. *Don't let him see you cry*, I tell myself. "Today really sucks, you know?"

He nods. He looks remorseful, but he's still a dick. *How could he?*

"But we slept together," I whisper. One time, two weeks ago. I didn't do it with him because he pressured me or anything. I did it because I wanted to, because every time we would hook up, I was left wanting more. I thought sex would make me feel amazing all over. I sort of liked it, but it didn't live up to the hype. I've heard it gets better and better over time, and I kept waiting for us to do it again, but he never made another move, and I didn't want to seem desperate by pushing to do it again.

"I thought you liked sleeping with me," I say softly.

"It was good." He scratches the back of his neck, looking at his heavy black boots. "But I want her. I've wanted her for a long time."

"Asshole," I say and storm back inside the garage.

"Maya?" Hannah asks, her voice trembling.

Ignore her. It's not like we're friends outside of the band.

Without saying a word, I pack my electric and acoustic guitars in their cases and carry them out to the road. I can't drive my bike with them, so I dig my phone out of my pocket and dial Dave. Barely holding back the tears, I tell him what happened with the band…and with Nate. Dave's the only one I told about hooking up with him.

"Babe, I told you he was no good," Dave says over the phone, and I hang up on him, even though he was right.

When his ancient Nissan Sentra rattles up to the curb, Dave parks, and his Abercrombie-model-lookalike-self storms past me to the garage, where he throws open the side door and yells, "Nate, man, you're a jackass! And to think I thought you were the hottest guy at school. No more!"

Slamming the door shut, Dave slips an arm around my shoulders and pulls me close. "C'mon. You need ice cream, stat."

I laugh at my friend's antics, but I'm struggling not to cry. I trusted Nate, and he betrayed me in every way possible. And now I've lost my band.

As a musician, I always thought the worst thing that could happen would be getting vocal cord nodules or arthritis in your hands. But I was wrong.

The worst thing is losing your band, the place where you belong.

Now what?

♪♫♩

Later that day, after my whole damned life went up in flames, I'm sitting on my front porch, cradling my guitar. I thought I had the energy to strum its strings, but I don't. What happened with Nate keeps playing over and over in my mind. It was almost as embarrassing as the time my knees locked during my "Scarborough Fair" solo in seventh grade, and I fainted in front of the whole school.

Dad pokes his head out the screen door. "You coming with us to your brother's for dinner?"

I shrug. Might as well. I have no other plans for tonight. Dave has a mini golf date with Xander—the college boy he met at Taco Bell—and my former bandmates are probably somewhere *not selling out*.

Mom, Dad, my little sister, Anna, and I load up in the truck to drive across Franklin to Sam's new place. He just turned twenty-four and moved into a house he rents with his girlfriend. Mom constantly complains that they are "living in sin" and wonders aloud why Sam doesn't propose already, but I don't really care how my brother chooses to live. I'm just excited I don't have to share a bathroom with He-who-leaves-wet-towels-on-the-floor anymore.

When my dad pulls into the driveway, we all shuffle out of the car. I can already hear the screaming through the open windows.

"I said take them off!" Jordan yells.

"It's my house too," my brother hollers back.

My parents look at each other and roll their eyes. Dad knocks on the front door, and as soon as Sam lets us in, Jordan storms out of their bedroom with a set of Detroit Lions bedsheets, wrinkling her nose like she's holding a dirty diaper.

"Those are three-hundred-thread-count sheets," Sam says. "Who cares what's on them?"

"You are a traitor not only to the Titans, but to the entire state of Tennessee!" Jordan throws the sheets onto the rug.

Dad lets out a low groan. When Sam and Jordan aren't making out, they're screaming at each other about sports. Growing up, they were both Titans fans, but during the time my brother went away to college in Michigan and Jordan went to school in Indiana, he became a Detroit Lions fan.

"The Titans are still my team," Sam will say, "but I root for the Lions when they're playing. Unless they're up against the Titans, of course."

Jordan's response is usually, "It's sacrilege!" She refuses to let him watch the Lions on TV. She even canceled their DirecTV package so he could only watch local games. One time, Sam snuck out to watch a Detroit game at a bar, and Jordan showed up and made a scene, dumping a beer on his head before storming out. My brother has a job working for the Titans, so I don't think he's actually a Lions fan. He just likes riling Jordan up.

I honestly don't see what the big deal is, because I've never understood the appeal of sports. Growing up, Sam was a football and baseball star. He even got a scholarship to play football in college. My little sister, Anna, who is tall and buff like Sam, is the best player on her elementary school basketball team. I'm barely five feet two, and the only muscles I have are from holding my guitar and plucking the strings.

My family always shows up for my performances, and I know they love me, but I get the sense that they would rather be tailgating at a football game. Then again, I'd rather be listening to music than watching a game on TV with them. And don't even get me started on how Mom tries to make me wear clothes that were made this century.

It wasn't until I formed my band that I felt like I really belonged. At first, anyway. Now I know I didn't fit in at all. Friendships come and go—I don't hang out with the same people I did in elementary school or even junior high. But I know that other people have managed to keep their friends. What am I doing wrong? Why don't I belong anywhere?

The minute my brother sees me, he knows something's up. "What's wrong?"

"Just tired," I lie, and he furrows his eyebrows. Sam has always been a protective big brother, and I know if I told him what happened with Nate today, Nate would get an ass-whooping. And as enjoyable as that sounds, I can't take any more drama this weekend.

We all head into the kitchen and sit at the breakfast bar while Sam and Jordan start fixing supper. Sam hands Mom and Dad beers, which they take readily following the Detroit Lions Sheet Incident, and Dad turns to his phone to check the Braves' score.

Jordan cracks an egg and lets the yolk plop into a mixing bowl. "We're having breakfast for dinner."

"In Michigan, we called it brinner," Sam says.

"Well, in Tennessee, we call it breakfast for dinner," Jordan snaps back. "And if you want some, you better call it by its proper name."

"Brinner," he teases.

Jordan throws an entire egg yolk at him, and he flips pancake batter at her. Then they kiss in the middle of their food fight with egg and batter on their faces.

Gross. I shift uncomfortably on my bar stool.

"You're disgusting," Anna tells them, and Mom doesn't even scold her.

Now that Jordan's teaching and coaching football at Hundred Oaks, I have to watch her being all lovey-dovey with my brother and then go to school and listen to her talk about safe sex in health class. Cringe.

We all usually sigh at Sam and Jordan's craziness, but secretly, I'm jealous. I hope I have a relationship like theirs one day. A relationship where there's love and happiness, but also the freedom to fight and say what's really on your mind. And, most important, trust.

"Are you sure you're feeling okay, My?" Sam asks. "You're not usually this quiet."

I shrug. "I didn't sleep well last night."

"And you probably spent all day practicing, right?"

"No, not today…"

"I didn't think you could go longer than five minutes without playing guitar," Jordan says as she grabs a package of hash browns from the freezer.

"Yeah, Maya not playing would be like if you didn't sleep with your football for one night," Sam teases.

"I'd rather not hear about your sleeping habits, thanks," I say.

"Maya was out late last night," Anna says in a sneaky tone. "That's why she's tired."

"A date?" Jordan asks with hopeful eyes, and Sam gives her a death glare. Like I said, protective big brother.

"Tell everyone about the concert, Maya!" Mom drums her hands on the counter. "Sam and Jordan are going to love this."

"It's nothing," I say quietly. I was so excited about the opportunity to spend time with a famous musician, but Jesse Scott is a certified country-boy ass.

"You won't believe what Maya gets to do for shadow day," Mom adds, wrapping an arm around my shoulders.

Sam licks pancake batter off his thumb and makes a face. "Are you shadowing somebody at Middle C?" He means the shop where I buy sheet music.

"No…I'm shadowing Dr. Salter's nephew."

"Who's his nephew?" Jordan asks.

"Jesse Scott!" Anna squeals.

Sam freezes in the middle of flipping a pancake, and it plops on the floor. Jordan stops stirring the eggs in the skillet. They look at each other, then at me, then at each other again.

"You're shadowing Jesse Scott!" Jordan shouts.

"I don't think so," Sam says. "Dad, you're allowing this?"

"Why wouldn't I?" Dad replies.

"Jesse Scott got drunk and fell off a boat," Sam explains. "I saw it on TV. That kid's a train wreck."

"A *hot* train wreck!" Jordan exclaims, and Sam's eyes might roll out of his head. "I want to come with you! Can I?"

"I'm not even sure if I want to go."

"That's crazy," she replies. "This could be huge for you and your music."

I ignore the mention of my music. They don't know that I got kicked out of my own band, and I really don't feel like facing a Sam and Jordan intervention.

"Jesse is kind of a jerk," I say. "And when I went backstage to meet him, he called me a 'sexy punk girl.'"

"You met him?" Jordan screams. She drops an egg on the floor, and it splatters everywhere.

Dad rips his eyes away from the scores. "What did that boy say to you?"

"I'll kill him!" Sam says, and pancake batter joins the egg.

"Will you get his autograph for me?" Anna asks, and I tell her I'll try.

"I love that song of his," Jordan says, looking wistful. "'Don't Cry for Me, Tennessee.'"

"I hate that song," Sam mutters. "Jordan sings it all damn day. I can't get it out of my head."

Jordan sighs dreamily. "Wow. I didn't know Dr. Salter is related to Jesse Scott."

I'm surprised that Jordan didn't know either, considering she works for the principal. "Dr. Salter asked me not to tell other students—he probably doesn't want girls storming his office every day," I explain. "And Scott is Jesse's stage name."

"Makes sense. The name Salter isn't near as sexy as Scott," Jordan says.

"Can we stop talking about how sexy Jesse Scott is?" my brother asks.

"Can you stop watching Detroit games already?" Jordan asks back.

Brinner is officially a disaster. Half-cooked pancakes are splotched on the floor. I can smell the eggs burning.

"Maybe we should order pizza," Dad mutters to me.

I whisper, "Mushrooms, please."

"If Dr. Salter arranged for Maya to shadow Jesse Scott, I'm sure he'll be on his best behavior," Jordan says.

"The school planned a whole schedule," Mom says. "Maya will be visiting Jesse's studio, going to lunch with him, and doing some educational tours at the Country Music Hall of Fame. His manager will be there the whole time."

"It sounds boring," I add.

"I wish I could go," Anna says, and Mom rubs her back. It probably would be more appropriate if Anna went, given that she's ten and has a Jesse Scott screen saver.

"If that jerk does anything to hurt you, My," Sam says, "I'm gonna rip his arms from his sockets, and then we'll see how sexy he is all armless."

Ignoring Sam's loud speech, Jordan starts cooking again, cracking a new egg into a fresh bowl. "I remember my shadow day. I said that I wanted to be an NFL player, and the school arranged for me to shadow the manager of the Athletic Superstore at the mall."

"And I said I wanted to become an exotic dancer," Sam says, "but I got detention."

My lips twitch.

Jordan points at me with a spatula. "I saw it! Maya smiled."

"If telling you about my most embarrassing moments will make you feel better," my brother starts, "I'll tell you about the time I fell asleep at a party and woke up butt-naked in a cow pasture with—"

"Whoa, whoa, whoa!" I wave my hands. "No more, please."

Anna is cackling hard, and my mom's face is red with laughter. Dad pushes buttons on his phone, lifts it to his ear, and says, "Delivery, please."

Being with my family makes me feel better, but I can't stop thinking of what happened this afternoon. I put my all into building The Fringe for an entire year, and it was for nothing. I won't fight to win my band back after they all made it perfectly clear what they thought of me and my musical tastes. I quit both the church and show choirs after I started my band, and since my voice cracks, it's not like I can go solo. How am I going to find a new group in time to record an audition video for *Wannabe Rocker*? It's due in less than three weeks! I already recruited the best musicians at my school for The Fringe. The only person left is Albert Cho and his upright bass, and he's told me a hundred times he only plays classical.

Maybe it's a good thing I'm not trying out for *Wannabe Rocker*, because that show is all about identity—about showing America why you are a talented, unique musician.

Without my band, I've got nothing.

Welcome to the Jungle

Showtime.

On Friday morning, Dr. Salter drives us up to a whale of a brick home surrounded by iron gates and lush green hedges in Brentwood, the Bel Air of Nashville. A sedan idles by the curb. I peer through my window at the unshaven man hunkered down in the front seat. Another guy leans against the passenger side door and snaps pictures of us.

"Paparazzi?"

"Always," Dr. Salter says as he steers the car to a security booth.

A beefy guard—he must weigh three hundred pounds—pokes his head out and tips his hat. "Dr. Salter," his deep voice rumbles. "He expecting you?"

"Yes." Dr. Salter sighs, drumming his thumbs on the steering wheel. "I guess he didn't tell you we were coming?"

The guard shrugs. "You know Jesse. Let me call and get clearance." He shuts the sliding-glass window and picks up a phone.

"Clearance?" I don't think I've ever heard that word used that way.

"Jesse's not—" Dr. Salter starts. "He doesn't have visitors often."

"Oh." I wipe sweaty palms on my dress. The corset top is black leather and red lace, the short skirt poufy black tulle. It looks awesome with my ankle booties. I wore my favorite outfit, because spending time with Jesse will probably be uncomfortable. Might as well feel good in my own skin.

Ten seconds later, the steel gates slide open. A paparazzi guy rushes to follow us in on foot, but the guard steps out to stop him from entering the property.

We park the car in the semicircular driveway, and I climb out, staring up at the ivy-laced brick façade. The brick is just like my house, but his is about ten times larger. We only moved out of a trailer two years ago, after my parents finally saved up for a down payment on a small house. By comparison, this place looks like Buckingham Palace.

I unfold today's schedule—I've read it so many times the paper is soft as a piece of cloth—and scan it one last time:

9:30 a.m. Arrival

10:00 a.m. Tour of Grand Ole Opry

11:00 a.m. Tour of Studio B

12:00 p.m. Lunch with Jesse and Mark Logan

1:30 p.m. Tour of Ryman Auditorium

2:30 p.m. Tour of Country Music Hall of Fame

3:30 p.m. Depart

"Come on," Dr. Salter says, clapping a hand on my shoulder

and steering me toward the door. "Jesse won't bite." My principal pushes the doorbell.

Seconds later, Jesse Scott opens the door wearing nothing but a pair of sky blue boxers.

Holy mother!

"Jesse," Dr. Salter scolds him. "Put some pants on for God's sake."

Jesse stifles a yawn. "Hi, Uncle Bob." He turns and goes back into the house, leaving the front door wide open. A woman with a tight bun, plain black dress, and fingers clamped over her mouth is left standing in the wake of Jesse's greet and run.

"I'm sorry, Dr. Salter," the woman rushes to say. "I tried to get here first."

My principal pats the lady's elbow. "It's okay, Grace." He gives me a reassuring smile as we enter the sunlit foyer filled with leafy green plants. "Don't mind him. Jesse's not a morning person."

"Based on how he treated me last week, he's not an evening guy either," I mutter.

The woman, Grace, disappears down a hallway, and Dr. Salter and I follow Jesse and his Celtic tattoo into the living room, where he flops down in a cushy brown armchair made of cowhide. I set my purse on the floor and take a seat on a leather sofa across from him. This room could be featured in the Pottery Barn catalog that Mom gets in the mail. I want to slip my boots off and dig my toes into the plush beige rug. Guitars of all makes and colors—including a double-neck Fender Stratocaster!—hang on the walls. Over by a huge picture window sits a gorgeous, walnut-colored Steinway grand piano covered by sheet music.

His Grammys are on the mantel, but I don't see any pictures of family or friends like at my house. Instead there are tasteful black-and-white portraits of the countryside: horses, cows, trucks, and tractors.

The only evidence that a person actually lives here is a drained coffee mug sitting on a glass table and sections of today's newspaper, the *Tennessean*, strewn across the couch.

"You didn't forget about Maya, right?" Dr. Salter asks Jesse.

"Nope." He leans back and closes his eyes. "How could I forget I'm giving up my day off to hang out with a groupie?"

"In your dreams I'm a groupie," I snap, shocking my principal.

"Why aren't you dressed?" Dr. Salter asks his nephew.

Jesse shrugs. "Maya wanted to shadow me, right? Well, this is what I do on Friday mornings. And Thursday. And Wednes—"

"Stop being rude." Dr. Salter shakes his head at his nephew. His cell phone dings. "Don't let him fool you, Maya. He works harder than anybody I've ever met and has a good heart too."

Jesse keeps his eyes shut.

My principal looks at his phone. "I need to get back to the school. Mark Logan just texted to say he's two minutes out. Mr. Logan will stay with you two the entire day, and Grace, Jesse's housekeeper, will be here until Mark arrives. Call my office if something comes up. Otherwise, Jesse and Mr. Logan'll make sure you get home. Okay, Maya?"

"Got it."

"Put some clothes on, Jess." Dr. Salter pats his nephew's cheek before leaving. As soon as the door clicks shut, Jesse checks me out.

"Wanna have sex?"

I gasp and glance at his boxers. And that line of hair on his stomach that leads down to places I shouldn't be thinking about.

"No, thanks. You're not my type."

Jesse looks surprised. "That's a first."

What the hell have I gotten myself into? I mean, someone who writes such sweet lyrics can't actually be such an ass in real life. Right?

"Everything okay?" Jesse asks. I look up to find him raising an eyebrow at me.

I shrug.

"Sorry—I shouldn't be talking about sex. We just met. Wanna get drunk?"

Why is he asking such weird questions? "Didn't you learn your lesson after you fell off that yacht?" I ask snarkily.

"You don't know anything about that," he snaps.

Ugh, I knew shadow day would be a stupid waste of time. Jordan probably learned more about being an NFL player from the Athletic Superstore manager than I'll learn about music from

Jesse. I swipe my phone on and look up the Hundred Oaks phone number. Maybe Dr. Salter hasn't left the neighborhood yet. I push dial, and the school receptionist answers. "This is Maya Henry. Can you please connect me to Dr. Salter?"

Jesse jumps to his feet, snatches my phone from my hand, and says, "Wrong number."

I reach to get my phone back, but he holds it way above my head.

"Give me that!" I leap up at my phone. "I want to leave."

"Already?"

"I didn't know it was your day off. I don't want to waste your time. Or mine."

He gives me a withering look. "*Your* time?"

I glare at him. "You know, before we met last week, I was really excited about this."

"A punk rocker chick was excited to spend the day with me? Yeah, I believe *that*."

"First of all, *buddy*, I wouldn't call myself a punk rocker. I'm into the eighties—I was going for Madonna. And second, I got my hopes up about meeting you. I thought it would be cool to watch you practice. Hell, I thought I might even get some pointers, learn something from you."

That's when I realize I've been shaking my finger at him.

After he looks into my eyes for several beats, he hands me my phone. "Last Friday, you said you play a Martin."

"Yeah, so?"

"Let's hear you play." He sits down and rests his elbows on his thighs. My eyes have a mind of their own and glance at his boxers again. He totally catches me.

"I didn't bring my guitar."

He purses his lips. "Why would you show up unprepared?"

"Well, why didn't you prepare by putting on pants?"

"You're not wearing any either." His eyes trail up and down my legs.

Some girls would've jumped him already, but not me. Even if he has a nice set of biceps and the cutest freckles I've ever seen, he doesn't deserve me after acting like a man slut.

"Where are your parents, anyway?" I ask.

"I dunno. Work? They don't live here."

"This is *your* house?"

"Yup. I bought it with my allowance."

That makes me laugh. But how is he ready to live on his own? I mean, Mom still has to remind me to set my alarm so I wake up in time for school.

He carefully lifts an acoustic guitar off the wall and hands it over. "Play a song for me."

I sit down and get it situated in my lap, studying it. My fingers tremble and itch to strum the strings. It's a Martin, just like mine, only a lot older and more valuable. "Is this from, like, the 1930s?"

"Yeah…it was Pa's—my great-grandfather's—before he died."

"You had a cool Pa."

His mouth twitches. "I know. Now play a song for me."

I run my fingers over the wood and bite my lip. If my own band ditched me, do I have any business playing for a Grammy winner? Despite my different musical tastes, I thought my guitar skills were top notch and that I would be a huge asset to any band. But they wanted that guy Bryan instead of me. Maybe I'm not as good on guitar as I thought I was.

He must sense my hesitation. "I'm gonna give you a bad grade if you don't play."

"You're not in charge of my grade."

"My uncle is, and if I tell him you didn't do what I asked, you'll probably fail."

I don't know if that's true or not, but I'm not willing to risk it. If I don't complete shadow day, I won't be allowed to graduate in the spring.

I pull my lucky pick (it's made of quartz and shaped like a teardrop) out of my purse. Taking a deep breath, I start plucking the first song that Jesse put out after he won *Wannabe Rocker*. He wrote "Mi Familia" when he was eleven. I played this song over and over in fifth grade.

After the first chord transition, I get nervous, my fingers tremble, and I accidentally mute the D string, then miss the next transition. Jesse and I cringe at the same time.

"Crap—I never screw up," I say.

"Maybe you haven't been practicing enough."

That's true. I haven't played much this week. Without a band to jam with, my heart hasn't been in it.

"Go on," Jesse urges, settling back into his armchair.

I start playing "Mi Familia" again, but after a measure, he waves a hand at me to stop. "Play something else. Know any James Taylor?"

"Obviously." I'm more of an eighties girl, but any serious guitarist should know the classics. I start strumming "Carolina in My Mind."

After I play two verses, Jesse holds up a hand again. "Are you gonna sing or not?"

I drum my fingers on the Martin's tuners. "I don't do solos."

He shakes his head at the ceiling. "I don't have time for this."

"I thought you have all the time in the world. You're quitting, right?"

The expression on his face could kill. "If you won't sing for me, you should leave right now."

"Fine, I'll sing," I shoot back.

"I promise I won't laugh at you," he replies.

"I'm not that bad a singer."

"Then prove it."

Game on, pretty boy, country jerk, I think.

I start in on the first verse, and I make it most of the way through before my voice cracks. Normally I'd be embarrassed, but I don't really care. A week ago, this would've been my big chance to show what I've got, but considering I don't really respect Jesse, I don't have anything to fear.

So I just keep belting out "Carolina in My Mind." Playing guitar feels so good, I find myself sinking further down into the soft couch, relaxing, and not wanting to cry. Which is good, because lately, I've been on the verge of breaking down. I don't want to waste a single tear on Nate or my band, but it's been getting harder and harder.

On the second verse, Jesse leans back and closes his eyes. He joins me in singing the chorus.

When we've finished the song, we sit in silence while he chews on his lip. Enough time goes by to play the song again before he speaks. "You could use some training. You're singing out of your throat, and it's making your voice crack, but you have a nice tone."

"So do you." *What a stupid thing to say.* "I mean, obviously."

He moves over to the couch, hip-checks me, and takes the guitar carefully by the neck, lifting it from my hands. I hold my breath and pretend I'm a mannequin.

"Watch." He places fingers on four different strings. "Your hands are super small. So when you're playing the key licks, don't play an open B7, because that makes the transition too tough. You should bar the B7 at the seventh fret, which'll leave your hand in perfect position to start the lick. That'll make it easier."

He demonstrates a riff, moving his fingers up the board.

"I'll do that," I reply, and we look at each other. If those caramel eyes weren't attached to Jesse Scott, I could get lost in them.

A phone beeps, and we both startle.

Jesse swats the newspaper out of the way and fumbles for his cell on the couch cushion. He swipes the phone on and checks the screen. "Mark got caught up in contract stuff. He says he'll be here in two minutes."

"Which is what he said five minutes ago."

Would Dr. Salter have left us alone with the housekeeper if he'd known Mr. Logan would be so late? I don't think Mom would mind me spending time alone with a cute guy—I'm seventeen, after all, and everyone knows that a huge part of being a seventeen-year-old girl is spending time with cute guys—but Dad and Sam would freak. My brother would beat up the three-hundred-pound guard outside, scale the fence, and put Jesse in a headlock just for looking at my legs.

"Have you eaten breakfast?" Jesse asks.

"Yeah. A strawberry doughnut." Dave made it especially for me when I dropped by the Donut Palace, where he's spending his shadow day. He used icing to spell "Rock it out" in squiggly letters.

Jesse makes a face. "That's so unhealthy. Come on." He places the guitar back on the wall and gestures for me to follow him into the kitchen. It's the biggest I've ever seen, but it's cozy with wooden cabinets and cast-iron skillets hanging on the wall. An old-fashioned butter churn sits next to a woodstove.

"Jesus." I stare up at the vaulted ceilings dotted with skylights. "You really live here by yourself?"

"Yeah...well, except for Grace and my cat. Casper doesn't like strangers though, so you probably won't see her."

He has a cat?

Jesse pulls the fridge open to reveal shelves chockfull of energy drinks and fruit and vegetables and milk. He takes out a carton of eggs, a pepper, and an onion and lays them on the marble counter. His fridge has more produce than the Quick Pick. Why would a health nut get drunk and fall off a yacht?

Grace hurries into the room, brandishing a pink feather duster. "Get out of my kitchen, young man!"

"It's *my* kitchen," Jesse fires back. "And your omelets are too salty."

"Last time you cooked, you burned chicken. It took days to get the stench out of here."

"I promise not to scorch the frying pan this time."

Grace mutters something in Spanish and feather-dusts her way out of the room. And I thought Sam and Jordan living together was drama.

I walk over to the French doors to check out the backyard. "Your pool is shaped like a guitar?"

"Big-time, isn't it?"

"I bet it would be fun to play Marco Polo in it. You swim?" I ask, thinking of the boating incident again.

"No. But I like guitars." As he slices up the pepper, he asks, "So why'd you wanna shadow me today? I mean, you're already a good singer and guitarist."

"Yeah, I'm being showered with record deals," I say sarcastically. "I can't keep the producers away."

He stops slicing and sets his knife down. "So you're after a record deal? Is that it?" he asks quietly. The sadness on his face surprises me. "It's always something," he mutters. "If you think you'll get a record deal from me, you're wrong. So if that's what you want, leave. Stop playing this 'I don't do solos' game with me, trying to make me feel sorry for you or whatever."

"Of course I want a record deal, but I want to earn it, not beg for it."

"Hmph."

"You don't know anything about me."

"Well, you don't know anything about me."

Talk about being guarded. I could barely follow all of his accusations. If he's this quick to judge, no wonder he doesn't get many visitors.

He uses the counter to crack an egg open, and the yellow yolk falls into the frying pan with a neat little plop. Unlike last week at my brother's house, it's quiet and orderly as Jesse cooks breakfast, and that makes me a little sad.

In an awkward silence, Jesse prepares two omelets and scoops them onto plates. He passes one to me. I pick at mine while he shovels egg into his mouth like there's no tomorrow, which softens me a bit: even though he's a big star, he still eats like a regular boy.

I say, "I thought Mr. Logan was supposed to be here fifteen minutes ago."

"He's been busy trying to get me out of my contracts. He must've got held up. So you didn't answer my question before. My uncle said you quit the school choir, so why'd you still wanna shadow me?"

Dr. Salter told Jesse I quit show choir?

The director spent weeks trying to change my mind, but I told her I couldn't commit to after-school practices anymore, not when I had a band to practice with. But it shocks me the principal knows, let alone cares.

I don't feel comfortable talking about my decisions with Jesse though, especially not the bad ones. Even if it wasn't my kind of music, I miss putting on my ugly green bodice-ripper gown and singing with my choir. Giving it up for The Fringe wasn't worth it.

"I wanted to shadow you because I was interested in learning from a professional," I finally say.

He chews. "A professional, eh?"

"Yeah, I mean, I haven't taken any lessons, except from my

choir teachers. And there wasn't much one-on-one instruction there, because I learned along with the whole class."

"Really?" he asks, surprise in his voice. "Where'd you learn to play guitar?"

"My dad and uncle. It's a hobby for them though, so they only taught me the basics. I taught myself the rest using online videos."

"Wow," Jesse says. "I can't believe you haven't had any formal training."

I focus on his castle's tiled floor. "I wanted to take lessons."

"But?"

I decide to tell the truth—it's not like I'll ever see Jesse again after today. "We couldn't afford them."

I used my dad's old acoustic Martin when I was growing up, and I wouldn't even own an electric guitar if not for my brother. One of the first things Sam did after he graduated college when he got a job working for the Titans was buy me my own guitar for my birthday. That meant I didn't have to use the crappy one in the music room at school or go sit at Middle C and play the floor samples until they kicked me out, which happened more frequently than Diddy changes his name.

"What do your parents do?" Jesse asks.

"Dad manages an auto repair shop, and Mom cleans down at Cedar Hill Farms, this big estate." Being poor must sound so foreign to the boy who lives here, but his expression never changes. I give Jesse a small smile, and he nods back, and it's a nice moment.

He wipes his mouth with a napkin and leans against the counter, holding his plate up by his mouth. "So what do you want to do today then?"

"Mr. Logan gave us a schedule, right?"

"I'm not following a schedule on my day off."

I pause. "So we'll do whatever you do on your day off."

"I usually play guitar and write."

"We can do that," I say eagerly.

"Nah—that's not good enough. My uncle asked me to give you a good day, and I don't want to upset him." He grabs up the phone and punches a button. "It's me. Meet me at the studio at ten thirty." Jesse rolls his eyes and raps his spatula on the marble counter. "No, no, you don't need to pick us up… I know we're supposed to be following a schedule. Mark, she's already seen the Opry—she doesn't need a tour… I wanna do something else." He pauses. "Can you call Holly and have her meet us there? Great." He hangs up. "I'm gonna show you what real voice lessons are like."

"That's really nice of you," I reply, not wanting to ruin his sudden about-face in attitude.

"Let me just get ready real quick."

He starts to jog up the stairs, giving me this great view of his Celtic tattoo, but stops and turns to smirk.

"Wait. Did you want to shadow me while I shower?"

Teach Your Children

Jesse comes back down the rear staircase, spinning a beige cowboy hat on his finger and wearing a plain white T-shirt and ripped jeans. Patches of tan skin peek through the holes.

"Those red cowboy boots," I say, shaking my head.

He looks down at them. "Most of the groupies think they're sexy."

Yes, they are. "They're not bad."

I'm fixing to stand up from my seat at the kitchen table when a ball of white fur lands on my lap from out of nowhere.

"Oh, hello," I murmur, petting the pretty white cat. "You must be Casper. Aren't you beautiful?" I scratch her ears, and she stretches her neck so I can get under her chin too. "Good girl," I whisper.

When I look up from petting the cat, Jesse is staring at me with his mouth slightly opened. He shakes his head, as if to clear his thoughts, then asks, "Ready to go?"

I nod. He gently picks up the cat from my lap, kisses her head before setting her on the floor, and leads me out to the garage.

The garage totally baffles me. It has six spaces, but only two are filled. I stare at a truck—a rusted ancient white Dodge, probably from the seventies—and a motorcycle, a black Harley-Davidson with orange flames licking its sides. He truly is a country boy.

"Where're the rest of your cars?"

"This is it," he replies, jingling his keys. "We taking the truck or the bike?"

Even though I'm wearing my black dress, I say, "The Harley, obviously!" Humming, I drag my hand across the leather seat, squatting down to check out the rear fender. "Love the dual exhaust."

"You like bikes?"

"Oh yeah. My Poppy—my grandfather—has an Indian."

"Big-time," Jesse says. "I'd love to see it. You ride it a lot?"

"He lets me take it out every time Halley's Comet flies by."

"So never?"

I stand up, dusting off my hands. "Last spring, I bought a '95 Suzuki 750 down at the junkyard for fifty dollars. Some guys at the shop helped me fix it up. That's what I ride."

"*You* fixed it up?"

I lean over to check out his transmission. Six-speed. "Well, I needed help, but I did a lot of it myself. A few years ago, my dad started running Caldwell Auto Parts in Franklin, and I work there as a receptionist part time. Sometimes I get to do oil changes, which is a lot more exciting than running a cash register."

"You like cars?"

"*Love* them. But not as much as guitars and bikes."

I tell Jesse about how when I was little, I'd hang out with Dad and Sam while they were tinkering around under the hood. Even before he quit his job driving a semi and started working at Caldwell's so he could spend more time with our family, Dad always loved fixing junk cars and bikes in his spare time and turning them for a profit. At first, I was interested in cars and bikes because it was a way to hang out with my dad when he wasn't on the road, but over time, I really started loving them. In a way, engines, carburetors, and transmissions are like individual guitar strings: each plays a part in creating a beautiful sound.

"So you're close with your family?" Jesse asks.

"Yeah. I mean, they drive me nuts, and we have nothing in common, but I love them."

Jesse goes silent for a long moment, seeming to forget where he is, then grabs two helmets from a workbench.

"You okay?" I ask.

He doesn't answer. He just takes his cowboy hat off and passes it to me. "You gotta hold my lucky hat while we ride."

Next thing I know, I'm wrapping my arms around his waist and locking my hips into his. I hold on to his hat, praying it doesn't blow away. Jesse fires up the Harley and steers it out of his garage and past the gates, immediately kicking it into high gear—probably because the paparazzi are already following us. Are they taking my picture?!

I close my eyes, and the wind whips around my body, freeing all the bad thoughts about the past week. It's a little weird having my arms and legs wrapped around this sexy guy who gets on my nerves. While wearing a short skirt. While on my way to a music studio, a place I've only dreamed of visiting. *Holy shit!* I, Maya Henry, am going to a music studio! Jesse speeds up to fifty miles an hour, and I feel like I'm taking off in a plane.

After about twenty minutes, we pull into a reserved parking spot on Music Row.

"Omni Studios!" I exclaim as Jesse yanks off his helmet.

He takes his cowboy hat from my hand and helps me climb off the motorcycle. We store our helmets in the Harley's saddlebags.

This is amazing. I pretend I'm heading inside to record my own album. I strut my stuff as we pass guitar statues and go through a security booth. Security guards wand the people patiently waiting in line, but Jesse waves at a guy and pulls me right on through.

Inside, people mill about the hallway. When Jesse appears, they scatter like ants at a picnic. He pays no attention, striding into a studio labeled with his name.

"You have your own studio?"

"I don't share."

Go figure.

Drums, a piano, and, like, a bazillion guitars and basses fill the brightly lit studio. I can't believe I'm here! My eyes dart from the speakers to the mikes to the control room and its mixing equipment. The "On Air" sign is off. Wouldn't it be amazing to watch it turn red and then dive into a session? I take a seat at the grand piano and drag my fingers across the keys.

"You play?" Jesse asks.

"Nah. But I've always wanted to learn." In the past at band practice, Hannah taught me a few easy songs on the keyboard. I slowly play a few low notes.

She texted me a few times this week, asking to talk, saying she had no idea the guys wanted to replace me, but I haven't felt like talking to her. Loyalty means a lot to me, and she just stood there and said nothing while the guys kicked me out of The Fringe.

Jesse squeezes in next to me on the bench, takes his cowboy hat off, and sets it on the piano. He cracks his knuckles, then stretches his fingers. "You know 'Heart and Soul,' right?"

"Nope."

He flashes a look at me. "Where did you grow up? Antarctica?"

"Actually, Franklin."

"Like I said, Antarctica."

I elbow him in the ribs. "It's not that bad."

"I know…I wish I still lived in the country. My parents live an hour away down in Hillsboro, but I need to live closer to my studio and the airport."

"You've got the money to build your own studio and the Jesse Scott International Airport out in the country, right?" I tease, and he gives me a look that says he doesn't know what to do with me.

He takes my right hand in his and guides my fingers to the keys. That's when I notice the blue ink stains on his hands. The ink is so ingrained that it looks as if soap doesn't do the trick anymore. He must spend a ton of time writing lyrics.

"You're gonna do the easy part—the upper register." He shows me which notes to play, then makes me practice it a few times. "I'm gonna play the lower register now. Keep the beat, okay?" His fingers effortlessly drum the keys. "Start…now!"

I join in, and the music seems to relax both of us. Jesse starts telling me that along with Garth Brooks, Tim McGraw, and Keith Urban, he's big into Neil Diamond, James Taylor, and Simon and Garfunkel—all the boys from way back. I confess that while I love badass girl musicians like Fiona Apple, most of the music on my iPhone is from the eighties. Prince, Madonna, Pat Benatar. My mom got me hooked on Queen.

"I love them so much I named my Twitter account QueenQueen," I tell Jesse.

He smirks. "A Tennessee girl who dresses like Madonna and sings Freddie Mercury."

Our musical tastes are very different, which makes me nervous, considering Nate never liked anything but metal, and I don't want to spend my entire day with Jesse listening to country. I want to listen to the music I like. So it's great that we discover a mutual love of Bon Jovi; he starts playing "Living on a Prayer" for us to sing along to, and I can hardly believe I'm practically doing karaoke with the king of country music. My voice stays steady through the song, just like when I sing backup.

"Your voice didn't crack that time," Jesse says. "That's good."

"I can relax more when I'm not the only one singing."

We play until a gorgeous blond woman wearing this long, flowing bohemian dress sails into the studio. She lifts her sunglasses and squints at us.

"Jesse?" she asks. "Who's this?"

Jesse and I stand. "Holly, meet Maya. Maya, meet Holly. She's been my voice coach for forever."

The woman beams as we shake hands. "Jesse's never brought a guest to one of our sessions before."

"She's not a guest. Maya's job shadowing me today."

"Ah. That's nice of you." Holly looks confused.

"Maya's a pretty good singer. No training."

Right then, Mr. Logan strolls in wearing a fancy navy suit, blue tie, and shoes so shiny they temporarily blind me. Two young women in crisp black suits carrying portfolios, iPads, and cell phones rush in behind him. Whoever they are, they need more hands.

"I told you, no press," Jesse says to the ladies. "It's my day off."

"At least let us put out a statement that you're mentoring a fan today," one woman says.

Jesse shakes his head. "This is a private favor for my uncle, not a stunt."

The other lady says, "We'll frame it that you're visiting important Nashville landmarks with a talented fan—"

Jesse responds by shooing the two ladies out of the studio, shutting the door with a click behind them. It's like watching a circus.

"Jess, I told you I was coming to pick you up," the manager scolds.

"We got sick of waiting on you."

"Did you really drive Maya here on your motorcycle? Your uncle is going to kill me."

"Maybe you should've been on time then."

I'd be flipping out at Jesse, but Mr. Logan stays cool and calm, adjusting his watch before shaking my hand. "Nice to see you again, Maya."

"You too, sir."

Jesse snorts. "Sir," he mutters, and Mr. Logan gives Jesse a noogie, then pats his back.

"You know you're not supposed to leave home alone without your security," Mr. Logan says.

"I didn't need it. Maya provided security."

"Is Jesse already driving you crazy?" Mr. Logan asks me.

"He's not too bad," I say.

"Hear that?" Jesse gives Mr. Logan and Holly a look. "I'm not too bad."

"Finally some good press," Mr. Logan says with a laugh, and Jesse scowls. "Well, don't let me interrupt. Just wanted to see how things are going."

"It's been, like, twenty minutes, Mark." Jesse begins to play the Charlie Brown theme song on piano. It's really cute.

"I'm going to make some calls," Mr. Logan says. He gives me another smile and goes to sit in the isolation booth where Jesse must do his singing. Through the glass, I watch Mr. Logan put a cell phone to his ear and pull a little book out of his jacket pocket.

Holly sits on a stool and arranges her billowing skirt around her legs. "So, Maya, sing something for me."

She's the voice coach to the biggest country singer there is. What if she thinks I'm terrible? "Um, I don't do solos."

The Charlie Brown music abruptly stops. "That's getting old real quick," Jesse growls. "You've got a world-class voice coach standing in front of you on my dime. So sing. Or I'm leaving, and you can tell my uncle why you didn't complete shadow day."

Crickets.

Holly says, "Okaayy."

"Fine. I'll sing," I tell Holly. "Thank you for the opportunity." I take a deep breath and try to relax as I belt out the first few lines of "Carolina in My Mind."

Like Jesse, her face gives away nothing. She taps her lips with two fingers as I sing and nods when I'm finished. "No one's ever taught you how to sing from your diaphragm?"

"Huh?"

She clucks her tongue. "Schools these days…"

Jesse stands up from the bench. "Sing like you normally would."

I sing a line from the song, and then he puts his hand on my stomach.

"What the?" I smack his fingers away.

Holly chuckles. "It's okay, Maya."

Avoiding my eyes, Jesse moves close to me again and lays his palm on my stomach, his long fingers splayed across the red lace and black leather of my corset. Wow, that feels intense.

"This time when you sing the measure," Jesse says, "try to push my hand off your stomach using only your breathing."

"While I'm singing?"

"Yup. You're going to sing from your stomach instead of your throat. It'll make the sound fuller."

I take a deep breath, and he waves a hand again. "No, no. Fill your stomach with air, not your chest."

I glance at Holly, who is staring at Jesse like she's seen a ghost. Inside the booth, Mr. Logan stands up, looks from me to Jesse, and pockets his cell phone. He rushes back out into the main room.

I inhale again, filling my stomach with air, and Jesse says, "That's it. Now start singing."

I rattle off another measure, trying to push Jesse's hand away from my stomach. It takes a lot more effort than usual, and I can't hear anything different in my voice, but whatever. He's the expert.

"Better," he says, one side of his mouth upturned.

Mr. Logan paces back and forth across the studio, staring at Jesse. He doesn't seem all that interested in me or my voice, just his star client. Is he as surprised as I am that Jesse is being kind to me?

Then Holly pulls out the big guns and the real work starts. For the next hour, she has me sing scales and melodies that are way out of my comfort zone. My voice cracks a couple of times, making Jesse wince again like when I screwed up on guitar. Harsh critic.

Holly hands over various sheet music for me to try, and Jesse makes me sing along with a guitar and then the piano and then a cappella. An hour later, my stomach is killing me. Holly is very clear I will not be singing from my throat anymore—I have to sing from my diaphragm—but it's tough to get used to. I take a break to sip some warm water.

"Maya sounds edgy," Jesse says.

Holly adds, "I love her raspy tone. She's got soul. You can't learn that."

"Thanks." It feels good to hear. But it also slices deep. It reminds me that I'm not a part of a band anymore. It's not like

I have anyone to sing with, and I won't be doing any shows anytime soon unless I find another band.

"You'll have to work hard on your mechanics," Holly adds, rising from the stool. Pushing on my tummy and back, she edges me into an uncomfortable posture. "You've started late in life."

"But Uncle Bob was right," Jesse says. "You have a good voice, but you need a lot of practice and training if you want to become something."

"Thank you." I smile at Jesse, and he nods, his gaze floating from my eyes to my nose stud.

"Let's have some fun," Mr. Logan says. He grabs a set of earphones. "Let's get you in a booth and see what you sound like on tape."

I take a step back. "No, no, no."

"Why not?" Mr. Logan raises one of his perfectly shaped eyebrows.

Ever since I fainted while singing "Scarborough Fair," and then the talent show "siren" incident, I've avoided being recorded. Those two are up on YouTube for all eternity. "I just don't want to hear myself, okay?"

Jesse takes my elbow. "It's okay. How about we do some scales instead? Me and you?"

I shrug. "Whatever."

Jesse sits down at the piano. "Use the breathing technique you just learned."

While Mr. Logan and Holly listen, Jesse and I sing for so long my stomach muscles feel like somebody's ripping them in two.

"How do you do full concerts like this?" I ask and sip some water.

"People think my life is easy. It's not. I work crazy hours, and when I'm not practicing or playing a gig, I'm writing or exercising. I never get much sleep."

"You have to truly love music, or you'll never make it," Mr. Logan adds.

Jesse begins playing piano again—something classical—slowly, not methodically, with lots of flavor.

"I remember when I first heard you sing on TV," I tell Jesse. "I must've been nine or so. I could tell how much you loved singing."

"Still do," he says quietly, softly drumming the keys.

"Want to sing your new song, Jess?" Holly asks.

He shakes his head. "Today's about Maya."

"I'd love to hear your song," I say.

He looks at me, pensive, as he stops playing piano, stands, grabs an acoustic Fender, and slings the strap over his shoulder. He takes a deep breath before beginning to pluck out a melody. Shutting his eyes, he sings in the purest voice, "Eight years old when we first went fishing. Now ten years on, I wish we'd never gone. They say to live in the moment, to live right now. But I'm back there, when you loved me for me."

Who's the song about? His dad? Or Dr. Salter? Or somebody else?

When he's finished, Holly pats his arm. He winces and opens

his eyes. He takes a step away from Holly, and with a sad expression, she begins stacking sheet music into a pile.

She and I glance at one another before I say, "That was gorgeous, Jesse."

A guy who clearly loves singing, who loves performing, and puts so much emotion and love into his songs—why would he quit? Give up something that is his whole world? The reason has to be big as life, right?

Jesse pulls the guitar strap from around his neck. "I'm starved."

Mr. Logan claps once. "Lunch sounds great. Then we can resume the schedule for this afternoon. The tour of the Ryman Auditorium should be fascinating."

Jesse sighs, grabs his cowboy hat off the piano, and puts it on.

"Mark." Holly clucks her tongue. "I don't know the rules of this job shadowing thing, but shouldn't Maya be spending time with Jesse while he does his normal routine?"

Mr. Logan straightens his jacket and tie. "How about Mere Bulles for lunch, then? It's fabulous. I got us a reservation."

"Sounds nice," I say, pretending I know what Mere Bulles is, but Holly shakes her head.

"Mark, how about you and I go to lunch together, and we'll leave the kids alone to get to know each other. Okay?"

"But," Mr. Logan blurts, and Holly gives him a monumental glare, so he quickly adds, "I think it would be great if you two went to lunch."

"Really?" Jesse asks, looking up.

"I'll send Gina and Tracy to handle any press who follow you and to deal with the restaurant. We'll meet up after lunch." Mr. Logan pats Jesse's shoulder. "You okay with this?" he asks quietly.

Jesse glances over at me. "Yeah. She's cool."

Mr. Logan goes from looking surprised to happy in record time. "Good. I'll have a car take you—"

Before he can finish his sentence about our ride, Jesse grabs my elbow and yanks me out of the studio and into the parking lot, where we jump on his bike and take off.

I Knew You Were Trouble

"We can't go to lunch here."

"Why not?" Jesse asks. "They've got the best steak this side of the Mississippi."

"I, uh, can't—" I look through the Mere Bulles window at the glittering chandelier and tables topped with white linen and lush flowers. "I don't make all that much down at Caldwell's."

"I'll spot you."

"But then you'll probably think I want a free lunch in addition to that record deal *I'm so desperate for*." Several older women with very structured gray hair are congregating near us on the sidewalk, trying to get a closer look at Jesse.

"Let's just go to Chipotle," I urge him.

"I know you're not trying to get a free lunch. And we can't go to Chipotle without my security detail." He keeps a close watch on the old ladies as if they are going to jump him. "There was a burrito incident."

"A burrito incident."

"Yeah."

"Well, we still can't go here. We're not...dressed appropriately."

He eyes my short black dress. "You look fine."

"I wasn't talking about me. Your jeans look like Swiss cheese."

Jesse looks insulted. "There's nothing wrong with my jeans."

"Your mother would not be happy if she saw you going to lunch in those clothes."

"We're not talking about her—" He stops midsentence and strides down the busy Nashville street. "C'mon. Let's get some barbeque instead."

My black skirt bounces as I hustle to catch up with him. "What about your publicists? Aren't they meeting us here?"

"Pfft." He waves a hand, and a couple of minutes later, I find myself at a restaurant called Finger Licking Good. It's not as fancy as Mere Bulles, but it's still nicer than what I'm used to. It's filled with well-dressed businesspeople who must love their barbeque.

Jesse opens the door, tipping his hat like a gentleman, and we go up to the empty host stand.

"Cover me," he says. He darts behind the stand and drags his finger across the reservation book.

"What are you doing?" I whisper-yell, keeping an eye out for the host.

"Ever seen *Ferris Bueller's Day Off*?"

"No."

"Watch and learn."

When the hostess walks up, her eyes trail over Jesse's dusty red boots, jeans, and ratty white T-shirt up to his cowboy hat. She pauses at his freckled face.

"Oh." Her hands fly to smooth and fluff her hair.

"We have a reservation for two," Jesse says. "Last name's Smith."

"Smith?" She raises an eyebrow.

"Yes, Smith," Jesse repeats, and I have to bite down on my cheek to keep from laughing.

"Tommy Smith? The owner of the Tennessee Titans?"

Jesse points a finger at her. "Yes, that's the one. I'm Tommy Smith."

"You had such a tough loss against the Jets last Sunday," I say. I only know the Titans lost because my brother and Jordan whined about it for hours.

"Don't you worry, darlin'. We're gonna bury the Dolphins this weekend."

The hostess raises her eyebrows at me, giving me a once-over and turning her nose up at my outfit. She grabs two menus and leads us to a table by a window overlooking the Cumberland River. The best seat in the house, just like at the concert last week. Getting the best seat seems to happen a lot when Jesse Scott is involved.

The hostess hands us our menus, winks at Jesse, and says, "Enjoy your lunch, Mr. Sco—I mean, Smith."

"Thank you," we say, and I dissolve into giggles. Jesse gives me his half-cocked smirk, the one on his most recent album cover.

I place a red and white picnic-patterned napkin in my lap. The tablecloth is made of paper, and a cup of crayons sits on the table.

"You and the owner of the Titans eat at a restaurant where you can draw on the table?" I ask.

"Wait till you try the brisket."

The smell is definitely making my mouth water.

Jesse chooses the brown crayon and starts drawing a horse.

"So why'd you pretend to be the owner of the Titans?" I ask.

He shrugs. "It's something to do, you know?"

No, I don't know.

He switches to a blue crayon, and I scan my menu. Should I get ribs or brisket? "So who's Ferris Bueller?"

He looks up from doodling a truck. "*Ferris Bueller's Day Off* is a great movie. I'm surprised you haven't heard of it since you're so into eighties music. It's about this guy who skips school and does all these crazy things."

"Like what?"

"He, like, commandeers a float during a parade in Chicago and sings 'Twist and Shout.' You know, by the Beatles?"

"I know who the Beatles are. I wasn't born in a barn."

"Oh, do they not have barns in Antarctica?"

"Stop." I laugh again. Jesse hasn't truly smiled once, but I haven't laughed this much in a while. "So what else did Ferris do?"

"He went to a fancy restaurant and stole somebody else's

reservation like we just did. Oh, and he convinced his best friend to steal his dad's hot red car for the day."

"What kind of car?"

"Does it matter?"

"Of course it matters!" I exclaim.

A server drops off a bread basket, and Jesse digs in. "I think it was a Ferrari."

"Nice. Go on then. What else?"

He rips into a roll with his teeth. "Um, Ferris went to a Cubs game and to an art museum."

"Sounds like a nice day."

He speaks as he chews. "You having a nice day so far?"

I loved sitting at the piano with him and just singing my heart out. And don't even get me started on how great it was to ride that Harley. But he's so guarded and on edge, I don't feel completely comfortable around him. He seemed so much happier in the studio, surrounded by music.

"It's been good," I say.

Jesse picks up a straw, tears off the paper from one end of it, puts it in his mouth, then blows the paper at me. I snatch the paper in midair and wad it up.

Out of the corner of my eye, I see an older man glaring at Jesse's straw paper antics. Is this why Mr. Logan wanted the publicists to come? To make sure Jesse doesn't play with his food?

Two ladies wearing Easter-colored dress suits, pearls, and heels saunter over and ask for Jesse's autograph. He tips his hat and fishes a black Sharpie out of his jeans pocket. "Who do I make them out to?"

The first woman speaks so quickly it comes out garbled and she has to repeat herself. "To Nicole. My daughter." The other woman wants an autograph for her niece. He reaches over to an empty table near us, snatches two white napkins, unfolds them with a flourish, and starts signing.

He seems completely bored by it all but acts like a gentleman the entire time, including when a waitress gets our drink order and the Finger Licking Good manager comes over to thank Jesse for "dining with us." Everything feels like a production, as if his life is stage-managed. Then he excuses himself to go to the restroom.

While he's gone, the two paparazzi guys from outside Jesse's house rush up and snap pictures of me. Where did they come from? Have they been following Jesse this entire time? I cover my face with a hand.

One of them rushes to ask, "Are you sleeping with Jesse?"

I shake my head and focus on the napkin in my lap. When my mother signed the permission slip for shadow day, she also had to sign nondisclosure agreements, stating that I would keep everything I learn about Jesse a secret. Confidentiality agreement or not, no way in hell would I hurt him. We didn't exactly get off on the right foot, but I know what it's like to be betrayed.

"You're friends with him then? Do you know why he's quitting the business?"

My breathing speeds up, and I can't catch it. Where is the manager? Why hasn't he thrown these jerks out? *Flash, flash, flash, flash. Click, click, click.*

"Give us something," the other guy says.

"I've got no comment," I say as Jesse approaches our table, his eyebrow raised. He stands there for a long moment, staring at me. *Flash, flash, flash, flash.*

"Come on guys, beat it," Jesse says nonchalantly, sliding into his seat. The paparazzi grab a few more pics of us—*click, click, click, click*—but they vamoose after Jesse gives them a stare that would scare the devil.

When we're alone again, Jesse chooses another piece of bread from the basket. He glances at me, giving me a smile. A genuine smile that lights up his face. It sends shivers rippling over my skin.

"I heard everything," he says finally.

"I'm sorry," I mumble.

"It's all good," Jesse says. "A lot of girls would lie to the press, say they're dating me or whatever, you know? It's happened before." He looks away and stares through the window at the choppy river. I know he thinks the worst of people, but does he not trust anyone?

"I get what that's like," I say.

"How could you possibly?"

"I understand what it's like to trust somebody… I know how bad it feels when they let you down or betray you."

He picks up a black crayon and starts drawing a night sky above the horse. "Go on."

For some reason, maybe because this is only for one day, I feel okay telling him the truth, which I haven't been able to tell my family. Maybe if I'm honest, he'll open up to me too. Isn't that what Dr. Salter wanted?

"I got kicked out of my band last week."

His caramel eyes meet mine. "Why would a band let a guitarist like you go?"

"Different tastes in music," I mutter and pinch my arm to distract from the pain in my chest. "They only wanted to play heavy metal and refused to branch out like I wanted. So they asked me to leave."

"That's silly. If you wanna be a musician, you gotta study a wide variety of music."

I peek up at him. That's what I think—a band should sample from different genres to find a unique tone. Like Queen. They started out with a hard sound and then eventually developed their own style. Hearing Jesse say that makes me feel better, but I'm still band-less, and *Wannabe Rocker* audition videos are due in two weeks.

"What are you gonna do?" Jesse asks.

I shrug, and that's when the server comes to drop off our

drinks. When she's gone, I change the subject. I doodle music notes and a flower. "You ever had a day like Ferris Bueller did? Where you did whatever you wanted?"

This mischievous grin sneaks onto his face. "So you really want to shadow me today, no matter what I do?"

I lift an eyebrow, smiling.

"Definitely."

♪♫♩

After gorging on brisket, we walk back to where Jesse parked his Harley. The two paparazzi guys from earlier are there, along with some new guys and even a lady, all snapping pictures of us while we climb on Jesse's bike.

"Jesse!" a reporter calls, his camera flashing and clicking. "New girlfriend?"

"Nah." He nudges me. "I'm not her type."

I run fingers through my bleached hair, mussing it, and focus on the asphalt so the press can't see my eyes. Suddenly a black town car pulls up right next to the press, and the two publicists from earlier, Tracy and Gina, climb out of the backseat. One of them rushes over to the paparazzi to do damage control. The other wobbles our way in her black high heels.

"Jesse!" she calls out. "Where have you been?"

"Hold on, Maya," Jesse says, revving his engine, and I throw my arms around his middle and grip his waist. The next thing I know, we're barreling down Second Avenue, with the black town car and half a dozen paparazzi on our tails. I feel like I'm in a chase scene from a movie. Hell. Yes.

He speeds down alleys and side streets and finally loses them by turning into a Food Lion parking lot. We hide beside some shopping carts. When the coast is clear, he drives his bike to the Maserati dealership, where he cuts the ignition.

"What in the world?" I ask. "Why did you do that?"

"I told you, it's my day off. I don't feel like dealing with Gina and Tracy and talking to the press about how much I loved eating brisket with my *biggest fan*."

I snort. "Why are we here?"

Jesse says, "Okay, in keeping with Ferris Bueller, first we're gonna do something I've always wanted to do."

"I thought this was my day," I tease.

"You'll like this."

"What about Mr. Logan? We were supposed to call him after lunch."

Jesse waves a hand. "Pfft."

I gaze at the Maseratis in the showroom. The few times Dad and I have been in this neighborhood, we slowly drove by the dealership and stared through the windows at the most magnificent cars on the planet. I always said, "Dad, let's go in and look around!" And he'd reply, "They won't even let us inside."

Jesse gives me an evil grin. "Let's do it."

"Do what?"

He nods at the window display. "We're gonna test-drive that red car."

"Oh, no, no, no."

"Why not?"

"That's a GranTurismo!"

"Yeah, and it's big-time. So we're gonna drive it." He takes my elbow in his hand, and the automatic doors swoosh open as he pulls me inside.

The salespeople lift their heads, then go back to their cell phones and paperwork. Then Jesse takes off his cowboy hat, and suddenly their sales team rushes over.

"Mr. Scott," a man says, sticking out a hand. "We're honored you're here."

Jesse ignores the man's hand and jerks his head toward the out-of-this-world sports car. "I'm interested in buying a GranTurismo."

"Of course you are," the man replies in this hoity-toity voice. "If I can see your driver's license, I'll have a test car brought around for you."

Jesse shakes his head. "Maya's doing the test-driving."

When Dad hears about this… He. Will. Die.

The man's grin melts. "And you are?"

I don't know what comes over me when I put a hand on my hip and pull out my attitude. "I'm Mr. Scott's senior adviser."

"Adviser of what?" the man asks.

"She tells me what I can and can't buy." Jesse crosses his arms, pretending to pout at me.

"Sometimes he doesn't know how to keep his wallet in his pants," I explain. "And that's where I come in."

"You help him keep it in his pants?"

Jesse and I burst out laughing.

"Yes, that's exactly what she does," Jesse says.

The man's face shines redder than the gleaming GranTurismo. "What, may I ask, do you know about cars?"

During my downtime at Caldwell's, I read all the car magazines, and I pay particular attention to the fancy ones that I will never be able to afford. "The 2016 GT goes from zero to sixty in five seconds, right?"

"Right…"

"Right," Jesse says, clapping a hand on my shoulder. "We'd like to test-drive it."

The man narrows his eyes but takes my license and steps into an office. The saleswomen lurk about, straightening their blouses while staring at Jesse, but he doesn't seem to notice.

My fingers caress a silver MC Sport as Jesse says, "You sure showed that jerk. Sometimes it's so great to stick it to people, you know?"

I shrug.

"What's wrong?" Jesse asks.

"Do you immediately think the worst of everybody you meet?" I feel bad for asking that, but it seems to be a Jesse Scott trend.

He goes silent for a long moment—so long I start to get nervous that I really offended him and he's going to abandon me here—but then he speaks. "When I got my first record deal, most of the guys at school teased me. Said I sang like a girl and stuff."

"They were jealous."

"Yeah…but it still hurt. And as I got more and more famous, people were around all the time. Girls wanted to date me, use me, screw me, whatever. And don't even ask about all the people who called asking for money or for help getting a record deal. The same people who had made fun of me."

"That sucks."

"Everyone always wants something."

"C'mon. *Everyone*?"

"It's more likely than not. Lately, I just like being alone."

"And you're happy with that?" I ask quietly, not accusing him or anything.

"I've got Casper."

"Oh God. You're like one of those old cat ladies!"

He laughs softly, then grows pensive again.

"What about your parents?" I ask, but he shakes his head. "You can talk to me. I mean, if you want to. You can trust me."

He rubs his eyes. "My parents don't—we haven't really been speaking to each other lately, okay?"

"What?" I blurt.

And that's when his phone rings.

He looks at the screen and starts pacing back and forth in front of the silver MC Sport. "Hi, Mark. No, we're done with lunch… I'm at the Maserati dealership… I forgot to call… Test-driving a red car… I dunno, I might buy it… We don't want to go on the tours… Please? No, do not send Tracy and Gina over here!… No, I don't need a stylist! I look fine," Jesse grumbles, and on that note, he hangs up.

"What'd he say?" I ask.

"He told us to have fun, go hog wild, and he'd check in later."

"Really?"

"No, he said he's on his way here now. He'll be here in five minutes. Which means we need to get out of here in the next hour or so if we want to miss him."

I grin. "How long has he been your manager?"

"I signed with him right after I won *Wannabe Rocker*…so eight years? He gets me. Lets me do my own thing."

The sales guy comes back and leads us outside to the shiniest, most beautiful piece of machinery ever built. "Holy shit," I whisper, dragging the tips of my fingers across the GT's hood.

The man hands me the keys. "Mr. Scott, I trust you'll have this car back in mint condition in twenty minutes, correct?"

Jesse claps the man's back. "You got it, Bill."

We slip inside the car. The leather seat is so soft it's like lying in sheets made of clouds. I groan.

"All my years of being a country stud and I've never made a girl make that sound," Jesse says with a laugh.

I smack him on the shoulder. "Would you behave?" I insert the keys in the ignition and test the clutch. "Any objection to me driving stick, or do you want to go automatic?"

"Whatever suits you."

"I like manual, 'cause then I'm in control."

"Figures."

I stomp on the clutch, start the engine, take my foot off the brake, give it some gas, and we shoot out of the parking lot. My head slams back against the seat.

"This thing's a rocket!" Jesse says as he turns on the radio.

I soar past the entrance to the Grand Ole Opry and sail onto Briley Parkway. I steer the GranTurismo onto I-24, shifting through all six gears, taking it up to ninety miles an hour, zigzagging across four lanes of cars. Eight cylinders roar.

"What do you think of her?" Jesse hollers over the music, drumming the dashboard.

"I've always wanted a Lamborghini, but I could get used to a Maserati," I joke as I near a hundred miles an hour, flying past a semi.

I rest my palm on the stick, and it surprises the hell out of me when Jesse reaches over and places his hand over mine for several seconds, then pulls it away.

Jesse Scott just touched my hand!

Trying to focus on the road, I glance at him out of the corner of my eye. *Don't freak out, don't freak out*, I tell myself.

He stares out the window. "Sorry. Just wanted to see what it feels like to have that kind of power and control."

He thinks I have control? Yeah, right. Remembering the first real smile Jesse gave me makes me wild inside. But this isn't a movie; this is a one-day thing with Jesse Scott, a famous star who's about to quit the business and give up all of his success.

And I'm gonna go back to my life, where I don't know what I'm doing anymore because I have no band. Where there is no control.

Live Your Life

I hand the Maserati sales guy my phone so he can take pictures of us with the red GT, and then we break it to him: we aren't buying a car today.

"I'll come back to check out the red car again real soon," Jesse announces, which somewhat placates the snobby sales guy. "Now what?" he asks me as we climb on his bike.

"Can we go back to your place and play guitar?" I ask. I'm itching to try that double-neck Fender I saw on his wall this morning.

"You got it. But first I have to pick up something for my concert in Atlanta tomorrow night."

"Fine," I say, wrapping my arms around his waist. But just before we take off, Jesse's phone dings. He swipes the screen to answer it. "Hey, Uncle Bob! No, no, everything's fine... No, we are not gonna do some stupid tour. I'm teaching Maya all about the business. We spent a whole hour talking about contract law. I even did a PowerPoint presentation... You're gonna give Maya detention unless she 'adheres to the schedule'?" Jesse rolls his eyes at his phone.

"We're fine, Dr. Salter," I yell over Jesse's shoulder into the cell.

"Maya, I'm going out on a limb here by letting you shadow Jesse," Dr. Salter warns loudly. "Don't make me regret it. You need to get back on the schedule."

"I want to stay with you," I quietly tell Jesse.

He looks into my eyes, and that's when he says to his uncle, "We'll catch you later, Uncle Bob!" and he turns off the phone and stows it in his pocket.

I groan. "What if I get detention? Or suspended?"

"If you want to go back to school, just say the word." Jesse says it matter-of-factly, but I can hear an edge in his voice. I know he'd be disappointed if I left, and at this point, I'd be disappointed too. Dr. Salter said he thought we could help each other, and I'm not gonna give up on Jesse just because I might get detention. When you think about how big this world is, how big this life is, detention is nothing. In ten years, I won't look back on this day and be pissed that I got detention.

I'd be pissed that I gave up the day.

"Let's go."

He gives me that famous half-cocked Jesse Scott smirk. "All right, put your helmet back on."

We take off on the Harley, zooming down the back roads surrounding Music Row, passing all the rustic mansions with their iron gates and green ivy.

I burst out laughing when Jesse kills the engine outside the Nashville Spur Emporium. The sign on the window reads, *Your One-Stop Shop for Your Cowboy's Needs!*

He must be kidding me. I can't go in here. I'll lose all my street cred.

Jesse and I climb off the bike, and I gaze through the window at a pair of green cowboy boots. "Oh my God, were those boots made from a snake?"

"Crocodile, I think." He leads me inside, a little bell dinging, and a small Asian woman comes rushing up.

She takes a deep breath. "Mr. Scott. They are here and they are *gorgeous*."

"Knew you could get them, Rosie."

The tiny woman goes to the back of the store, leaving me and Jesse to browse. "Jolene," that Dolly Parton song I hate, is playing, and there must be thousands of cowboy boots. Horrifying.

I pick up a black leather boot covered by flames. "You need these."

"You think?"

"Yes. They'll match your Harley."

"We could get matching boots."

"Like those old people who wear matching clothes on vacation?"

"Exactly."

"Sorry to disappoint you, but I'm not getting married anytime soon."

He picks up a hot pink boot and studies the sole. "You got a boyfriend?"

"No boyfriend…I was into this one guy, but it didn't work out."

"How come?"

"He liked another girl more."

Jesse studies my face so hard it makes my cheeks burn. "He sounds like an idiot."

More like I was the idiot. Back in middle school when I had my first crush, Mom gave me a piece of advice that I listened to but never actually followed. She said that I should never waste my time pining for a boy, because the boy I'm meant to be with will want me so bad, I won't have to pine at all.

I've known Nate since elementary school, but I developed feelings for him after we started The Fringe last year. I'd look for him in the halls between every class, and at night, I'd clutch my phone and wait for his texts. I knew it wasn't healthy to obsess like I did, but I wanted him. Just being in the same room with him made life seem sharper, more intense, like adding a splash of whiskey to a Coke.

During spring break earlier this year when we were firmly in the just friends zone, we road-tripped to Myrtle Beach with Hannah and her ex-boyfriend. Her ex was older—like, twenty-one—and she'd sworn us to secrecy so her parents wouldn't find out who she was dating. Anyhow, Nate and I spent a lot of time on the beach while Hannah and her boyfriend mostly stayed in their hotel room, and at night, Nate and I shared a bed.

Lying next to him in the dark, knowing Hannah was next door having sex, drove me wild: I wanted to hook up with Nate. My body felt as if it had been zapped by electricity. I finally got some guts, rolled over, and rested my head on his chest. He sucked in a breath and lay still, and my fingers roamed all over his chest, and when I straddled his waist and pressed my mouth to his, he didn't stop me. He gripped my hips and flipped me over onto my back, his weight heavy between my legs. Excitement rushed through me. Thanks to my courage, we were finally going to make out.

We did, and the next day, I asked him if we were officially dating.

It must've been the beer he'd been drinking on the beach, or maybe it was just Hannah and her animal noises, because he laid it all out for me: "I liked hooking up last night, but we can't have a relationship because of the band."

The rejection hurt like nothing I'd ever felt. But over the next few months, we kept fooling around anyway. But I really thought we would become more one day. He said the reason we couldn't be together was the band; I figured he would eventually want to take the risk. Because I was worth it. I should've known better. If he had really wanted me, he wouldn't have let being in a band together stop him. I hate that I went down on him—slept with him—when he never had any intention of making things serious.

I examine a pair of blue boots. "How about you? Do you have a girlfriend?"

"I don't date," Jesse replies. "My last girlfriend? Turned out she was selling secrets about me to the tabloids."

"I remember hearing about that last year."

Rumor had it Jesse was dating Stacey Oliver, the daughter of his drummer, and she told a reporter that Jesse was obsessed with doing freaky things in bed. The story was on the cover of every magazine down at the Quick Pick.

When Jesse found out Stacey had betrayed him, he fired his drummer. Walked right into his studio and told him to get the hell out. And then Stacey showed up outside Omni, crying for Jesse to give her dad his job back, and security made her leave. An article detailing the drama filled the front page of the *Tennessean*.

"She sounds like an idiot too," I say. "Did you get in trouble with Mr. Logan or your record company for all those rumors?"

"Some major stores threatened to drop my records because they didn't like what Stacey said about me. The stores said I need a clean image, considering my audience is mostly teen girls."

"Oh, I thought your audience was the old lady convention from lunch."

Jesse gives me a look. "Mark said any publicity is good publicity, but my parents weren't happy. The story embarrassed them in front of their church friends...and my dad's boss at his accounting firm wasn't happy. They're all about 'family values.'" Jesse makes finger quotes. "And honestly, I was pretty embarrassed myself. I'm glad my pa wasn't around for it..."

"But it wasn't true, was it?"

"Wouldn't you like to know?" he flirts, and I playfully slap his hand. "Of course it's not true. I want what every normal guy wants in bed."

"Oh." I feel my face burning hot. I can't help but wonder what normal guys want in bed. I've only done it the one time with Nate. And he finished before the song we were listening to was over. He didn't cuddle with me or tell me how nice I felt; he just put his clothes back on and asked if I wanted a snack.

When he cut things off between us last week, I can only assume it was because I wasn't what he wanted.

I spend a lot of time thinking about what great sex with a guy must be like. Nate never gave me goose bumps. Maybe I should've paid more attention to my body when it was trying to tell me it wasn't getting what it needed from him. But when all your friends are hooking up, you want to do it too, to be normal, even if it doesn't feel exactly right.

"So you haven't dated since then?" I ask.

"I trusted Stacey, and then it turned out I couldn't. I thought I could trust my parents too."

"What do you mean?"

He pulls in a deep breath. "They were excited when I first started out in the business. They wanted me to be a Christian singer, but that just wasn't me. I thought they'd support me no matter what."

"Go on."

"Mark said that I'd be a lot more famous and make more money if I went mainstream, and honestly, I wanted to sing about fishing and family, not God. My parents were fine when I was singing about horses and how much I love Tennessee, but they hated when I started writing about girls a couple of years ago. It was like they'd rather I fail than embarrass them in front of my dad's boss and their church friends. They stopped wanting to spend time with me and started making excuses..." He taps his finger on a pointy spur. It looks painful. "If the music I perform is going to continue to create this rift between me and my parents, then I need to give it up."

"Is that why you're retiring?" I ask.

After a long moment, Jesse nods. "Partly. I want a normal life too. I love music more than anything, but not if it costs me everything."

"I'm sorry," I say quietly. I can't imagine giving up music for any reason, but I've never had to experience pressure like he has. It sucks that his parents aren't supportive of his musical choices. It sounds like a complicated situation, and I don't understand, because my family has always been there for me. Family should support you no matter what, but I guess sometimes that doesn't happen.

Jesse points at some fire-red boots. "I think you need a pair of those."

"Don't be ridiculous. I can't color-coordinate my boots with my corset lace."

Jesse considers this, then points across the room. "You're right. You're getting those purple python boots instead."

"Oh, hell no."

The woman comes out of the storeroom carrying a box, which she hands to Jesse. He pulls out a spur covered with skulls and diamonds.

I crack up. "Why do you need those?"

"Why *don't* I need them is the question. They match my belt buckle." He lifts up his T-shirt, revealing the skull he wore at his concert.

"My fault," I say, rolling my eyes. "I was unaware the belt buckle had diamonds on it. The spurs make perfect sense now."

Jesse sits down, rolls up his jeans, and slips the spurs over his red boots. "Big-time."

Smiling, Rosie folds her hands together, lifting them to her chin.

He adds, "Rosie—can you grab me a pair of those Laredo boots with the flames? I'd like to try them on. And a pair of those purple Dingos for my friend. Size?"

"No way," I say.

Jesse grabs my leg and yanks off my ankle bootie in one movement.

"Hey!" I shout.

He peers inside my boot. "She wears a seven, Rosie," Jesse says, and the saleslady scurries to the back.

I grab my bootie from his hand. "If you're retiring in two months, why are you buying new spurs to perform in?"

He shrugs. "I like helping out local shops."

A couple of minutes later, Rosie has me sit down on a plush bench as she opens a long brown shoe box and pulls out the purple boots.

"These are so not me," I say.

"Stand up and model," Jesse replies, so I put the boots on and walk back and forth in front of him like when Mom took me shoe shopping as a kid.

"I don't like how they look, but they feel almost as awesome as the leather in that GT," I tell Jesse, which makes him smile.

"Then you're getting them."

"How much?" I ask Rosie.

"Five hundred."

"About four hundred and eighty out of my price range."

"If you change your mind, just come back," Rosie says. "Those boots were made for you."

Just like that GranTurismo? I'm sorry, but these boots and that Maserati weren't made for me. They were made for country music stars.

Jesse admires the boots with flames. "Oh boy. I'm getting these Laredos though."

"But the spurs don't match," I say with a laugh.

"Guess I'll have to order some more spurs then. Rubies, maybe?"

I shake my head with a smile, glad that his temper seems to have cooled.

But how damaged is he?

♪♫♩

"I miss doing stuff like that," Jesse says and nods at the playground across the street. He tucks his Nashville Spur Emporium box into the Harley's saddlebag.

The playground is filled with toddlers and chatting moms. There's a jungle gym, a merry-go-round, swings, and a sandbox. A little girl is throwing pennies into a marble fountain with a fish statue that's spurting water.

Maybe the key to helping him feel better is to make him feel like a kid again. I grab his arm. "Come on."

"Where're we going?"

"To swing." I grin at him, and he returns it.

"You gonna push me?"

"You're a big boy. You can pump by yourself."

We sit on the swings by the sandbox, where four little boys are building a castle. I swing higher and higher, my short black skirt flapping in the wind. Jesse starts laughing as he zooms higher than me. I pump harder to beat him. It's a nice moment—just me and him and the blue sky. I hum the Charlie Brown theme song; it's been stuck in my head since Jesse played it on the piano.

"Can I ask a personal question?" he asks.

It makes me happy he's starting to open up. "Of course."

"So you didn't want Mark to put you in a recording booth, but you want to become a musician?"

"I do. More than anything."

"Then why not let us record you so you could have the experience? I thought that's why you wanted to spend today with me."

"I'd love to be recorded, but I need a band for that."

"What for?"

"I can't do solos."

He stops pumping his legs, and his swing begins to slow. "You sang just fine on your own this morning."

"But that was just for you and Holly. When I'm in front of big crowds, something always goes wrong. I like it when the audience has somewhere else to look besides me."

"You have a good voice. You don't need a band to perform."

"You don't get it. You've always performed solo. I like being part of something, you know? That's why I started The Fringe."

"Which turned into a heavy metal band?"

"Yeah…"

"Do you even like heavy metal?"

"No, not really," I say quietly.

"Then why were you playing it?"

Okay, so maybe I don't want him asking hard personal questions. "Because I love performing."

"Then why can't you do it by yourself?"

"I just can't."

I jump off the swing and go over to the hopscotch court. He follows me. I start skipping through the numbered squares to try to escape, but Jesse reaches out and grabs my elbow. He puts his hands on my shoulders and bores into me with those caramel eyes.

"You okay? I talked to you about my life. You can talk to me."

Do I really want this big star to know the most embarrassing thing that has ever happened to me? No, I don't, because I'm ashamed of what happened. I don't want him to think I'm a talentless loser and decide I'm not worth his time. But he told me about his ex-girlfriend and his parents…and when you think about it, what happened to me is nothing compared to Jesse's ex telling the tabloids that he gets freaky in bed. As someone who has had his secrets shared, I bet he'll keep mine.

"In seventh grade, I was singing a solo at a concert at school. It was awful because I locked my knees and fainted."

Jesse cringes but gestures for me to keep talking.

I take a deep breath. "When I fainted, I busted my chin on the stage and had this terrible bruise for a long time. But what really hurt was how much kids made fun of me. After that, I never wanted people to look at me while I was performing. I quit the choir for a while too, but I ended up rejoining."

"What made you go back?"

This is embarrassing to admit, but I told myself I would tell the truth. "I kept with it because of you."

"Me?" he blurts.

I suck in a deep breath. If Nate or Hannah or anybody from The Fringe heard me say this, they'd make fun of me for all time. "Your second album came out around the time I fainted. 'Agape' was on the radio all the time, and my dad said, 'if that boy can do big concerts for thousands of people, you can sing in the choir.'"

Jesse turns his gaze away from mine and rubs the back of his neck, furrowing his eyebrows. "I had really bad stage fright when I first started performing. But I worked through it. Did you?"

"I rejoined choir," I say. "But I didn't sing another solo until the talent show last spring. I was upset that my band wouldn't perform, so I decided to go for it by myself. But my voice cracked...and I felt like this big joke. I sucked."

"Your voice isn't a joke. Up until it cracked, your performance in the talent show was pretty good."

I trip over my feet as I'm hopping from block number 4 to 5. "How do you know that?"

He grins. "At first I wasn't sure about you shadowing me, but then Uncle Bob showed me your 'Bohemian Rhapsody' video."

I groan. "He showed it to you?"

"Yeah—it was big-time. You should put it on YouTube."

"It's *already* on YouTube. It's called 'The Siren.' Ugh." I jump through the hopscotch blocks again. "So when did you see the video?" I ask.

"Right after you left my dressing room last week."

"You were so mean to me that night!"

He looks over at the merry-go-round, watching it circle in place. "I'm sorry. I figured you'd be like all those other screaming girls, and I was in a grouchy mood, I guess."

"Because of your parents? Because they didn't show?"

He nods and hops through the numbered blocks. "You were mean to me too, you know. When you stormed out of my dressing room, I thought, *Who is this mean, sexy punk girl?*"

"I am not mean!"

The side of his mouth quirks up. "You're mean as hell. Always yelling at me and telling me what to do."

"Someone has to." I step closer to him and shove his stomach. He retaliates by grabbing me around the waist. His cologne smells so good, and I can barely fight the urge to rest my cheek against the white T-shirt covering his strong chest. He tickles my side, and I jerk away, laughing, and that's when he pulls me up against him for real. His body presses to mine, and his warmth radiates down to the tips of my toes.

"Seriously though," he whispers. "If you want to sing on your own, just keep working at it, and don't worry if people make fun of you. There will always be critics, but you have to trust your instincts. If you're serious about being a musician, you can't let other people decide what music you should play… You could end up going down a path that you were never meant to take… and then you could end up living a life that's not *yours*."

He suddenly takes a step back and looks away, putting distance between us that somehow feels greater than when we first met.

That's when he jerks his head at the two reporters who have been following us. Behind them, a few moms with toddlers are taking pictures of Jesse with their cell phones, nudging each other and pointing at us.

"I can see the headlines now," he says. "Jesse Scott Plays Hopscotch with Mean Sexy Punk Girl."

I stick my tongue out at him and start hopping through the blocks again, and then Jesse jumps in too.

"You don't care about being in the tabloids?" I ask.

"My parents care." He hops through the blocks again. "But Mark says nearly any kind of publicity is good. You know, except joining a cult or hiring a hit man."

"Don't you think Mr. Logan is worried since you just took off after lunch?"

At that, Jesse takes out his phone, pushes a button, and puts the receiver to his ear. "Guess what I'm doing?… Playing hopscotch… No, I'm not making that up, Mark… Yes, I'm wearing my boots… No, I'm not telling you where I'm at… I don't care if Uncle Bob's mad—we're having a nice time. He called *eight* times?… Tell him not to worry. We haven't done anything against the law. Yet."

That's when I remember to check my cell—I don't think I've ever gone so long without checking it—and discover four missed calls from the school number I dialed earlier, two missed calls from my mother, a text from Dad telling me I'm grounded (I wasn't aware he knew how to send texts), ten texts from my brother demanding an explanation for why I went off the grid on shadow day, and one from Jordan telling me to disregard everything my brother says and enjoy myself.

I can't believe Dr. Salter told on me to my parents! I am going to be in such deep shit when this day is over. I text Jordan and ask her to tell my family and Dr. Salter that everything is fine and put my phone back in my purse as Jesse ends his call.

Jesse walks over to the marble fountain, fishes a penny out of his pocket, and lobs it into the water.

"What'd you wish for?"

"If I tell you, it won't come true."

I'm so glad he seems happier than this morning. Maybe he needs more fun in his life. Fun, without a rhythm. Like how he ditched today's schedule. We should do more of that.

I slip my ankle booties off. "Here's some publicity for you!" I step into the fountain and start splashing around in the chilly water. I shriek at the cold and the joy.

The reporters aim their cameras at me, and Jesse grins and pulls his red boots and socks off. He rolls his jeans to his knees and hops in.

We splash and throw coins at each other, and I try to push him down, but he escapes through the water. The little kids rush over and squeal and try to join us. Their moms scoop them up, horrified, but not so horrified that they can't snap pictures with their phones.

A cop gallops up on a massive brown horse, and Jesse and I tear out of the fountain and grab our shoes. The cop is on our tail!

Laughing, we dart across the street to his bike, water dripping off us.

"I like your job, Jesse Scott!"

Crash Into Me

We take off on Jesse's bike to escape the horse cop and then drive at, like, seventy miles an hour down back roads in Brentwood until we lose the paparazzi. When he pulls over to the side of the road so we can regroup, we're both out of breath when we take off our helmets.

"I don't think we can go back to my house," he says. "I bet my uncle and Mark will be waiting there."

"That sucks. I was really looking forward to playing your double-neck Fender Strat."

He scratches the back of his neck. For a second, I expect him to say the polite thing—that maybe I can play his guitar another time. But then I remember who I'm talking to. Somehow over the course of the afternoon, Jesse Scott started feeling like a regular ole guy. But he's not.

It's only three o'clock. The schedule said shadow day is over at three-thirty, but I'm not ready to leave my new friend yet. Is that what we are? Friends? I would like that, but how can I make it happen?

"What do you want to do now?" I ask.

He shrugs.

"Let's just drive," I tell him.

As he zooms down country roads, my heart finally begins to slow. Did I really just run from a cop? I laugh at the idea, vibrations filling my chest. Jesse must feel it, my happiness, because his back relaxes against my front. I hold on tight as he dips around curves and flies over hills. He slides to a stop at a small gravel path leading into some woods. We're *way* out in the country.

After exchanging his helmet for his cowboy hat, he takes my elbow and leads me up the gravel path into the woods. Birds chirp and sing, and I can't hear anything man-made. No traffic, no tractors, no talking. It's just us.

The gravel turns into a dirt path, which winds through the dense green trees. We walk for about five minutes until the path empties us in front of a sparkling lake. It's tiny—not anywhere as big as Normandy Lake—but it's a beautiful blue.

"Where are we?"

"My pa—my great-grandfather—used to bring me here as a kid. It's his fishing hole. It was our secret."

"And you brought me here?" I whisper.

Avoiding my stare, he adjusts his hat. "You said to just drive… and this is where I ended up. It felt right."

I gaze out at the calm, blue water. "Do you come here a lot?"

"When I need to be alone, yeah. I write a lot of my songs here. I feel closer to my pa, you know?"

"So you were really close?"

He nods sadly. "He taught me to play guitar. He always encouraged me, but he never got to see me make it big. He had a bad hip, see, and one day…one day, he fell down the stairs, hit his head, and didn't wake up."

I touch Jesse's elbow. "You must miss him, huh?"

"Yeah." Jesse's voice sounds raw with emotion. "To be honest, I've kinda felt alone ever since he died."

"I get that. I've never really felt like I truly belong…with my choir, and now my band, and even my family."

"Nothing wrong with being a solo artist," he says with a small smile.

If there's anything I've learned today, aside from the amazing lesson from Jesse and Holly, it's that singing by myself is not as scary as before. I stayed calm when I sang for him, and my voice didn't crack. Maybe one day, I could try a solo on my own again. I do prefer being part of a band though, where I don't have to carry all the weight all the time.

Seeing Jesse all on his own and lonely, I can't help but wonder if being a big star would be easier for him if he was part of a group. If he were part of something larger than himself.

"This seems like a good place to write," I tell Jesse. "I usually write on our back patio."

"You write too?"

"Uh, well, I write, but I don't write well."

"You got any of your stuff?"

Crap. I didn't expect he'd actually want to read it. With a trembling hand, I reach into my purse and pull out my tiny Moleskine journal, the black one with gold trim that my brother gave me for Christmas. The small songbook is too pretty for my crappy songs, but I love writing in it. It makes me feel special, like the music I put in the notebook is important.

Jesse sits on the grass, takes his boots and socks off, and rolls up his jeans to dip his feet in the water. As he opens my tiny songbook, I skim my fingers across the lake's surface. It's cold but not freezing, so I copy Jesse and take off my booties. It reminds me of how we jumped in that fountain a little while ago. But this lake is quiet and intimate, and what we did at the playground feels like a million years ago.

He flips from page to page in my Moleskine. He stops on a page and holds it out to me. "You got a melody for this?"

I nod.

"Sing it to me," he says. "But make sure you sing from your diaphragm, okay?"

He wants me to sing a song *I wrote* without a guitar? No piano for backup? Just my voice? That's crazy.

But Jesse put himself out there for me today, telling me about his life. Not judging me when I told him that my family couldn't afford music lessons. He didn't laugh when I told him about fainting onstage or when I told him about losing the band I started.

I can put myself out there too. I take a deep breath. I tap out a beat on my leg, then sing the song I wrote after Nate turned me down at the beach last spring. Jesse drags a hand through his floppy brown hair when I sing my favorite line, "I tell you again and again, but only the darkness hears."

The words aren't lyrical—some are choppy even—but my chest burns every time I sing this song, because it's filled with my feelings.

When I'm done, Jesse doesn't say anything about the song. He just takes the songbook out of my hands and turns the page. He truly is a tough critic. But that only makes me want to work harder. I may not like country, but the guy knows his stuff, and I respect his opinions.

Jesse reading my lyrics makes me nervous, so to distract myself, I stand and wade out a few feet into the fishing hole.

He reads part of another song aloud: "I'm a tiny swatch of quilt, and I want to be sewn into your heart."

"Ugh, that's terrible. I don't even remember writing that. I plead insanity."

Jesse yodels the line Dolly Parton style. "I want to be sewn into your hearrrrrttttt," he croons, and it makes me snort.

"Stop making fun of me!"

He sets my songbook on the ground, jumps to his feet, and starts serenading me with a pretend microphone in hand, "I'm a tinnnnnnnnnny swatch of quillllltttt."

I giggle. "Stop it!" I push his chest as hard as I can, causing him to stumble backward. Realization dawns on his face right before he splashes onto his butt.

Oops.

He pulls himself to his feet, water sloshing around him. His clothes are soaked from neck to ankles. He fumbles for his hat as it floats away from him.

"Are you crazy, Maya? It's September. It's freezing!"

"It's seventy degrees outside, you big baby."

He wades over, shaking the water from his hair, and I'm thinking *God, water makes this boy even sexier* when he grabs me by the wrist. I try to escape, but he playfully yanks me toward him. I scream so loud you could hear me on the moon. The water goes up to my waist. My dress billows and I have to hold it down to make sure my underwear stays covered.

"You jerk!" I yell.

"Tell me something I haven't heard before," he says, smiling down at me.

"Fine. I think your new spurs are ugly."

"Oh, you did not."

"Did."

"That's it." He chases after me, but I quickly wade back onto the banks and throw my arms around a skinny tree trunk so he can't pull me in.

Breathing hard, he pushes the wet hair out of his face and

follows me to the shore. He reaches over his shoulder and pulls his T-shirt off in one movement, and then he removes his jeans, revealing a pair of navy blue boxers.

Confident, much?

As he's laying his clothes on the grass to dry, I let go of the tree and smooth my wet dress back into place, staring at him. His Celtic tattoo is giving me heart palpitations. "What is it with you and hanging out in your underwear?"

"I told you this is what I do on Fridays."

"And Thursdays," I reply.

"And Wednesdays." With a laugh, he starts to move toward me again. I dart away through the grass. Is this really happening? Is Jesse Scott chasing me in his boxers?

"Marco," he calls out.

"Polo."

Soon, my only escape is back into the water. It hits my knees as I splash away from him. "Turn around," I say.

"Why?"

"I'm gonna ditch my dress—it's too heavy when it's wet—and then we can go for a swim." *Did I just ask Jesse Scott to go swimming in our underwear?* Yes, I think I did. I reach around to pull my zipper down, and that's when I see his face fall.

"I told you I don't swim," he says.

I slowly take my fingers off my zipper and move closer to him. He grabs the back of his neck, staring down into the water, which barely reaches his shins. Is he scared to come deeper?

"What happened on the yacht?" I ask quietly.

He turns, giving me a view of his tattoo. "It was stupid."

"You can talk to me."

He stares up at the sky, his back still turned toward me. "You know *Wannabe Rocker*?"

Just thinking of the show and what The Fringe could have been—and won't be—makes my heart start racing so hard it hurts. I sweep my bleached hair behind my ears. "Of course," I say, calmly as I can. "That's how you got your start."

"Mark wanted me to become a judge for the show next season. You know, to improve my reputation?"

"What's wrong with your rep? I mean, besides the whole falling off the yacht thing."

"Ha ha," he says sarcastically, giving me a look. "I wanted to be seen as an adult artist, so I said I didn't wanna do any more photo shoots for those tween bop magazines. And Mark got scared I'd lose my fan base if I gave them up."

"Was this before you decided to retire?"

"Yeah." He musses his wet hair.

I stretch out on the banks to warm myself in the sun. "What does this have to do with falling off a boat?"

Jesse gives me an amused shake of the head. "You are obsessed with me."

"I know...and with the pending shortage of tween magazines featuring your face, I have no idea what I'm gonna do with my spare time. Can we get back to the boat already?"

"Last June, Mark invited me and all these Hollywood types to a party on his yacht so we could seal the deal for me to become a judge on the show. So we're on the yacht with all these people I don't know, and all I can think about is this field trip I took in fourth grade. My class went on a riverboat cruise on the Cumberland."

"Oh yeah! We did that too. There was even a swing band. It was fun. We're having our graduation cruise in June on a riverboat too."

"Well, during my field trip, I loved hearing that band. I thought it would be cool to sing on the Belle Carol one day."

I smile. I can't believe Jesse Scott got his inspiration from the Belle Carol Riverboat.

He goes on, "So after the field trip, I told my pa, and he signed me up for singing lessons. After the first session, Holly said I was a prodigy and should be singing professionally. She encouraged me to try out for *Wannabe Rocker*, so Pa helped me make an audition video, and a few weeks later, I was accepted onto the show. That's how it all started. Life hasn't slowed down since."

"Being on the yacht made you think about all this?" He nods, so I add, "And this isn't what you wanted out of life?"

He shakes his head. This must be what he was talking about

earlier, how you can end up leading a whole life you were never meant to lead. For me, it was letting Nate take over my band that landed me on the wrong path. But I don't buy that Jesse wasn't born to showcase his talent.

"Jess, you were meant to perform. Other people would kill to have your voice—"

He interrupts, "I'm about to turn nineteen. I can't go to the grocery store without getting mauled—Grace has to do everything for me, or I have to have stuff delivered. You saw what happened earlier—I couldn't even go to lunch without being interrupted for an autograph. My manager basically raised me. I have no friends—"

Suddenly he picks up a rock from the shore and hurls it into the water. He watches the surface ripple and wave until it smoothes. Then he sits down next to me on the grass. "I just sat there on the yacht that night, thinking all I wanted was to perform on the Belle Carol Riverboat. Now no one I used to know from school will talk to me anymore, 'cause I won't give them money and record deals…not that I wanna talk to them anyway. And my parents were still angry with me because my girlfriend blabbed about our sex life."

"So you were lonely?" He nods, and I swallow hard and ask with a shaky voice, "You weren't trying to die or anything, right?"

"Of course not." Jesse bends over and drops his forehead onto his crossed arms. "I drank, like, half a fifth of Jack Daniel's and slipped and fell off the boat."

"Half a fifth?" I exclaim.

"I'd never actually drank before—or after—that night."

"Wait—why did you ask if I wanted to get drunk earlier today?"

He tousles his wet hair, peeking up at me. "Maybe I was testing you a bit."

I stick my tongue out at him. "You sure know how to do things up the first time. You practically get a record deal during your first singing lesson, and then you totally wipe out during your first alcoholic experience."

"I always say go big or go home."

I stretch out my legs and wiggle my toes, drying them in the sun. "Do you still love singing and playing guitar?"

"More than anything."

"So what are you gonna do when you retire?"

He looks to the opposite shore. "No idea."

"Then why would you quit?"

"I don't have a choice, Maya. I can quit or never have a real life. Right now, I don't have anything but my music. Not friends, not family."

"Haven't you ever tried to make friends with other people in the industry?"

He nods. "It's hard though. You never know if someone likes you for you. I used to spend time with Candy Roxanne, you know, the country singer? Then I realized she never wanted to hang out at home, watching a movie or listening to music. We always had to be seen somewhere together, like at a party or a restaurant, and people were always taking pictures that ended up in *People* and *Us Weekly*. It was never about friendship. She just wanted to be seen with me. And you know what happened with my ex, Stacey."

"But not everybody will use you. Some people *are* good, Jess..."

We sit, listening to birds singing, to wind blowing through the trees. To the beautiful song of Tennessee.

"Marco," I say.

"Polo."

I tentatively scoot his way. "Marco."

"Polo."

I crawl over next to him, touch his forearm. His brown eyes look so pretty and warm in the late afternoon sun. He touches my dress, twisting the black tulle in his hand. "I ruined your outfit."

"I know."

"I've liked getting to talk to you today. You're different."

"So are you."

His lip upturned, he leans back onto his hands, squinting at me, and I pull my eyes away from the line of water trickling down his flat stomach into places I still shouldn't be thinking about.

He catches me looking. "Sure you don't wanna have sex?"

I slap his arm. "Would you behave?"

He grins. "So what's up next?"

"As soon as our clothes are dry, I'm driving your Harley."

♪♫♩

Jesse tells me that his favorite part of being a musician is writing. It makes him feel calm and excited all at once. Calm, because it's quiet, and he gets the opportunity to think. Excited, because he never knows what might come out of his pen onto the paper. I've never been much of a writer, but I love that feeling of success, like when I figure out how to play a particularly hard transition.

"So you do all your writing at your Pa's fishing hole?" I ask.

"I've got a few other places too. My studio is one. The other is a secret."

"Tell me!"

He grins. "Are you serious about driving my bike?"

"You better believe it."

"I trust you after seeing you drive that red car earlier. You know the way back to Second Avenue in Nashville?"

As I climb on his Harley, I feel like I'm hitting a high C, the note that, as an alto, I always have problems singing. With Jesse securely behind me, I kick-start the bike and carefully steer it back onto the road. It's a lot bigger than my Suzuki, but I manage it okay. I head toward downtown Nashville at seventy miles per hour. Jesse clutches my hips as I speed through yellow lights.

Zooming down Franklin Road, we pass by Vanderbilt University and the Frist Art Museum. I honk and wave at the NashTrash Tour's Big Pink Bus as I drive down tree-lined stretches of road, passing by Music Row and heading for the waterfront.

At Second Avenue, I pull over and park. Jesse takes off his helmet and sits on the Harley, panting for several seconds. "Good God, woman. Never again!"

"You're just jealous I'm a better driver."

He leads me to a Chinese restaurant, and I'm about to ask if he's craving dim sum when I see a small sign with an arrow pointing down to a place called the Underground.

Is he taking me into the sewer? When we reach the bottom of the mossy, crumbling stone steps, he pushes open a door, and I gasp. A used record store. It's totally hidden away. How has it stayed in business?

I feel like I've stepped into a time machine. Band posters and magazine articles coat the walls, and tables filled with used CDs, DVDs, magazines, records, VHS tapes, video games, and cassettes stretch the length of the room. Cardboard cutouts line the aisles: Eddie Vedder, Mariah Carey, John Lennon, Cher, Jimi Hendrix, Aretha Franklin, Jim Morrison.

Jesse nods at the guy running the cash register. The boy salutes Jesse, then goes back to plucking away at his bass. The place is empty except for a few customers who are digging through stacks of magazines and DVDs. I wonder if they're looking for something in particular or just browsing, because I could spend my whole life looking through everything that's here.

Jesse wanders over to the classical section as I beeline for the rock. In a relaxed silence, he and I dig through milk crates and boxes full of cracked CD cases and old records coated with dust. I discover a Queen Christmas album that I might buy.

"Got it," Jesse says, slapping a CD against his palm.

He'd been fishing around in a milk crate for a couple of minutes. With his gaze fixed firmly on mine, he grabs my hand and leads me to a rope ladder in the corner. It goes up to what looks like a loft.

"That's the listening room," he says. "You can take records and CDs up there if you want to relax and listen to music. I write there when I need to get out of the studio."

"This is your special place?" I ask.

"Yeah."

We climb up into a cozy crawlspace with a low ceiling. I scoot across the floor and rest on an elbow. The loft is dark, only lit by black lights and a glimmer of sunlight streaming through a peephole. It smells like patchouli and incense. Patterned pillows and velvet cushions are everywhere.

"Do you like it?" Jesse asks, taking off his hat.

"I might have to steal your secret spot. I would love to hole up in here with my guitar."

He puts the CD in the stereo while I take a look at the case: *The 50 Most Essential Pieces of Classical Music*. The first song is Adagio in G Minor.

I relax onto a purple quilted cushion and listen to the violin as Jesse writes in his notebook. It's insane to think he could be composing the next Grammy-winning song of the year right next to me. I'm glad he's getting a chance to write, since this is what he likes to do on his day off. He's taught me so much today, I want to do something for him.

I swipe my cell screen and check the details for the Belle Carol Riverboat online, then find a text from Dave: Saw pics of you on Access Hollywood!!!!!!

There are pictures of me online? Dr. Salter is going to kill me. I won't just get a detention; I'll be in detention until I graduate. I scroll through the rest of my messages. My sister sent no fewer than twenty texts reminding me to get Jesse's autograph for her.

I hold my breath when I read a text from Hannah, asking if we can talk. I don't know what there is to say. She just stood there while the guys kicked me out of The Fringe. Not to mention that she's with Nate now. Granted, she didn't know I had feelings for him and we'd been fooling around, but still. I don't feel like talking to her.

I text Dave back: Best day ever.

Today really has been the best day. We're getting to be real friends. But what if that feeling is one-sided and I never see him again? What if he cuts off all contact with everyone after he quits the business? It's not like people will suddenly stop mobbing him just because he doesn't record albums anymore. How will he feel when he's no longer playing music full time, after he's given up his heart? He loves singing and playing guitar and loves being onstage, but that's being drowned by all the drama offstage.

Maybe all he needs is a real good friend.

And then my cell buzzes. Dave is calling.

"Is it okay if I take this, Jess?" I ask, and he nods. "Hi," I answer.

"Hey. I saw you almost got arrested for jumping in a fountain with Jesse Scott. There's a video of you running from a cop."

I cover my mouth. Yup, detention is definitely in my future. "Yeah. Jesse's kind of crazy. How'd working at the Donut Palace go?"

"I learned how to make a bear claw!"

"Would you shut up about the bear claw already?" I hear a guy say in the background. It must be Xander, Dave's college boy he met at Taco Bell.

I take a peek at Jesse. He's very interested in the purple cushion all of a sudden. Is he sad?

"How's it going with you, My?" Dave asks.

"It's been a great day," I reply, and Jesse looks up at me.

"Tell whoever it is I said hi," Jesse whispers.

"Tell him yourself. His name is Dave." I pass the phone to Jesse, who takes a deep breath.

"Hello?… I'm not gonna lie, she's pretty nuts. She hijacked our whole day. We were supposed to go on these educational tours, and then Maya kidnapped me and made me go test-drive a sports car, and then she made me play hopscotch and go shopping for boots… Yeah, I'm being totally serious… Oh, and she won't have sex with me either."

I snatch the phone out of Jesse's hand and put it to my ear, giving him a look. He lies back on a cushion, dying of laughter. "Pay no attention to Jesse Scott. He's ridiculous."

"Girl, he wants to have sex?" Dave blurts. "Take your clothes off!"

I tell Dave I'll text him later and hang up, setting my phone on the floor. It makes me happy that Jesse was willing to talk to Dave on the phone. Maybe Jesse's not as closed off as he thinks he is.

The classical CD switches to a new song—a piano medley. It's really relaxing, and I can see why Jesse loves writing in this loft.

And that's when it dawns on me.

I'm lying next to Jesse Scott.

This is a far cry from when I used to lie on my bed at home and stare at the poster of him tacked to my ceiling.

I suck in a deep breath.

"So," he says and props himself on an elbow, looking down at me—like a real-life-size poster.

"So."

His eyes trail over my legs, and he softly sweeps a hand up my arm. It makes me shiver, even though the loft is nice and toasty and I'm feeling warm all over. A sliver of sunlight streams through the tiny window as I stare into his beautiful eyes and he looks back into mine, and I wonder how it would feel to dig my fingers into his silky brown hair that curls around his ears down to his shoulders. He slips his fingers in between mine and rubs my palm with his thumb. This feels even more personal than seeing him in his underwear, and that makes me laugh nervously.

His mouth lifts into its signature smirk. "What?"

"Nothing," I say, struggling for air.

He edges closer, tangling his boots with mine, and my mind goes to war with itself, wondering if I want him to kiss me—of course I do!—but also liking who he is as a person and not wanting to mess up something that might become a friendship, especially when we both need a friend.

"Jess, I told you you're not my type."

"You're not my type either, Maya Henry."

A voice calls from downstairs. "Jesse, man, the store's starting to fill up. School's out, you know?"

"Thanks, P.J.," he calls down, then turns to me. "We should get out of here before people discover we're up here and mob us."

I let out a long breath, glad that the moment—whatever it was—is over.

We start to climb down the rope ladder. A few girls see Jesse and start freaking, but we rush out of the store and up the crumbling stone steps. As we walk back to his bike, Jesse asks how I got to be friends with Dave.

"In third grade at recess, this totally bitchy fourth grader, Shelley Cross, was talking to a bunch of the girls about how this guy liked her, but she didn't like him. I asked a question, and she yelled in my face, 'It's none of your beeswax!' I started crying, and Dave told Shelley that she had boogers, even though she didn't."

Jesse smiles sadly as we walk up to his bike. "I've never had a friend like that."

I squeeze his hand. "You can have me. I'll be your friend."

His lips part, but he doesn't respond, and I'm kicking myself inside for being so forward. I probably scared him off. Thank heavens my phone beeps and the moment is over.

"No more calls." He snatches my cell from my fingers and pockets it. "This is our day, and I'm not sharing you."

Our Song

"I have a surprise."

"Oh yeah," Jesse replies. "What is it?"

He straightens his cowboy hat, and I scan the boats lining the banks of the Cumberland River. *Good, it's there.* "We've still got some time."

"You're not gonna make me swim in the river, are you? Like as therapy or something?"

I giggle. "Yup. To get over your fears, you're going to meditate and become one with the water."

"Smart-ass," he says, his lips forming an amused smile. "What are we gonna do in the meantime?"

"Not sure."

"Let's go up to Gibson then." We take the brick walkway toward Second Avenue. He doesn't try to hold my hand again like in the loft, but our shoulders rub against each other. "So. You and Dave. You're not together, right? From the way you talk on the phone, it doesn't sound like you have chemistry."

"I would hope not. Dave is gay."

"I figured you weren't with him. I can tell when people hit it off," Jesse announces. "I have precognitive relationship skills."

I snort. "And who have you used your so-called precognitive relationship skills on?"

He pauses outside the door to Gibson. "Holly and her husband, Jay. And I just know Uncle Bob has a thing for Mark."

"Get out! Dr. Salter is gay?"

"Yeah."

"I'm cool with it; I just had no idea. No one at school knows that."

"My parents know." Jesse's body deflates as he leans against the store's brick wall. "They reacted badly when they found out. My dad hasn't spoken to Uncle Bob in almost five years."

Poor Jesse. And poor Dr. Salter.

But jeez—if anyone at school finds out that Dr. Salter is gay, I bet some closed-minded parents would storm the school carrying torches like in some kind of medieval crusade. I hate that about our town, that a lot of people are so closed-minded.

"My parents and grandparents stopped talking to him when they found out," Jesse says. "And I told my grandparents I wasn't coming back for Christmas or Thanksgiving until they let Uncle Bob come, and well, I haven't been over there in years."

"Wow," I say, shaking my head.

"It hasn't been the same since Pa died anyway."

"Good for you standing up to your grandparents like that. But it must be hard not being part of their lives."

Jesse nods. "It's complicated."

If his parents are this judgmental, I have no idea why he values their opinion so much. He must really love them if he's willing to retire from the music business so he can rebuild their relationship. But then again, I stuck with The Fringe for a whole year, even when I didn't want to play metal. I just wanted to belong, to be a part of something.

"Jesse," I whisper. "How will I find another band? What if I can't find people who want to play the same music as me? Should I just settle and play whatever?"

And right there in front of Gibson, on the busiest street in Nashville, he folds me into his arms. A whisper in my ear: "I don't know what's right for you, but even after I retire, I'm not gonna stop playing guitar and writing. Because that's who I am."

Me too. Even if I have to sing stuff like "When the Saints Go Marching In," I love performing, so I might rejoin the show choir. And regardless of whether I find another band, I'm gonna sit on my front porch and play awesome covers of eighties songs. Because that's who I am.

I wrap my arms around his waist and hold on tight. A cacophony of cameras sounds around us as people take pictures with their phones, but I don't care. Even if he didn't answer my offer to be friends, I know we are.

"Can we go in Gibson now?" I ask. "I'm dying to see the new Les Paul."

He pushes the door open, making the little bell on the doorknob jingle. We step inside a music utopia, and I feel crazy lust for the guitars.

A middle-aged man darts up, buttoning his gray suit. "Jesse! It's a pleasure." He keeps his hands folded in front of him.

"Nice to see you, Max," Jesse replies. "Maya, meet Max—he's the manager here."

Max gives me a warm smile and a firm handshake. "I didn't know you were coming or I would've closed the store," Max says to Jesse, swallowing as he looks around at the other customers. Some of them are already staring.

"It's okay. We're just looking around."

Jesse and I head over to the Les Paul section and look up at the new Jimmy Page limited edition electric displayed on the wall.

"Amazing, huh?" I say.

"I like the archtop series myself."

"Want to try it out?" Max calls from across the room.

"Maya wants to," Jesse replies.

A minute later, I find myself cradling this heavenly $15,000 guitar. Max even hooks it up to an old-time Fender amp, so I can hear what it truly sounds like. I pull my lucky pick out of my purse. With trembling hands, I play the first few measures of the Eagles' "Hotel California," and then I start blistering through the guitar solo—one of the toughest there is—and Max's eyes grow wider than supper plates. Some of the other customers crowd around us, staring and beaming at me.

"She playing backup for you now?" Max asks.

"She could be," Jesse replies, taking the Les Paul from my hands. "My turn." He throws the strap around his neck and adjusts the guitar in front of him, and the other customers scream.

Jesse pays them no attention as he starts playing Bon Jovi's "Wanted Dead or Alive." It's like a little concert in the Gibson store, and everyone cheers and claps when he's finished.

He hands the Les Paul to Max. "I'm gonna go look at the Citation for a sec." He strides across the room to look at a guitar that must be worth more than my house.

Max says, "You're welcome to come back and play anytime, Maya."

I look over at Jesse. "Yeah, maybe sometime."

"You don't have to come back with him," Max says. "You just drew a crowd playing solo."

That makes me feel really good. "Thanks! I've always wanted to come in your store—I was excited when Jesse suggested it." I smile over at him. He's staring at the Citation's toggle switch like a scientist examining a molecule under a microscope.

Max lowers his voice. "I've known Jesse for a long time, and he's never brought anyone here but his manager, and even that's rare. He usually makes appointments and comes by himself."

Wow. So coming in here with me was a big change for him. Maybe he would be open to getting out even more. How can I show him he doesn't have to stay holed up, alone and friendless?

"He's such a nice person," I say.

"I'm sure he is. It's a shame he's quitting...I've never had a student who's that good."

"You give lessons?"

Max folds his hands in front of him. "I teach advanced guitar to a few talented people. Some of my students have gone on to get scholarships at Vanderbilt."

"Wow." I would love to go there to study music, but it's very expensive, and the only way I could go is if I win one of those scholarships. I've been planning to try out for one later this fall, but if that doesn't work out, I'll go to Middle Tennessee State. It's more affordable, and the music program is pretty good.

"Are you still in high school?"

I stare down at my boots, then nod.

Max pulls a card out of his wallet and passes it to me. "If you're interested in some lessons, email me. I could help improve your technique."

My hand shakes as I accept the card. "Thank you."

Jesse finally tears himself away from the Citation. "Gotta go, Max. I've got some sort of surprise waiting."

Outside the store, we walk beneath a pink sky toward the waterfront. The sunset gives his face a rosy glow.

"That video Uncle Bob showed me doesn't do you justice. You're really good on guitar."

"Thank you." I tell him about Max offering to give me lessons and how some of his students went on to get big music scholarships. "I'd love to win a scholarship to Vanderbilt, but I don't have the money for lessons…and I doubt I'd do well in auditions, you know, by myself."

"You have to take chances to get a chance at your dreams."

I pause. "Did you graduate high school? Would you consider going to college?"

He stops. "I got my GED, but I have no idea what I'd even study in college. I don't really have other interests besides music. And with my life, it's like I have nothing left to go for. I have all the money I'll ever need. My goal was to win a Grammy, and now I've got three."

"You need a new goal."

"Like what?"

"Figure out how to be happy again."

His face hardens into a frown. "I've been happy today, you know, talking to you about music and your life."

"You really helped me with my technique. And you said you thought something was missing in your life…maybe you could give music lessons?"

He takes a step back. "No way. People don't really want to

learn; they'll just want record deals and favors and shit. They're not like you."

I get right back in his face. "You can't lump all people together like that."

That's when the boat whistle toots. It's time. Shit, we're gonna be late. I start sprinting down to the docks as best as I can in my booties.

Jesse calls out, "Where're you going?" but I keep running. I wait until I've made it to where the boat is docked and turn around. He chases after me in his cowboy boots, holding his hat on his head so it doesn't blow away. When he's close, I run up the plank and hop down onto the riverboat's deck. A sign reads, "Private Party." I can already hear the music.

"No," he says, still on land, out of breath. His eyes glisten as he stares at the Belle Carol Riverboat from the docks. "No way. I can't."

Suddenly the engines roar to a start.

"Come on!" I yell and wave at him to join me. Giving me a desperate glance, he rubs the back of his neck and jogs up the plank and jumps down onto the deck. Seconds later, a boat hand comes up to retract the plank as the boat casts off.

"Remind me to run next time the word 'surprise' comes out of your mouth," Jesse says.

Darkness is beginning to dye the blue sky. I sneak down the hallway, heading for the stairs that lead to the upper deck where music is blaring.

"Maya!" Jesse whispers. "What are you doing? You're gonna ruin the party."

I turn as he catches up to me. "*Au contraire*," I reply, poking him in the chest. "Whoever's party this is will love me forever."

I dart up the steps and find, like, ten thousand purple and pink balloons.

And a hundred young teen girls.

A "Happy 13th Birthday, Katherine!" banner stretches across the wall behind the band.

Jesse emerges from the staircase and swallows hard. "Shit." And the screaming starts.

Girls encircle Jesse, and he looks at me, shaking his head, his lips pursed. I expect him to flip out or be a jerk like the night we met in his dressing room, but then he cracks up. We laugh at each other as the girls swarm him and separate us.

I head toward the stage to approach the band. "Know any Bon Jovi?" I ask the lead singer.

"Sure." The man nods past my shoulder. "Is that Jesse Scott?"

"Yes. And it's his dream to sing on the Belle Carol Riverboat."

"Well, get him up here then."

I grab the mike and say, "Happy Birthday, Katherine! My gift to you is a performance by Jesse Scott!"

I swear, the shrieking is so loud, you could hear it on Pluto. Jesse makes his way up to the stage, the girls hanging all over him like barnacles. Narrowing his eyes at me, he grabs the microphone out of my hand. "Where's Katherine?" he asks, and this skinny girl with glasses pushes her way to the front of the crowd. She raises a trembling hand.

"I also got you a gift," Jesse says. More screaming. Girls are holding cell phones above their heads, taking pictures and recording.

"Thank you," Katherine says, so happy, tears are rolling down her face. She'll be the most popular kid at school after this.

"My gift is a duet," Jesse says and grabs my hand.

"Oh no." I shake my head as I back away. He keeps a firm grip and pulls me close.

He whispers in my ear, "Surprise."

The band starts playing "Livin' on a Prayer." The drums make the stage vibrate, and the guitar's squeal causes my arm hair to get staticky. I love it.

"Nice choice," Jesse says. A mosh pit forms around the stage. We start to sing together, and Jesse's face is happier than I've ever seen it—in person or in the tabloids. Together we belt the lyrics into the microphone, and the girls point at me and take pictures with their cell phones. The back of my neck is damp with sweat, and I shut my eyes, drowning in Jesse's beautiful voice.

On the last verse, Jesse stops singing. I stop singing too, but Jesse elbows me.

"Keep going," he says, dancing to the beat. "You can do this."

I can't let him—or myself—down. I fill my stomach with air like he taught me, and I'm careful not to sing out of my throat. I control my voice, and somehow, it doesn't crack. The new technique works! I can't believe I'm singing a solo in front of an audience. I don't faint, and my voice doesn't crack—I just sing. And, God, it feels good to hear those cheers. It's just like in my dreams.

When the song's over, I whisper-yell in Jesse's ear, "That was so fun!"

"You were great," he replies, helping me off the stage. "Really great."

"Did you have a good time?"

The sun disappears behind the horizon as he whispers in my ear, "Definitely."

"Jesse, how can you give this up?" I ask, grasping his T-shirt.

"Not every day is like this one." His voice breaks. "I want to live."

He gives a bunch of autographs and takes pictures with the kids. And it shocks the bejesus out of me when some girls ask to have their picture taken with me. One who recognizes me from the Access Hollywood video of me running from the horse cop asks for my autograph. News travels fast when it involves Jesse Scott.

"I love your dress," one girl says.

"Are you Jesse's girlfriend?" another wants to know, bouncing on her toes.

"No."

"But he's so great!" another girl squeals.

With my blood still pulsing like crazy, I turn to stare at him as he gets a photo taken with the birthday girl. "Yup, he sure is." I try not to think about what'll happen when this day's over.

When Jesse gives up his love, his music.

When I go back to my life in Franklin.

He looks up from signing an autograph and grins. It's a smile just for me.

Suddenly, I get the feeling this doesn't have to be a one-day thing. That maybe the best day ever can develop into a lot more. Maybe it can become a life where I'm friends with Jesse Scott, where I can sing solos on a regular basis, where I can take chances.

I'm going to work for it.

Story of My Life

Neither of us is ready for our day to end.

When Jesse's sick of schmoozing with the girls (only five minutes later), he gets the boat captain to make a special detour to drop us off at a dock near his motorcycle. The girls wave at us from the deck of the Belle Carol as the captain toots the horn.

Jesse hooks an arm around my waist. "Now what? Dinner?"

A text from Dave says he and Xander are heading over to the Coffee County Fair. It only comes once a year, and I usually go waste my money on the Ferris wheel and bumper cars. I also like to check out the biggest pumpkin contest and the mule races. And it could be another chance to help Jesse feel normal!

His phone rings right then. He pulls it from his pocket and checks the screen. His eyes grow wide as he answers. "Hey, Dad."

The hope disappears from his eyes as he listens. I can hear the shouting. I hear the words "motorcycle" and "riding around town" and "blond floozy."

At that word, Jesse steals a horrified glance at me before darting several feet away. Did his dad really just refer to me as a floozy? I bite down on my lip.

When Jesse hangs up, he lets out a long sigh and looks up at the dark sky.

"You all right?" I ask.

He shrugs, and we just stand here awkwardly. I have no idea what to do. Is Jesse okay? He doesn't look okay.

"Want to hit up the fair? I'm craving a funnel cake," I say, scared because his dad insulted me. I know Jesse wants to make nice with his parents, but I hope he doesn't compromise by ending our day.

Jesse's eyes darken. "I used to go to the fair with my parents when I was little."

I wrap an arm around his side. "I have an idea. Let's invite Dr. Salter and Mr. Logan to meet us."

Your true family.

♪♫♩

At the fairgrounds, we walk through cakey mud to the entrance. The smells of corndogs and popcorn and funnel cakes waft through the cool night air. Lights from the Ferris wheel and booths brighten the inky sky.

We see Dr. Salter and Mr. Logan in front of the arts and crafts booth before they see us. The publicists, Gina and Tracy, are with Mr. Logan, and Jesse's manager and uncle are going on and on about something, hands flailing around. Jesse throws me this pompous knowing grin as we walk up.

My principal gives me the look he saves for kids who get high behind the woodshop at school. "Maya Henry, you have two weeks of detention."

Mom and Dad will kill me. "I might want to rejoin the show choir."

Dr. Salter smiles. "Okay, but you still have two weeks of detention."

"But not tonight, right?"

"No, not tonight."

Then Mr. Logan and Dr. Salter are all over Jesse about our afternoon. He tells them everything. Dr. Salter seems nervous that the press took pictures of us jumping around in a fountain and is worried about repercussions of us running from the horse cop. He's worried the school board will cancel shadow day going forward. Mr. Logan and the publicists think it's all great, of course, because any press is good. And my principal *does* seem pleased that Jesse is smiling. I was worried after the call with his parents, but he seems okay.

"You wore a suit to the fair?" Jesse teases Mr. Logan.

Mr. Logan adjusts his gold watch and ignores Jesse. "What's first?"

"Funnel cake, then the Tilt-A-Whirl."

Later, the four of us do bumper cars, and Jesse keeps ramming us. Mr. Logan yells at him when his gelled hair gets messed up, which makes Jesse laugh so hard he snorts. Then we all ride the teacups and the Ferris wheel.

Jesse and I slide into the seat together, and the fair worker secures the bar in front of us. My shoulder nestles against Jesse's, and he looks over at me. His hand grabs mine as the wheel soars toward the sky.

I pretty much love sailing over Franklin while holding Jesse's hand. Thinking back to this afternoon when we were lounging on the purple cushion, I still can't believe what happened, that he looked deep into my eyes and gently touched my arm. I felt sparks then, and I'm still feeling them now as the Ferris wheel plunges through rushing air back to the earth.

I decide right then that I'm going to take Mom's advice this time: if Jesse really wants me, he'll let me know. *He'll show me.* I haven't had time to pine over Jesse, and I don't want to start. But his calloused fingers—rough like sandpaper from playing guitar—feel so warm and solid in mine. I can't ignore that. I don't know what I'd do if I had the chance to be with him, and that scares and excites me.

There's this anticipation I get when I'm about to strum guitar strings. I get a similar feeling when I look at Jesse. It's a feeling of *I want to be near him*, and *what's next?!*, and I crave that sensation as much as playing guitar. My interest in him has nothing to do with the fact that he's a star. I like him for his temper and his sweetness, his pranks, his protectiveness, his laugh. And damn, when he sings, my skin tingles as if he's kissing me all over.

After the Ferris wheel, we go through the funhouse of mirrors, where Jesse gets trapped by a bunch of younger girls who want pictures and his autograph, so he gets his black Sharpie out and starts signing shirts and scraps of paper. An elementary school girl tells him, "I love 'Agape.' The way you played piano makes me want to learn how, but my parents say I can't right now 'cause they just had a baby and piano lessons...aren't as important." Her voice trails off.

Does that mean her parents can't afford lessons? Jesse looks over at me, and I wonder if he's thinking the same thing—that this little girl's story might be similar to mine. The publicists snap pictures of Jesse with the girl for his website.

And then the four of us head over to the Harvest Dance at the fairground's barn, where a slow Tim McGraw song is playing. Groan.

Bales of hay and large pumpkins fill the barn, and it smells like campfires and hot apple cider. I do love the way the fair people decorated, using wheelbarrows and hay and rusty farm equipment and wildflowers and gourds. Strings of white lights droop from the wooden rafters.

I'm standing elbow to elbow with Jesse when his hand slides into mine. "Wanna dance?"

I swallow and nod.

He leads me onto the dance floor and wraps his hands around my waist. I smile up at him as we dance junior-high style, two feet apart. Lots of gaping kids from school watch us dance. Connor Crocker—a junior at my school—pumps his fist at me, laughing, and I smile back at him.

The paparazzi who've been following us today snap pictures, and Gina and Tracy are managing them, but Jesse doesn't seem to notice. If he's happy, I'm happy. Dr. Salter and Mr. Logan buy cups of hot cider and sit on a bale of hay together, chatting, but they both keep looking over at Jesse, checking on him as if he's a kindergartner.

"What are you thinking about?" Jesse asks quietly.

"You."

"Yeah?" His voice is gravelly and thick, and we go from dancing far apart to having no room between us at all. His chest presses to mine, and I tighten my arms around his neck.

"I'm thinking about you too," he whispers.

The music changes from Tim McGraw to Roberta Flack's "Killing Me Softly."

"This is my favorite song ever," I say.

"You have good taste," he replies, and my heart swells because he respects my music choices. He rests his nose against mine. It's like we're in our little cocoon beneath the brim of his cowboy hat. He softly sings the song to me in the most romantic moment of my life.

And that's when I hear, "Maya, we need to talk."

I turn to find Nate looking mighty pissed. He stumbles back at the sight of Jesse.

"Can I cut in?" Nate asks.

"No, you may not," Jesse says and twirls me away, leaving Nate dazed. I can't help but snort. But what did he want?

We dance until I hear Dave shouting my nickname: "My!" He hugs me, and then I introduce him to Jesse, and I meet the famous Xander of Taco Bell, who is quite cute with his styled blond hair and tight polo shirt.

Mr. Logan and Dr. Salter come and clap Jesse on the back. "We're old," Dr. Salter says with a yawn. "I've gotta hit the sack. You kids okay to get home?"

"We'll be fine. Thanks for coming," Jesse says.

"We should do this kind of thing more often," Dr. Salter replies, patting Jesse's cheek, and then the two men take off for the parking lot.

Jesse nudges me. "Think they're going to get it on?"

"Ew! Too much info." I laugh, and he curls a hand around my waist. It feels really nice to be in his arms. What's happening between Jesse and me isn't lost on Dave and Xander, and they share a knowing look.

"You guys want to get some food at Foothills?" Dave asks.

Jesse looks nervous at the invitation. "I can't. I have a show tomorrow and need to get to sleep soon."

When I hear his words, I stare into the distance at the Ferris wheel as it slows to a stop. Does this mean our night is over? It's barely ten o'clock.

"I'll get her home safe," Jesse says, and Dave excitedly whispers that I need to call him as soon as I get there. I turn to leave with Jesse, and a bunch of kids from school, those annoying publicists, and the press all trail behind us, but really, it's just me and him walking under the sparkling fair lights, my arm curled around his elbow.

♪♫♩

I wrap my arms around Jesse's waist and rest my cheek against his back as he drives me to my house, going extra fast to lose anyone who's still following us. We pull into the driveway, stirring up gravel. Neither of us speaks as I take off my helmet and hand it to him. We still haven't talked about what happens after today. Is this the last time I'll ride his bike?

The last time I'll see him?

Jesse leaves his cowboy hat on his bike, and we walk slowly to the porch, rocks crunching beneath our boots. The stars sparkle down on us, and moths do figure eights in the air.

I stop next to the screen door. "Thank you so much, for everything. I had such a good time."

He squeezes my shoulders. "Me too."

"You never answered my question."

"What question?"

"If we can be friends…"

That smirk of his fills his face. "I hope so. I mean, I'd like that."

My knees wobble in relief when he takes my phone and enters his number, then calls his phone so he'll have mine.

Then he clears his throat. "May I give you a kiss good-bye?"

I smile and lean back against the house. "You may."

He places a hand against the brick above my shoulder, leans in, and gives me a quick peck, his lips barely brushing mine. I let out a soft moan. I've been kissed before—thoroughly—but none of those kisses felt as amazing as this tiny peck. This must be the rush everybody talks about, the rush that makes it impossible to breathe.

When he pulls away, he stares at my mouth.

"Wow," he whispers, burying a hand in my hair. With the other, he runs a thumb across my lower lip. His breathing speeds up, and right when I think he's gonna kiss me again, my stupid brother slams open the screen door.

"What's going on out here?"

"Nothing," Jesse sputters and pulls away from me. Jesse is tall—at least six feet—but my brother is huge, a six-foot-four former football player, so I can forgive the sputtering.

"Who's this guy?" my brother asks, even though he knows damn well who it is.

"Get out of here, Sam! What are you doing here anyway?"

"I was waiting on you to get home so I could have a few words with this country buffoon for running off with you—"

Jordan bursts through the door and grabs my brother by an ear. "Are you insane, Sam? Get your ass back inside now."

"But that jerk is touching my sister!"

"Oh, as if you never touched a girl when you were his age. You touched every girl you saw."

"Quiet, Jordan, or you're going in time-out."

"Time-out, my ass!" She tugs him inside, then pokes her head back out the door. "Nice to meet you, Jesse. I love your work. Especially 'Ain't No City Boy.' No one else can sing about making love on a tractor like that. I love—"

"You only like it 'cause it's about sex," Sam hollers.

"It's not *only* about sex. It's a metaphor! You probably don't even know what a metaphor is, you dumba—"

"Now you're really going in time-out!" my brother says, and I let out a long sigh as they disappear back inside.

Jesse's mouth has fallen open at their spectacle.

"That was my brother and his girlfriend."

He scratches the back of his neck. "I guess I'm glad I'm an only child..."

"Come this way," I say, grabbing his hand and tugging him toward a towering oak tree at the edge of the property. It's swallowed in darkness where we can be alone. Jesse presses me up against the bark, the force stealing my breath away.

He nuzzles his cheek to mine and murmurs, "What are we doing?"

"I'm not sure." I run my fingertips along his strong jaw, unable to keep my hands off him, and I guess that's all the encouragement he needs.

He nudges a knee between mine, threads a hand through my hair. He takes his time, slowly peppering my throat and cheek with kisses. Making my knees weak, making my breath catch. I steady myself by wrapping my arms around his neck as our lips meet again.

The encore blows the first kiss out of the water. His body melts against mine, and his lips feel so soft, his breath warm, his hands strong as they glide over my sides and settle to grip my hips. I kiss the freckles on his face, trying not to miss any.

"You're so sexy. Your nose stud drives me crazy," he mumbles, and the pleasure of his words makes me kiss him harder. "I'd ask if we could do this inside, but your brother's kinda scary."

"It's probably better that we stay out here anyway."

"Oh yeah? Why?" He dives in for another long kiss.

I come up for air. "I'm afraid I wouldn't be able to stop."

"You'd take advantage of me, huh?" I can feel him smiling as he kisses me. "Maybe we can hang out again soon?" he asks.

"What are you doing tomorrow night?"

His lips trail along my neck. "Concert in Atlanta."

I slip my fingers inside the waistband of his jeans, right behind the skull belt buckle, and pull him hard against me. "Atlanta's not far. I could drive down to see you—I'll sit backstage. That'd be so fun."

Suddenly he pulls away from me. He furrows his eyebrows.

"What's wrong?" I ask, pressing a hand to my heart, trying to slow it down.

"You want to come backstage? Why?"

"To be near you." I move to take his hand, but he shoves it into his pocket.

"This was stupid."

My heart practically stops. "What?"

"You don't actually like me, right? You just want to come to my concert and sit backstage. You're shadowing me and want a record deal."

"Jesse, that's not it at all."

"Stacey did shit like this. She always wanted to come backstage, but she only cared about being seen with me. Only cared about what I could get her."

"I don't care about that at all. I just want to be around *you*." I reach to take his hand, but he steps back, wincing like when I first met him. What in the world?

"But why do you want to be near me? 'Cause I'm famous? Because the press was all over you today?"

"You're funny, and you're interesting. You're a great musician… I can't stand country music, but I guess I can deal with a shortcoming or two." I grin. "You're cute as hell. Why wouldn't I want to spend time with you?"

"You said I'm not your type."

My smile disappears. I feel the blood drain from my face. He doesn't trust me. After we spent a day telling each other our secrets and dreams, he still doesn't trust me.

A truck zooms up on the road, getting closer and closer, its white lights blinding me momentarily until it disappears the night.

"And you're thinking the worst of me," I say. "Comparing n to Stacey—which is insulting by the way—and pushing me away, 'cause that's what you do, right? So you can be alone."

He glares. "You should try it. Going solo. It's better that way."

I lean back against the tree's rough bark so I won't slip to the ground. Why did I let him kiss me? It's like being betrayed by Nate all over again, only a million times worse. Kissing Jesse was totally different. I felt that spark, the one everybody talks about. But on top of that, I told Jesse all my secrets, I let him in, and he's ditching me already. Why is it that as soon as I place my faith in others, trust disappears in a second?

"I didn't mean to upset you, Jesse," I say with a shaky voice. "I don't need or want anything from you."

"I didn't mean to upset you, either…it's just that you and me? We'd never work out."

"We haven't even tried to be fr—"

"I guess I'm not ready for this… I don't wanna get your hopes up. I'm sorry."

First he gave me his number, then he kissed me, then he freaked. He's all over the place. I hate that we're losing what could've become a really good friendship for a kiss. Why did I let that happen? Just because today has changed me doesn't mean stuff would change for him too.

"ɪ had a great day," I whisper as tears burn my eyes.

"I did too, darlin'."

I pinch my nose and sniffle.

"Bye, Maya Henry."

"Bye."

He walks backward to his Harley, staring at me, and climbs on. Turns the ignition. His engine roars to a start. The wheels crunch gravel on the way out of the driveway.

I hate that today is ending like this. Hate it. I dart toward the road, waving my arms to get him to stop, but he's too far gone.

I bring my phone to my lips and watch the Harley's lights disappear in the distance.

Bad Day

Saturday, 5:45 a.m.

It's hard to believe that yesterday I played an electric Les Paul in the Gibson store and sang a solo on the Belle Carol Riverboat, and now I'm up to my elbows in grease at Caldwell's. I hope working at the garage will keep my mind off how the best day ever crashed and burned like Axl Rose smashing a guitar.

I shut the back of the Volkswagen bus Dad and I are taking a look at. It's such an old model that the engine is tucked beneath the trunk.

"Want the good news or the bad news first?" Dad asks.

"Bad," Garrett Wainwright replies, pacing back and forth in the shop like it's a hospital waiting room. Garrett is a guy I know from school. I need a new geometry tutor now that Nate and I are no more, and Garrett agreed to tutor me if we'd fix his orange bus. Hence Dad and I are up at the ass crack of dawn, before Caldwell's officially opens.

Some people describe Garrett's orange bus as "the setting of a bad 1970s porn movie." Wooden beads hang over the side windows, and instead of standard bench seats, he installed jump seats on the side. A tie-dyed beanbag sits atop a faux bearskin rug stretching across the floor.

Normally something this heinously amazing would cheer me right up, but not today.

Yawning, I wipe the grease off my hands with a rag. "The bad news is your transmission slipped out of gear."

Garrett stares at his bus like it's an injured puppy. "And?"

"When a transmission slips out of gear, it has to be replaced," Dad starts, "but since your VW is so old, they don't make transmissions for them anymore, so you have to rebuild them."

"The whole thing?" Garrett exclaims.

"Yup."

He rubs his eyes and looks at me. "Expensive?"

"Six hundred dollars or so, parts and labor included," I say.

"Crap. What's the good news?"

Dad gives me a smile. "Since we're fixing it, you only have to pay for the parts. Probably about two hundred dollars."

"I'll have to see if I can come up with it."

Garrett and I make plans to meet after school on Monday—after I've served detention—to talk about where we can buy the parts for cheap. I feel his pain. To some people, the kind of cash he needs is pocket change, which sucks, but it is what it is.

My coworkers who always open on Saturday mornings appear

Side B

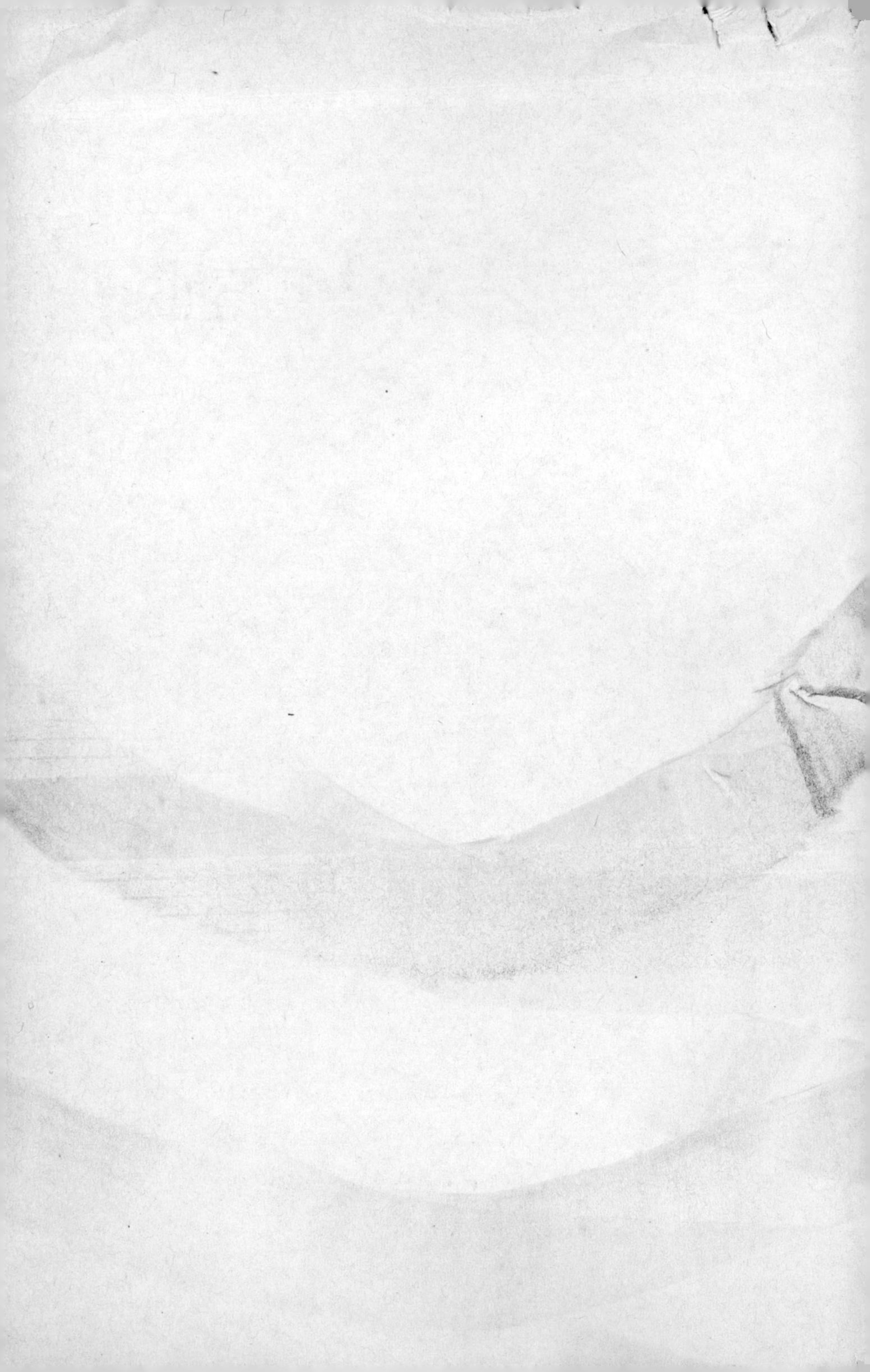

in the garage carrying cups of coffee and a box of doughnuts. Nick and Evan graduated from Hundred Oaks a couple of years ago, and both are really cute and funny. They always make the workday go by more quickly.

"If it isn't the famous Maya Henry!" Nick holds out the box of doughnuts and a napkin. My greasy hands are gross, but I don't really care at the moment. I'm starving and cranky, and I want a doughnut. I take a napkin and choose a strawberry glazed one from the box. If Jesse were here, he'd complain about how unhealthy it is. I sigh and take a huge bite.

I didn't cry over him last night, but my body feels like it did. I was up half the night thinking about what went wrong.

"Check it out," Evan says, passing me a rolled-up newspaper.

"Will you sign it for me, My?" Nick jokes.

"What is it?" Dad asks me.

With a shaky, grease-covered hand, I take the newspaper from Evan and unfold it. A picture of Jesse and me singing together fills the front page. It's from the Belle Carol. In the photo, he and I are hovering above a microphone, our noses an inch apart, smiling as we stare at each other.

The headline reads "Jesse Scott Retakes Nashville."

Hello, corny headline.

Dad pats my back. "That's a great picture of you! Your mom will go crazy when she sees this. I'm gonna tell her to buy a bunch of copies."

Dad goes to call Mom, and I eat my doughnut and dig into the article. It talks about how "after spending nearly four months out of the limelight following an incident in which he fell off a yacht on the Cumberland River, Jesse made an impromptu visit to a fan's birthday party with a spunky girl, seventeen-year-old Maya Henry of Franklin, Tennessee."

Spunky? Seriously? I need to write a complaint letter to the editor, because that is beyond dorky. My eyes drift back to the picture of Jesse and me, to a moment in time when we were both happy and free and loving life and music. *Forget about him, Maya. The same thing happened with Nate. You always get your hopes up, and guys just let you down.*

I fold the newspaper in half, hand it back to my coworker, and grab my clipboard. Time to get this day started. I'll be working reception later when it gets busy, but first up is an oil change for a 2005 Toyota Camry and then cleaning an air filter on a Mazda.

"Bo-ring," I sing to myself, because these are pretty lame cars—at least compared to a Maserati—but completing the two tasks clears my mind. Then I change the oil on my next two cars: a Nissan Sentra and a Ford Focus (double boring), and that's when the mayhem starts.

During his break from bussing tables over at the Roadhouse, Dave comes rushing into the garage wearing his uniform: a neat brown apron and crisp blue button-down shirt. Evan and Nick stop hammering out a dented fender to greet Dave, probably hoping he brought biscuits from the Roadhouse.

"Look at this!" Dave says, holding out his phone. He presses play on a YouTube video of me and Jesse singing on the Belle Carol Riverboat.

"Does that say 715,000 views?" Nick asks, leaning over my shoulder to watch the video.

"Maya, this is so, so cool. You sound amazing," Dave says.

"Finally, a YouTube video where I don't sound like a banshee!" I reply, and that's when reporters from the *Tennessean*, NBC, ABC, the *Franklin Times*, the *Nashville Scene*, and the *Tullahoma News* arrive to interview me, like I'm some sort of celebrity. I'm mortified when I look down at my greasy white T-shirt and jeans. The reporters thrust microphones up to my mouth.

"How'd they know where to find me?" I ask Dad.

"They came by the house first," he replies quietly. "Your mom got excited and sent them here. I hope Mr. Caldwell doesn't get angry."

"Mooooom," I whine, and Dad gives me a sheepish shrug.

The first question the press asks is, "Do you know why Jesse's quitting the business?"

"No, I'm sorry, I don't." Can they tell I'm lying?

When they realize my mouth is glued shut to talking about Jesse, they start asking questions about me.

"Jesse Scott's manager Mark Logan told our producers you

are skilled on guitar and have a nice voice," a lady from Channel 4 news says, holding a microphone up to my mouth. "So what's next for you?"

"School on Monday, I guess." I shrug, smiling. *Mr. Logan said that?!*

The reporter's question strikes a nerve, and I can't stop asking myself that same question. What's next? Rejoining show choir and the church choir? Trying to find members to start another band?

I gaze around Caldwell's, from the oil spots on the floor to the guys covered with grease, and let out a long sigh, trying to keep it together. I like working here, but it's just a job for me. I want to perform.

It sucks having a once-in-a-lifetime day, a day that changes you, only to hear the same old song repeated on the radio over and over.

I don't want yesterday to wither away and die.

♪♫♩

When I get home after work, I plop down on a bar stool in the kitchen, exhausted from not having slept last night and having to fend off reporters at Caldwell's. Dad had to kick them out because no work was getting done, and he sent me home three hours early to stop the press from coming back. I really could've used that money.

I swipe my cell on to find a ton of texts from Mom, Dave,

Hannah, *Nate?*, and everybody I've ever met. Foolishly, I had been hoping Jesse might reach out to me.

I rest my head on the counter and sigh. I shouldn't have invited myself backstage to Jesse's concert tonight. It spooked him. What is it with me and guys? Do I come on too strong? Why do none of them want to stick around? I'm gonna be forty years old and out on a date with some man, and we'll make out, then he'll tell me we're not meant to be, and I'll go home to my fourteen cats.

"Hey, baby girl."

I look up to find my mother has appeared in the kitchen. She fills the teakettle with water and sets it on the stove.

"So did you do anything interesting yesterday?" she asks with a coy smile, and I give her my look of death. "What's wrong?"

"It was all going really well…"

When my voice breaks, Mom wraps me in a hug, and her familiar smell of lavender and dryer sheets calms me. There's no way I can admit that I thought I had a chance with a boy like Jesse Scott. What was I thinking? She pats my back and soothes me.

"This might make you feel better. Something came for you." Mom releases me from her embrace and passes me a large brown box. The handwritten label reads *Maya.*

"Where'd this come from?" I ask.

"A messenger dropped it off this morning."

"A messenger?"

"Yeah, a guy in a fancy town car."

"Brown paper packages tied up with string, these are a few of my favorite things," I sing softly, dragging my fingers over the crisp paper.

"Open it already," Mom says.

I unlace the string, and the paper falls away from the box. With shaking hands, I lift the lid. It's those purple boots I tried on yesterday. I gasp and trace my fingertips across the soft leather/python/whatever it is.

"Those are beautiful!" Mom says. We're the same shoe size, and I can tell she's desperate to put them on and dance around the house to Dolly Parton.

A card sits wedged between the boots.

Dear Maya,

These boots could belong to no one but you. Holly will be in touch to discuss voice lessons. Thanks again for the great day.

J

Is this a parting gift or a mixed message? I push the card into my back pocket, then open the fridge for a Diet Coke. What did he mean Holly would be in touch to discuss lessons? Does she want me as a client? Because I can't afford that.

"What'd the card say?" Mom asks. "Anything about how good of a kisser you are?"

"Mom! Were you spying on me?"

"Of course not. Your brother told me."

"He was spying? Ugh. Sam is the worst."

She presses a comforting hand to my forearm. "So what happened with Jesse?"

I'm trying to figure out what to tell Mom when a knock sounds on the back door. It's Hannah. My mother motions my former bandmate—former friend?—inside. Hannah plays with her lip ring and looks at me with big, sad, brown eyes.

"Hey, Maya."

"Hi."

The teakettle rattles, hissing and spitting out steam.

Mom pours the hot water over a teabag, then wraps her hands around the cup. "I'll be in my room."

"You don't have to go," I say, because I don't want to talk to Hannah. Especially not alone. I'm afraid I'll want to yank the extensions out of her hair or worse, cry.

With a smile, Mom takes her tea and leaves the room, and then it's just me and Hannah. I lead her to the couch in the living room. Why is she here? I lean my head back, close my eyes, and sigh.

"Bad day?" she asks.

"Not the best." Most kids would probably love the attention I got from the press this morning, and truthfully, normally I would too, but it only reminds me that Jesse left me last night.

"I figured your day would be going pretty great since you hung out with Jesse Scott yesterday." Hannah smiles shyly. "Are you gonna see him again?"

Does she not care that I *sold out*? I ignore her question, because I'm still really upset at how last night ended. "What are you doing here?"

Hannah sits on the edge of the couch and ruffles her dark chestnut hair. I want her to leave so I can practice. And listen to a bunch of sappy eighties love ballads. And maybe eat a bag of Cheetos.

"You haven't been answering my texts or calls," she says. "I need to talk to you."

"So talk."

"I'm sorry for what happened—I had no idea Nate wanted to replace you."

"Why didn't you say anything when he kicked me out?"

"I was shocked, honestly, and I had just gotten together with Nate and didn't want to piss him off. I was confused, I guess. I know I should've spoken up."

"Well, it's too late now."

"Maybe it's not."

"Huh?"

A smile appears on her face. "I told the guys that unless they get rid of that dickwad Bryan Moore and bring you back as lead guitar, I'm quitting. Nate has been trying to reach you too."

That must be why Nate texted and why he tried to cut in when I was dancing with Jesse last night.

I can't believe this. "So basically the band *that I started* said they'll take me back because they don't want to lose *you*?"

"That's not how I meant it, My. I love performing with you—*you* are what makes our band special, not any of those guys."

I sigh and sink deeper into the couch, sipping from my can. "Would the guys be willing to play other kinds of music besides metal?"

"We didn't talk about that," she says softly.

Yesterday on the playground, Jesse pulled my body to his and told me that if I keep letting other people decide what kind of music I play—if I let them tell me how to live my life—I will end up leading a life that's not *mine*.

Yesterday changed me. Before Dr. Salter suggested I shadow Jesse, I thought I knew all there was to know about singing and playing guitar. I never considered I might learn something. And now I know several new techniques to sing from my diaphragm, to better play a B7.

Hell, what if there's even more stuff I should learn?

Regardless of how the day ended with Jesse, he gave me the biggest gift ever. I'm motivated again. If I want to become something, I need to work a lot harder. Which makes me want to start practicing right away.

After my solo on the Belle Carol, I know that I can do things on my own. I don't need a band to move forward. If you love something enough, want it bad enough, you should be willing to go after it on your own.

I stand up from the couch and stare down at Hannah. "Tell the guys I said thanks but no thanks. I'm going solo."

After I let Hannah out, I go to my bedroom. I swipe on my cell, take a deep breath, tap Jesse's name, then type: Thank you for the boots.

And leave it at that.

♪♫♩

This afternoon, I napped for hours, and I feel a lot better after clearing my head. I glance over at the clock. It's nearly eight.

I hear arguing, so I drag myself out of bed, quickly rinse my face in the bathroom sink, then head out to see what drama my family has cooked up for this evening.

Before I even make it to the kitchen, I smell it. Mom's beef stew. I find my parents and Anna, Sam, and Jordan crowded around the breakfast table, spooning stew into their mouths, laughing at a story Anna is telling about how her friend named her new betta fish "Sam."

My brother puffs out his chest. "I bet it's a very good-looking fish."

"I bet it looks just like you," Jordan replies.

Dad makes a puckering fish face, and Mom and Anna laugh at Sam's expense.

"You're awake!" Anna squeals at me. "I want to hear about your day with Jesse!"

Like the ten-year-old she is, she bounces around the kitchen, waving the newspaper that features my picture.

"It was fun," I say. "I learned a lot from him."

"Is he cute in person? Did you get his autograph for me? Can I go with you to one of his concerts? Did you find out what his favorite color is?"

"Yes, yes, no, no," I reply.

"Why can't we go to a concert?" Anna asks as she pouts, clutching my arm. "He likes you! I can tell from the picture!"

"We just can't," I snap, and Jordan and Sam exchange a look. Thankfully, nobody presses me about what happened last night, even though I'm positive Mom told them I was upset earlier.

Gossipy. If I had to choose a second word to describe my family after sporty, it would be gossipy.

"Let your sister sit down, Anna," Mom says. My sister collapses dramatically in her chair and shovels stew in her mouth, throwing me dirty looks.

Jordan stands up. "Want some stew, Maya?"

"Yes, please."

I take a seat as Jordan spoons stew into a bowl for me and talks about the upcoming homecoming game. It's her first year coaching at school, and she is very nervous and upset because her record is 4–1 so far. I don't follow sports, but apparently the whole town is pissed we lost last night's game, which hasn't happened since the Stone Age or something.

"I haven't lost a game at Hundred Oaks in…well, ever," Jordan says quietly. "When I played here in high school, I mean."

"Don't let any of the nincompoops around here get you down," Mom tells her. "Everybody knows you were the best person for the job. You just don't have a strong quarterback and offensive line this season."

"The team's doing very well, considering," Dad adds.

"That's what I've been saying," Sam says, pointing at Jordan with his spoon. "You should start hunting for a new QB for next year. Like now."

Mom looks over at me. "Maya, when Dr. Salter called to discuss your detention next week, he mentioned you might rejoin the choir. I'm so glad."

"I'm not sure," I say, shoveling the last bite of stew into my mouth. I was so starved, I finished in two minutes. "I think I might try going solo for a while."

My family starts grinning, and Sam whoops.

Dad serves me another helping, and we move on to discussing Sam's job as a scout for the Titans. Last night may have sucked, and my former band members are dicks, but at least I have my family. I am beyond lucky. I scoop another heaping spoonful into my mouth and smile around at everybody.

But when I imagine Jesse at his show in Atlanta tonight, a

show his parents most likely didn't show up for, I wonder if he's okay.

I finish my second helping of stew, scraping the bottom of my bowl.

I'm sure he's lonely.

♪♫♩

I never sit alone at lunch, and if there's a school dance, a guy or two will invite me. But I've never been one of those girls who gets elected prom queen, runs the student council, or has plans every Friday and Saturday night. But considering the reception I get when I walk into school with Dave on Monday morning, you'd think I'm the most popular girl of all time.

"Woooo, Maya Henry!" screams Alec O'Malley, the star wide receiver of the football team. He throws an arm around my shoulders. "Do you have a date for homecoming?"

My mouth falls open.

Justina Carr, the captain of the dance team, pushes Alec out of the way to walk beside me. "Tell me all about him!"

"Who? Alec?"

She laughs as if I'm Jimmy Fallon, not a girl she's never spoken to. "Do you think Jesse could introduce me to True Balance?"

True Balance is a boy band that I can't stand. Their biggest hit is called "I Love Your Saucy Sauce, Hot Mama." Nuff said.

"I'll get right on that and ask Jesse," I tell her, just so she'll leave me alone. It works—she skips off down the hall to brag to her real friends, who probably sing the saucy sauce lyrics in the shower.

As soon as she's gone, Alec the wide receiver tries to Heisman his way through the crowd that's formed around me. Dave blocks Alec, thank goodness. Jordan should recruit Dave as an offensive lineman for the football team, because Alec gets the point. He adjusts his shirt and strolls away as if he can't be bothered with me any longer.

"That was enjoyable," Dave says. "Alec has a nice chest."

"Don't let Xander hear you say that."

Nate walks up and gives me a dirty look. If Hannah actually quit the band because of me, I bet he's pissed. Whatever.

"Are you really not rejoining the band?" Nate asks me.

I shake my head. "I seem to recall you kicking me out. I'm going solo for a while."

"When I told the metal clubs in Nashville you're not with us anymore, they wouldn't book us. We need you back."

"I'm done with heavy metal." I turn away just in time for a freshman girl to squeal in my face.

"Are you dating Jesse Scott?"

"Do you think he'll come visit you at school?" another girl asks.

I have a sudden urge to spend the day hiding in a bathroom stall. I wish Jesse's security guard were here, because I feel like I might get swept away any second. Unlike Jesse, I've only had to deal with two days of this nonsense. I can't imagine dealing with this for eight years.

"Hey!" Dr. Salter separates the crowd. "If you aren't in class in two minutes, you get a week of detention!"

Everybody scatters, and I swallow. I do not like people mobbing me like that.

"You okay?" Dr. Salter asks, patting my shoulder, and I nod. "Good. Drop by my office during homeroom later this morning so we can discuss your behavior on shadow day."

Great. Just great. I take off for my first-period Crucial Life Lessons class, which I have with Dave.

I enter the classroom to massive applause, and I can't help but smile. It's all so ridiculous that it's becoming funny. I take a bow, and the cheering gets louder.

"Okay, okay, settle down," Coach Lynn tells the class. "Take a seat, Maya and Dave."

As soon as everybody is quiet, Coach Lynn starts teaching. "What's the number-one secret to financial success?"

"Shred all credit card offers the moment we get them in the mail," the class drones.

"What's the second most important secret to financial success?" Coach Lynn asks.

"Always balance your bank account."

"Good," she says. "Today, everybody is going to give a brief oral report on what they learned during shadow day."

I groan under my breath. While the other students talk about how they spent the day—one guy helped a vet deliver a foal and another rode in a news helicopter—I sink farther and farther into my seat.

"Maya? Care to tell us about your shadow day experience?" The way Coach Lynn enunciates the world "experience," you would think I've been riding roller coasters at a theme park.

I walk to the podium. "Um, I had the opportunity to shadow Jesse Scott."

Suddenly, Dr. Salter appears in the doorway.

I go on, "During shadow day, I got to visit the studio where Jesse records his music, and he gave me some singing and guitar tips." I lick my lips and take a quick glance at the class. "I had the opportunity to play a Les Paul electric guitar. I—"

"Did you fool around with him?" Zachary Painter asks, getting lots of laughs from other kids.

Dr. Salter's face goes redder than his bow tie, and I wonder if it's that obvious that I made out with Jesse Scott.

"Zack," Coach Lynn reprimands. "Not in my classroom." She focuses on me again. "What's the most important thing you learned from Jesse, Maya?"

I think back to what he said when we goofed around on that playground. "I learned that I have to take chances if I want a chance at my dreams."

That shuts the class up. Everybody, including Dr. Salter and Coach Lynn, seems to be thinking about my words. Jesse's words.

Back at my desk, I pull my phone out of my pocket and search Jesse's name. I stare at the cover of his greatest hits album. It's him leaning against a blue pickup truck, staring at a field of sunflowers. If I had an album, what would be on the cover? How many tracks would it have? Would it be a mix of rock and pop?

That's when I decide.

I'm going to take a chance. A big one.

Don't Dream It's Over

"My name is Maya Henry, and I'm the next *Wannabe Rocker*...I mean, winner of *Wannabe Rocker*!"

I cringe and hit the stop button on my phone. *Wannabe Rocker* audition videos are due in less than a week, and this is take #147. I am not exaggerating. I really have messed up that many times. Even with the singing tips Jesse and Holly gave me, my voice still cracks from time to time.

Anna pounds on the bathroom door. "I need to go bad, Maya! Let me in!"

"*God*, just use Mom's bathroom!" I yell. Can't she understand that the acoustics in this bathroom are necessary to my future success?

I adjust my guitar strap and get situated for take #148. *I'm doing this*, I tell myself. *I'm going solo. I can do it.*

That's when my phone buzzes. I read: Hi.

Holy crap. It's Jesse.

When I first thanked him for the boots, he wrote back: NP. No problem. I figured it was his parting gift for being an ass, and that would be it between us. I mean, besides our ongoing YouTube relationship where the number of views continues to rocket.

One day during lunch, Dave broke out the *People* magazine blurb about Jesse and me performing on the Belle Carol. Together we pored over the article, which talks about how Jesse made a young fan's dream come true when he crashed her party. It also has a picture of us and notes that more than five million people have watched the video online so far.

But it's been nearly two weeks since shadow day. Two weeks since I've heard from Jesse. And now he texts me?

Whatever. I don't have time for this.

I fluff my hair, adjust my guitar, then reach over and press record on my phone. "My name is Maya Henry, and I'm the next winner of *Wannabe Rocker*!"

I launch into "Somebody to Love," and I make it through the song with no issues, but it still doesn't feel special enough. Should I go for a more soulful performance, or should I rock it out? I slip in my earbuds and listen to the original Queen version, wondering if I should switch the melody up to make my performance more interesting. Maybe I should choose another song. I'm no Freddie Mercury.

Another message from Jesse pops on the screen. It's a link to a YouTube video, along with a text:

been thinking of you

I take a deep breath and push play. It's a video of him at one of his concerts. The stage lights dim, and he begins plucking an acoustic guitar. He stares at his fingers as he plays each note, and he licks his lower lip, concentrating.

Then he starts singing my favorite song.

Suddenly, my knees go wobbly. I grip the edge of the bathtub and sit as his rendition of "Killing Me Softly" plays. God, it's beautiful, the way his tone crests and falls, making me teary-eyed one second and smiley the next.

He performed it just for me.

Do I respond? What do I say? I'm still pissed at him and embarrassed, but I can't ignore how good the excitement feels, my heart hammering, my hands clutching my guitar for dear life.

The entire song goes by before I make a decision. Hi.

Seconds later, he texts, How are you?

Fine.

What are you doing?

Listening to music. You?

Just got home from Seventeen mag photo shoot

Exciting

They made me pose shirtless by my Harley. I felt like a piece of meat.

poor baby

And then I found Casper had unrolled a whole roll of toilet paper.

lol. good job, Casper.

Can we talk?

I stare at the blinking cursor on my phone.

Then I stand and go back to rehearsing in front of the mirror.

♪♫♩

Jesse keeps sending texts over the next couple of days. I haven't responded, because I didn't know if I want to talk. I still don't know.

Besides, I have a bigger problem I need to deal with: my audition video sucks ass! I haven't been able to figure out which song I should sing, nor have I recorded a clip that I can stand behind. And it's due by October 5. By midnight tonight.

In total crisis mode, I drive my bike a mile to Dave's house, and when I get there, his mother lets me into the foyer.

"He's upstairs with Xander, dear." She must be the most trusting mom in the world, or she hasn't figured out that Dave is seeing Xander, which makes no sense, because everybody knows Dave is gay.

I hustle up the stairs to his room, moving faster than I ever have in gym class, knock once on Dave's door, and hurl myself in. Xander and Dave startle apart from kissing on the bed and scramble to sit up.

"Maya, what the hell?" Dave asks, flattening his mussed hair.

"Emergency! I need your opinion. And your MacBook." I sit

down at his desk, open his computer, and plug in my phone. The boys untangle themselves and come lean over my shoulders.

"What's going on?" Dave asks.

"Tell me which of these videos you like." We run through the best of the clips I recorded in my bathroom. There's lots of shrugging and "hmmm-ing," which does nothing for my self-esteem. I try to keep in my mind that I interrupted their hookup and they'd like to get back to it, but this is my life we're talking about!

After watching my sixth video, Dave drums his fingers on his desk. "Can't you use a real live performance? A video of you in the bathroom is just so…"

"Unhygienic?" Xander offers.

"Amateur," Dave says.

"And unhygienic."

I roll my eyes.

"Why don't you send in your talent show video from last year?" Dave asks.

"Because my voice cracked!"

"But before it cracked, your guitar playing was so badass. People at school were talking about it for weeks."

"What? All I heard was them calling me 'the Siren.'"

"Only because they were jealous. Seriously, everyone was way impressed with your guitar playing. That's the video you gotta send in. We'll cut it before you start singing."

"But I have to send in a singing sample too," I whine.

"Can you send in two videos?" Xander asks.

"No," Dave and I say at the same time.

"I mean, can you splice together sections of your different performances?" Xander asks. "Like, one where you sound good singing?"

I shrug. "It's not a bad idea. But my audition video can't be longer than three minutes…and I don't really have any recorded live performances that are good."

"You do with The Fringe," Dave says, leaning over Xander's shoulder to pull up my former band's YouTube channel. "We can show you singing backup, and if we have to, we can use one of the unhygienic bathroom clips."

"But I'm singing metal in our Fringe videos."

"It's what we have to work with," Dave says.

"Here, scooch over," Xander says, squishing into the desk chair with me. Over the next hour, the boys help me splice together my video. And by the end, I'm pretty happy with the result. With my talent show "Bohemian Rhapsody" performance making up most of the video, it screams eighties…with a small amount of metal. But it's not terrible.

"I still think you should send the video of you on the riverboat," Dave says. "Your voice was amazing."

"Seriously," Xander says, nodding.

I shake my head. "This audition is about me and me only. I don't want any special favors because I sang once with Jesse Scott."

I'm doing this on my own.

♪♫♩

A few days later, a weird sound wakes me up. Th-dump.

I sit up straight and look around my room. Shimmering moonlight flows through the window and bathes the room in a soft white glow. Th-dump. Th-dump. That noise again.

Something's in the yard. Maybe I should get Dad? I push my covers away and pad toward the window, then pause when a rock hits it. I look out into the yard and place a hand to my chest.

"Jesse," I whisper.

When he sees my face, his hand falls to his side, and a few rocks tumble from his fingers. I stare into the caramel eyes I never thought I'd see again in real life. Not breaking eye contact, he walks closer. I struggle with the latch, then yank up the window up and lean out toward him.

"Hi," I say breathily.

"Hi." He smiles that wicked smile, and then he does the worst possible thing. He sings, "I'm a tiny swatch of quilllllllllt, and I want to be sewn into your hearrrrrrrrt."

I cover my face and start laughing my ass off.

That's when my bedroom door slams open. "Who are you talking to?" my dad demands.

"Nobody."

He stalks over and looks out into the night. As my heart gallops away from me, I gaze into the yard. I see nothing but trees and grass. Where did Jesse go?

"I was looking at the stars," I lie.

"Riiiight," Dad says with a yawn. "Go to bed, My, and tell whoever's outside to beat it. Now."

He shuts the door behind him.

I whisper-yell, "Jesse!"

He pops straight up. I yelp and stumble back.

"Can you come out?" he asks quietly.

I shake my head. "I can't walk through the house—Dad'll hear me."

He holds his arms out. "C'mere, then."

For the first time in my life, I'm happy with my super-short, nonathletic body. Jesse lifts me out the window and drops me to the ground in front of him. He smoothes my bleached hair behind my ears and gazes down at me. I cross my arms over my chest. I don't want to give him a show: I'm not wearing a bra. My tank top is thin, and it's a chilly night.

"What are you doing here?" I ask.

"You weren't answering my texts, so I came to serenade you."

"With the worst song I ever wrote."

"I got stage fright. I sang the first thing that came to mind."

"Jesse Scott got stage fright," I say in a monotone voice.

"That's right." His eyes twinkle at me.

"For real though," I whisper. "Why are you here?"

A cricket chirps a few times, filling the silence. Then he replies, "I missed you."

I have no response to that. I missed him too, but he'll never hear that from my mouth. I hug myself harder, to protect my heart.

"I'm sorry about the way I acted that night."

"Yeah, me too," I say snarkily.

He takes a deep breath. "The way I was feeling…about you… it was all new to me, and I didn't know what to do."

I just stand here, because I have nothing to apologize for and too many things I want to say but shouldn't.

"I was thinking," he says quietly. "I don't have a show on Friday. Do you want to hang out?"

I glance up. "What?"

"Friday night?"

I thought he said things couldn't work out between us, and now he shows up at my bedroom window after midnight to serenade me with terrible lyrics and ask me to hang out? I swear.

"Like as a date?" I ask.

"I was thinking as friends… I'm not sure I'm ready for something more yet, but let's see where this goes."

It's like with Nate all over again. He said we couldn't officially be together because of the band, but he had no problem with hooking up on the side. And now Jesse Scott is saying we can hang out and "see where this goes," but he isn't offering any assurances beyond that. I don't want to place my trust in a guy who doesn't know what he wants.

"Jess, this is a bad idea. You freaked out because you thought I'd treat you like your ex-girlfriend did."

He lowers his eyes. "I was wrong, and I'm sorry."

I worry my lip. Fold my arms more tightly around my body.

"We can do whatever you want," he says. "I only want to spend time with you."

The moon disappears behind a cloud, leaving his face in shadow. He's scared I'll say no. I *should* say no. I should use my Friday night to practice, just like I've been doing every other night. But I'm interested to know how far Jesse will go to spend time with me.

"I want to see a movie," I announce.

"You probably want to see *Hot Wired*, right? The car chases look awes—"

"I want to see *The Commander in Chief Who Loved Me*."

His nose crinkles. I don't blame him. I don't have any interest in seeing it either—it's a romantic comedy about political rivals who fall for each other on the presidential campaign trail. I just want to know if he *will* see it. Of course I would rather see *Hot Wired*, which is about stealing fancy cars, explosions, sex, and stealing even fancier cars.

"I can probably get it," he says.

"What do you mean you can get it? You mean tickets?"

"No, I mean I'll have Gina or Tracy get a copy of the movie, and we can watch it in my home theater."

Of course he'd be able to get a copy of a movie that hasn't come out yet, and he doesn't even have to download it illegally.

I appreciate that he drove to Franklin because he missed me. But if we're going to see a movie, we're gonna do it on my terms. If he wants a real life, I'll give him one.

"I want to see it in an actual theater. And I want to invite Dave and Xander. We'll double."

Jesse swallows hard. "We can do that."

"Text me with the details." I turn on my heels and march toward the front door. My dad's gonna kill me, but I won't give Jesse the satisfaction of helping me get back in the window.

Love Is a Battlefield

"Just act normal."

"You're asking me to do the impossible," Dave complains. "I don't see how you can act normal around him."

That's a fair statement. Jesse and I have been texting on and off for the past couple of days, but I haven't caught my breath since he showed up at my window.

Tonight, I may get so nervous that I spill my Coke or drop popcorn down inside my top. Oh God, is my red leather halter cut too low? I look down to make sure I'm not wardrobe-malfunctioning.

Xander opens the door for Dave and me, and we walk inside the theater, which smells of popcorn and nachos. Gazing around, I anxiously adjust my bracelets. There he is.

Jesse is holding court by a cardboard display for an animated movie about a bicycle that wishes it were a car. If Jesse were any other guy, he'd be standing alone, probably checking his cell or deciding which candy to buy at the concession stand. But no. He's surrounded by girls and signing shirts and napkins with a

Sharpie. Some girl yanks the collar of her shirt down and motions for Jesse to sign her chest. With barely a glance, he turns away to sign a little girl's popcorn bag.

One point for Jesse.

The hulking security guard from the booth outside Jesse's house stands sentry over the group of girls. I never imagined I'd go to a movie with a guy and his security detail. *How romantic.*

Xander grabs my elbow. "Are we sure Jesse isn't bi?"

"I told you, I'm much more his type than you are," Dave tells him.

"Keep it in your pants, boys," I say, pulling down on my white skirt that won't stop riding up.

When Jesse looks up and sees me, a true smile breaks across his freckled face. The crowd around him parts like the Red Sea as he makes his way over and hugs me.

"Awww!" The younger girls gossip about how romantic we are.

"It's so good to see you," Jesse whispers in my ear, making me shiver.

"You too." I gently pull away from him and turn to face my friends as Jesse places a warm hand on my lower back. "You remember Dave and Xander?"

"I do." He reaches out to shake their hands.

Dave squeaks out a "Hi!"

"It's nice seeing you again," Jesse says, sounding as awkward as my preacher when he greets me after services. (My nose ring mixed with poor church attendance make for a sin cocktail.) At least I know Jesse doesn't care that we're doubling with two gay guys; he's nervous because he doesn't hang out with people his own age that often.

"You brought your security guard?" I whisper.

"I want you to have a good time and not worry about people bothering you." With his hand still locked in place on my back, Jesse steers me to the concession stand. "Want something to eat?"

"I dunno. This all seems pretty unhealthy. Am I allowed?" I joke.

He grins. "You're allowed."

He buys me some Twizzlers and a cherry ICEE for himself, and we choose seats in the last row. Jesse's security guard sits next to me, and Xander and Dave scramble to get the seat next to Jesse.

"I want to sit by him!" Dave whisper-yells and plops down in Xander's lap, trying to get him to move.

"Your ass is bony as hell!" Xander exclaims, which makes Dave wiggle his butt more intensely. Xander pops up, launching Dave off his lap, and Dave steals the seat.

"Fine," Xander says, straightening his polo. He takes the spot on the other side of Dave.

I burst out laughing, happy for the distraction. I'm not nearly as nervous as I was. At least until a bunch of girls rush to sit in our row, and while the previews fill the screen, people blatantly look back at us. Some even snap pictures. *Flash, flash, flash.* White spots dance in front of my eyes.

I sneak a glance at Jesse. His back is rigid, and he grips his ICEE tightly with both hands. Maybe coming here was a bad idea. He wanted a normal life, a life with friends. Going to the movies is as normal as it gets, but I'm scared he's gonna realize he can't handle this and get up and leave me.

He's still holding his ICEE like he expects someone to steal it from him. I lean over and sip from the straw without asking.

"You're welcome," he says.

"Thank you." I wipe a drop of ICEE off my lip. "Twizzler?" I hold one out to him, and he takes a bite.

Dave leans over to Jesse and grumbles, "I can't believe we have to watch this crap. We should've seen Channing Tatum in *Hot Wired*."

"There's still time to sneak into it," Jesse replies.

I elbow him hard. "Excuse me?"

"ICEE?" He tries to placate me by sharing his yummy drink, and yeah, it works. I wrap my lips around the straw and stare into his eyes, but he looks away to focus on the screen. He smells delicious, like soap and leather and boy, and all I can think about is how much I want to feel his lips against mine again. Our elbows touch on the armrest, and it makes me gasp with excitement, but he moves his arm so our skin isn't touching.

Then I remember he's not sure what he wants yet. What does it say that I'm willing to wait to see what he decides? Is it going to be like with Nate again, six months of waiting, waiting, and waiting for something more while continuing to fool around physically?

But that doesn't seem to be a problem: even though I'm resting my hand on my thigh, palm facing up, he never once reaches for it.

♪♫♩

The four of us head back to Dave's house because he has a rec room in his basement, and his parents are out for the night at some party. Sure, Jesse has a mansion, but none of us suggest going there.

After raiding the kitchen for candy and chips, we sprawl out on the couches and flick on the TV. Xander thumbs through the channels.

I decide to cause some trouble. "Let's watch that movie *My Mother Married a Gigolo.*"

"God, yes," Xander says.

"No!" Jesse and Dave say at the same time.

"We already watched that terrible *Commander in Chief Who Loved Me* movie for you," Dave says. "God only knows why you wanted to see it."

"I'm considering a career in politics," I lie.

"You are not," Dave drones.

"The sex scenes were steamy."

"That was the least sexy sex scene I've ever seen," Xander complains.

"Right?" Dave laughs. "I find it hard to believe the president would have sex with the lady he's running against."

"And that they'd do it on the White House lawn," Xander says.

"For real," Jesse replies. "My manager always says, whatever you do, don't have sex outside, because somebody will see and take pictures."

Dave and Xander gape at him. Then at me. Then back at Jesse.

Dave licks his lips. "Are you sure you're not bi—"

"How about we play a game?" I ask loudly.

Jesse then proceeds to kick our asses at Dance Dance Revolution and Guitar Hero, which totally sucks, because I always win these games. I get that he does this for a living, but I've always been the best at DDR!

He sits down next to my pouting self and whispers, "You're cute when you're in a bad mood."

"Hmph."

"This is really fun."

"Really?" I raise an eyebrow at him. "We're just hanging out in a basement. I figured you'd think this was boring."

Jesse looks at Xander and Dave battling on DDR. "I haven't done anything like this in a long time."

Dave screams "Nooo!" when he loses to Xander, then perches on the armrest and speaks low to me, "Do you care if I go up to my room with Xander?"

I don't mind if they want to make out. "Have fun. Don't do anything I wouldn't do!"

"Yell if you hear my parents' car, okay?" he says, and they disappear up the stairs.

"So, are they serious?" Jesse asks.

"They just started seeing each other a few weeks ago, but it seems to be going well, even though Xander's a freshman at MTSU, and that makes Dave kind of nervous because they don't see each other at school every day," I ramble.

We sit in silence, picking at the M&Ms until he speaks up again. "I'm glad we went out tonight. I was worried you'd say no."

"I nearly did." I lean my head against his shoulder, but he stands and leaves me sitting alone on the couch.

Which doesn't make any sense. The first thing he said to me on shadow day was "Wanna have sex?" and now he doesn't want to hold my hand?

"What's wrong?" I ask.

He leans against the staircase railing, crossing his arms. "I haven't dated anybody in a while, you know?"

"I haven't either. Not for real, anyway."

"I need time," he says quietly. "Just to make sure."

"Sure of what?"

He points back and forth between us. What does that mean? He wants to be sure of me? Of dating in general? What if he leaves me standing alone in the dark night again?

"Jess, why did you come back?"

A tiny smile starts on his face. "Everywhere I went, I kept thinking of you. I'd put on my spurs for a show and remember how you said they're ugly. I'd drive past a playground and want to swing with you. I went to the listening room at the Underground to write, and when I closed my eyes and tried to think of words, all I could see was your face."

I suck in a breath. "Those are the most beautiful lyrics I've ever heard."

He laughs. "They're nowhere near as good as 'I'm a swatch of quilt and I want to be sewn into your heart."

I scowl, then pause for a long moment to think. "You aren't going to get my hopes up and leave again, right?"

He chews on his lower lip, his eyes never leaving mine. "I don't want to. That's why I need to take things slow." He drags a hand through his hair. "I'm goin' out of town for ten days. I'm on *Saturday Night Live*, and then I've got some appearances on the talk shows and photo shoots to do before I start my last tour. Can we go out again when I get back?"

I nod, pulling a couch pillow to my chest. The situation doesn't make me feel comfortable, but if this is what he needs, then I should support him. But it's a lot of trust to place in him. I trusted Nate, and he let me down. I survived it.

But I don't think my heart will survive being broken by Jesse.

He finally breaks the silence. "Want to play another game of Guitar Hero?"

I hop to my feet. "You're so going down this time, Jesse Scott."

♪♫♩

On Halloween, Dave follows me home from school because he says he needs girl talk.

"I'm just not sure what to do about him," Dave says, letting the screen door slam behind us. We go to the kitchen in search of snacks.

"You like him, right?" I pull a box of crackers out of the cabinet.

"I like Xander more than anybody I've ever met."

"And he likes you too. He can't keep his hands off you, bud."

"I've never felt like this before…and he wants more. Like, he wants to have sex."

I squeal and get excited. "And?"

Dave's face heats from pink to a dark maroon. "He doesn't think it's a big deal. To him, it's something that just happens when people are dating. And I kind of get that, but I don't know whether it will be a big deal for me or not. It feels like a big deal…like, I hate to bring it up, but it sucks what happened with you and Nate."

My heart begins to pound at the memory, and not in a good way. "Only do it if you want to, Dave."

My friend reaches into the cracker box and pulls out a handful. "Would you do it with Jesse?"

Considering we didn't even kiss after the movie, I don't know if sex will ever be on the table. "If we were in a relationship and I was certain we were solid, then yeah, I'd do it with Jesse. But…"

Dave pops a cracker in his mouth. "Hmm?"

"We've only texted a couple of times this week. I guess he's been busy on his trip."

"My, he's always going to be busy. Until he retires, anyway."

"I'm afraid…it's not that I think he'll forget about me…" Reporters have been speculating as to what's going on with us. Some magazines say we're dating; others say that I'm not Jesse's type and I'm just a flavor of the month. *Us Weekly* wrote that a source very close to Jesse Scott said I'm his *good friend*. Who is this source? Could it be true that he only considers me a friend?

"I worry he'll find somebody better," I say softly. "Like Nate did with Hannah."

"Everybody worries about being let down. Even famous people."

Dave and I smile at each other and dig into the crackers until Mom comes home and drops a stack of mail on the table. I sort through it, tossing coupons and credit card offers to the side, and come across a crisp, white envelope with my name on it. I check the return address and my heart stops. *So You Wanna Be a Rocker?*

My pulse thumps wildly. I rip open the envelope and scan the letter.

Rêve Records and NBC studios are pleased to invite you to the semifinal auditions of Wannabe Rocker*! You are one of a select group of five hundred contestants who have been chosen…New York City…December 1–4… Our producers love your country accent and eighties vibe…*

I scream and dance around the kitchen. I made it to the top five hundred on the show!

Dave rips the letter out of my hand and reads it, then starts to dance and scream with me. "Holy shit! Holy shit!"

"Holy shit! Holy shit!" I yell back.

"What's going on?" Mom asks when she comes back in the kitchen, folding her Cedar Hill cleaning uniform. "I heard all that foul language and figured Sam and Jordan were here."

"Look at this, Mrs. Henry!" Dave shows her the paper, and Mom freaks out. She hugs me and says she's so proud.

I collapse to the floor with a thud to go over the letter in more detail. That's when I read the fine print: the top five hundred singers are invited to New York City in December to perform in person. From there, the show will whittle the number of contestants down to thirty. But the show won't pay for the top five hundred to come to New York for the weeklong auditions, and since I'm not eighteen yet, I have to bring a parent or guardian.

"What a cheap show!" I complain. A cheap show I desperately want to be on. Several of the artists who've won and even those who only made it to the top ten have gone on to get huge record deals. Jesse has his three Grammys, Tammy Goldstein is on Broadway, and Minka Carlton even won an Oscar!

Dave pulls out his phone and swipes it on. "Let's see how much flights and a hotel would cost." A minute later, a shadow crosses his face. "Flights are pretty expensive…probably because it's between Thanksgiving and Christmas…hotels are steep too. Looks like it'll cost you between $1,500 and $2,000."

"I have about $150 in my bank account," I murmur.

"What about driving?" Dave asks.

"I don't think my car will make it," Mom says. "It needs a new carburetor." She looks at me. "And don't even think about it. We're not riding your motorcycle to New York."

"Damn."

At the beginning of each season of *Wannabe Rocker*, they show snippets of audition week in New York. Normally they only show the horrible people and the best people—the contestants they want to win. There's a chance I may not even be featured. Unless I'm one of the horrible people…

"We'll figure it out," Mom says and hugs me again.

After Dave leaves to put on his costume for tonight's Halloween field party at Morton's (he and Xander are going as Mario and Luigi, and I'm going as Princess Peach), I wait anxiously for Dad to get home from the shop. When he pushes open the screen door, wearing coveralls covered in black grease, I pounce on him with the news.

"Congratulations, baby girl," he says, wrapping me in a huge hug. "I'm so proud of you for going solo." Dad yawns and goes to start a pot of coffee.

"There's a catch," I say. "We have to pay for travel. It's expensive to get to New York. I've got $150, and I bet I can save up another hundred or two in the next month, but I'll need a lot more for two plane tickets and a hotel…maybe a thousand."

He stops scooping grounds into the coffeemaker and turns to look at me. "Baby girl, you know that I used every spare cent we had toward the down payment on this house…and I can't miss a mortgage payment. I might be able to spare a couple hundred, but not a thousand."

"But, Dan," Mom interrupts, placing a hand on his chest.

"I'm sorry, love. I don't think we can save up enough in a month. Maybe if I'd had a bit more warning, I could've put some aside, but I just don't have it right now."

I hurry out of the kitchen to my bedroom, blinking back tears. Sometimes it really sucks that my family doesn't have money. My brother played football for Michigan for four years, but we only made it to two games because we couldn't afford to travel. Dave's dad works out at the Air Force base and his mom is a teacher, and while they aren't rich or anything, they could afford a trip to New York. And don't even get me started on Jesse Scott. I'm not jealous of being rich, but I wish I had the chance to have options. Even if I pick up a ton of hours down at Caldwell's, I could never save up this kind of money in a month. I lie down on my bed and clutch my pillow. What other options do I have?

My brother only recently started making money, and while Jordan's family is wealthy, I'd never ask her for help. If she or her family found out about it, I know they'd butt in and pay to send me to New York, but that would embarrass my father and brother. They are both very proud men.

Do I have anything I could sell? The only things I own of worth are my two guitars, the boots Jesse gave me, my Suzuki I fixed up, and the Bose iPod dock I saved and saved for.

Mom knocks and comes in my room to join me on the bed. We sit in silence together for a while, her holding my hand.

"Are you gonna call Jesse and tell him the news?"

I shake my head. "I can't tell him."

"Why not?"

We're not in a relationship. I don't have any idea what we are, we haven't talked in several days, and I don't want him thinking I'm asking for favors. He hates when people do that.

"I have to do this on my own."

Mom smiles and squeezes my hand. "That's my girl."

Dare You to Move

Dave comes with me.

We meet the guy in the Walmart parking lot—a safe place with lots of lights.

"I'll give you $300 for it," the man says, eyeing the Suzuki I slaved over for six months, the motorcycle I ride every day. I spent hours working on the fuel line; it took three months to find the right parts to upgrade the transmission. I put my heart into this bike.

"How about $350?" I say in a strong voice, not letting my voice waver, not letting a tear fall down my face.

"$310?"

Dave just looks at me. He doesn't know what it's worth. I swallow hard and run my hand across the seat, feeling the care I poured into it.

I guess, in a way, the bike is getting me to New York for the auditions—even if I'm not riding it there. I can only pray that the time and money I'm dedicating to this trip will amount to something as cool as this Suzuki.

"$330?" I ask.

"$325."

"Sold."

♪♫♩

With three weeks until the semifinals in New York, I'm working my fifth shift of the week at Caldwell's. I've clocked nearly twenty hours, and boy, am I exhausted. It's a good exhausted though. With the money I got for the Suzuki and my Bose iPod dock, plus the cash I have saved, I'm up to $750. Even though they are so not me, I would never consider selling the boots Jesse gave me.

After taxes, this week's paycheck will probably be about $125. I'm getting closer, but I still can't afford five nights staying in a $200 per night hotel, and every time I check online, the cost of plane tickets goes up, up, up. It must be so expensive because everyone's heading to New York to see the decorations after Thanksgiving.

My phone rings right as I'm finishing ringing up a customer. I glance around to make sure Mr. Caldwell and Dad aren't in the lobby and answer my cell.

"Jesse!"

"Hey, My."

We've barely spoken since that night we went to the movies, and it's good to hear his voice. I jog in place and grin. "How are you?"

"Good. I get home tomorrow. This was a hell of a trip."

"You did great on *SNL*."

"I'm never doing that again. It was way past my bedtime," he jokes, and I smile into the phone. "I've missed you," he says.

"I miss you too."

"Can I take you out tomorrow night?"

"Definitely," I say, trying not to sound overeager, but it's impossible. I'm anxious to see him.

"I'll pick you up at seven. And I'm deciding what we're doing this time. No more sappy movies."

"You loved it!" I tease, and I stay on the phone with him until another customer comes in.

At lunch the next day, I can't stop dancing in my chair and smiling to myself, but Dave isn't talking. He's poking at his pizza with a fork.

"What's wrong?" I ask. "Is everything okay with Xander?"

"Everything's good—we went back to his dorm after homecoming! I ended up sleeping over."

I throw a french fry at him. "Get out!"

Dave dishes up all the details, and while I'm happy for him, I'm also jealous. Jesse was still out of town on Saturday night, and I had no date to the dance, so after cheering for Jordan at the football game and watching them win, I went home and practiced guitar.

"If everything's so great with Xander, what's wrong?"

"I have something to show you." Dave reaches into his backpack and removes a magazine: a shiny issue of *Us Weekly*. He flicks through a few pages and passes it to me. A picture of Jesse and Natalia Naylor—a famous model—stares back at me. Natalia is clutching his elbow and smiling at something he's saying as they walk down the street. Or should I say stumbling? How can she walk in those four-inch stilettos? The caption says they're in Santa Monica. I flip to the cover and check the date. It's this week's issue.

"He didn't mention anything about her," I say quietly, rolling the magazine into a tight coil.

"Didn't you say he was in California?" Dave asks.

I nod. "He was in LA for a few days at the American Music Awards and shooting a music video."

It's not like we're official, but it hurts seeing him with another girl. While he wasn't ready to dive right in, he wants to see where this goes, and to me, that means we are starting to explore a relationship.

"What should I do?" I ask with a sigh.

"Just ask him about it," Dave says. "I'm sure there's an explanation."

"But what if the explanation is that he's dating somebody else?"

"My, I saw the two of you dancing at the fair and at my house that night. I doubt Jesse looks at any other girl the way he looks at you. Are we sure he's not bi? I want him to look at me that way!"

I throw a baby carrot at Dave's face.

My cell beeps. Jesse sent a text: Can't wait to see you tonite. I'm dying here.

Part of me wants to play it cool. Play it hard to get. But I decide to be honest. I text back: can't wait to see you too.

♪♫♩

Jesse picks me up on his motorcycle and somehow survives meeting Mom, Dad, and Anna. My mom and sister are all over him like white on rice, and Dad is channeling Sam, looking like he wants to kill Jesse or at least put him in a headlock. Men.

We climb on Jesse's bike, I wrap my arms around his waist, and we zoom to Nashville. The whole way there, I think about how I'll raise the subject of the picture of him with Natalia Naylor. Do I even have a right to ask?

He parks in front of a restaurant called the Spaghetti Factory, and we head inside.

"I'm gonna wash my hands," I tell him, and he agrees to get the table.

In the bathroom, I examine my outfit to make sure nothing is out of place following our ride. It's totally me, this sleeveless, purple tartan minidress covered with leather accents and silver zippers. I'm wearing a cropped leather jacket over it. I look good. *Take that, Natalia Naylor, you silly supermodel, you.* I inhale deeply. Who am I kidding? She's a supermodel! How can I compete with her?

After I'm done using the bathroom, the hostess leads me to

the back of the dark restaurant, past a classical pianist, to a cushy, circular red booth. Jesse is signing autographs for a bunch of younger girls. He scribbles his name on a white cloth napkin with his black Sharpie and hands the napkin to a little girl.

"Thank you," she squeals.

I slide into the booth next to Jesse. The girls recognize me from the YouTube video and beg for my autograph. Ever since Jesse started following me on Twitter, lots of random people have been talking to me online, but this is a whole new level.

"Can I use your marker?" I ask Jesse.

"Get your own Sharpie." He passes it to me with a smile. Taking a deep breath, I sign my name on two cloth napkins and hand them back to the girls. A photographer snaps pictures of us before the restaurant manager chases him out.

Will I ever get used to being out with Jesse? I'm not jealous of the attention he gives other people or that it takes away from our time together, but I want to help him lead the normal life he wants so bad. How will that ever happen if we can't go to dinner without being disturbed? Before I can feel too down about the situation, a waiter pulls a thick velvet curtain around our booth, leaving us in candlelit privacy.

The second we're alone, I can't help it—I have to be near him. I scoot over and burrow against his side, expecting him to pull away like he did at Dave's house that night. Instead, he gently traces my jaw and kisses my cheek.

"How are you?" he asks, searching my eyes.

Much better now, after that kiss. "Things are okay," I say slowly.

"Hungry?"

"Starved."

He doesn't even look at the menu. "We're splitting the Spaghetti Vesuvius. I'm addicted to it."

I clutch his hand. "You seem happy."

"I am happy." He drags a fingertip from my wrist to my elbow, making me shiver. "It's really good to see you, My. Uncle Bob and Mark took me out for lunch today. The concert in Memphis last night went well. Just finished writing a new song. I'm working on a secret project too."

"Oooh, what is it?"

"I can't tell you until Mark gives me the go-ahead," he says, shooting me his famous half-cocked smile. "Besides, why should I tell you my secret if you won't share yours?"

When Jesse asked why I've been working so many hours, I told him I'm saving money for something, but it's a secret. I will not put him in the position of feeling like he has to offer me money. Also, since he won the show as a kid, I don't want him to feel obligated to help me in any way. I am doing this on my own. Plus, what if he thinks I'm asking for favors? I don't want to be somebody who takes, takes, takes.

"I'm not sure if it's gonna work out after all," I say slowly. I leave his arms and choose a piece of bread from the basket.

"Why not?"

"My plans have a lot of moving parts." Specifically, I haven't made enough money to buy plane tickets. "I don't think I'll be able to make it happen...at least not without help." *And my family can't afford to help me.*

"So you've got a decision to make then."

"What's that?"

"Decide if you wanna give up and move on to something else, or if you wanna make it work." He picks up a straw, rips the paper off the end, and blows the straw paper at me. I catch it. "If I want something, I tell people. Even if I don't end up getting what I want in the end, at least I've put myself out there."

"But you're Jesse Scott."

"And you're Maya Henry."

I tap the table with my fork. I already asked my mom and dad for help, and that didn't work out. But I do have other people in my family. My older brother, who I love so much, even if he is an overprotective ass. He doesn't have money either though.

Mom always complains about Sam living in sin and wishes he'd propose to Jordan already, but I know the real reason he hasn't. It's pride. I find it hilarious that Jordan has asked him to marry her several times, but he always says no. He wants to buy Jordan an engagement ring she'll love first, but he's still working to save up for one. He's nearly there.

To ask him for help would just set his plans back even further.

I can't do that, certainly not for something so selfish, something that's all about me. I guess Jesse is right in a way though—I could at least tell Sam what's going on.

Our food arrives, and we dig into our spaghetti. Jesse even tries the *Lady and the Tramp* move, you know, where we're both eating the same strand of spaghetti and kiss? It doesn't work out so well—we end up with spaghetti sauce all over our faces.

Jesse nudges my nose with his. "I missed you so much. It seemed like everywhere I went, I heard a Queen song that made me think of you."

"I thought about you too," I say. "My sister will not stop playing 'Ain't No City Boy' on repeat. I can't stand that song."

He laughs, and my body aches for him to take me in his arms, but I can't get the *Us Weekly* photo out of my head. Every time I think about it, I wince.

"You okay, My?"

"I'm all right," I reply. "You?"

"I'd feel better if you'd kiss me already."

He edges closer and rubs my cheek with a thumb. Then we're kissing like crazy. His lips become my lips. They're warm and soft—slow, but hungry. And his hands—rough and calloused from playing guitar all the time—feel nice against my neck.

"You've got spaghetti breath," I tell him, burying my fingers in his wavy brown hair.

"You too."

One hand drifts downward as he rubs my stomach through my dress. The piano music crescendos. I keep kissing him, but his hand is making me tremble all over. I don't want to mess this up, but I don't want to go any further, at least not without knowing what we are to each other. Last time we were together, he didn't want anything physical, and now he's all over me. And that's confusing. I suck in a deep breath, my body tensing all over.

"It's okay," Jesse mutters, biting my earlobe. "Relax."

"I saw the magazine," I blurt. "*Us Weekly*. There's a picture of you with Natalia Naylor."

"Who?" he mouths, scrunching his eyebrows together.

Great. He can't even remember his conquests. What am I even doing here?

"The model? You were walking down the street with her. She was holding your arm. Wearing a tight jean skirt and white halter top…"

Suddenly his eyes light up. "Oh! Nat. I haven't seen her since we worked together on a Levi's campaign last year. *Us Weekly* printed a picture of us together?"

I nod.

He goes on, "They're probably just trying to get some gossip going. They know I'm interested in you, and since neither of us is talking to the press about it, they're trying to bait us."

"Oh. So you're not seeing Natalia?"

"No. I'm sure my publicists would love that, but I've never been into her. I'm glad you asked me about the picture."

"I'm glad you're not dating a supermodel."

"Me too. Because then how could I go on dates with a mean, sexy punk girl?"

We kiss, and he clutches my dress with both fists as the pianist begins playing a new song.

"I love kissing you." He leans into me as he peppers me with kisses that make my whole, and I mean whole, body buzz. But the guy's about to go on a six-week tour. That's a long time, and we haven't even talked about what's happening here.

I gently push a hand to his chest to stop him.

"You okay?" he asks.

"Can we get dessert?" He smiles at that, but it doesn't reach his eyes.

I leave his arms and open the dessert menu, pretending to read it.

After dinner, Jesse insists on paying the bill, and even though it wasn't expensive, he leaves a fifty-dollar tip. A few photographers take pictures of us as we walk over to Gibson. Turns out Jesse actually had the store shut down this time, because he wants to play his new song, "Waiting for Christmas," for me, and he's been thinking about buying that archtop Citation, the one that's worth more than my house. A guitar of the gods.

"I want a special guitar for my last tour," Jesse explains with a wobbly voice.

Max greets us warmly, paying just as much attention to me as to Jesse.

"I've already got her set up for you," Max says, ushering me over to the Les Paul section. "I knew you'd come play this guitar again."

"Thank you," I say as I throw the strap over my shoulder, running my fingers up and down the neck. My hips swaying to the beat, I begin to pluck out "Eye of the Tiger," an eighties song that has one of my favorite guitar riffs. I pretend I'm playing this guitar in front of thousands of fans. Fans who've bought my single from iTunes.

Max's face grows brighter than the first time I played here.

"Hey, hey," Jesse calls out, cradling the new Citation. "What about me?"

I wave a hand at him. "Would you hold your horses?"

Then Jesse starts playing his new song. He closes his eyes, plucking out a beautiful melody. He sings,

Meeting her was Christmas, on a sunny September day.
Her lights, her smile, I want to celebrate her every day.
I waited for her, for her twinkling voice.
Waiting for her, waiting for Christmas.

By the time Jesse finishes the song, a tear is rolling down my face.

"Max," Jesse says, drumming his fingers on the bridge with one hand, touching the tuners with the other. He finds my eyes. "I think I'll take her."

♪♫♩

I take a deep breath and knock. A few seconds later, Sam opens the front door.

"Hey, My, what're you doing here?" He peers over my shoulder into the driveway. "And why are you driving Mom's car? Where's your bike?"

"Long story. Can I talk to you?"

He gestures for me to follow him inside to the dining room, where I find Jordan, her brother Mike, and a pretty lady sitting at the table playing the loudest game of war ever. Each time they slap down a card, the house rattles. Jordan slams down a king to beat her brother's four, winning the game. She jumps to her feet and dances while Mike grumbles.

"Do you want in the next round?" Sam asks me. "Maybe with four of us, we might have a chance at bringing Jordan down."

"No, thanks," I say. "I didn't mean to interrupt. I can come back tomorrow."

"Maya wants to talk," Sam tells Jordan.

"C'mon, we'll talk in the living room," Jordan rushes to say, and she pulls me and Sam out of the room and to the couch.

"Seriously, I can come back—I didn't know you'd have company."

"It's totally fine," Jordan says, and in a low whisper, she adds,

"I'm trying to fix my brother up with our friend, and I want to give them some time alone. So let's have a very long conversation about whatever you need to talk about. Please tell me it's about Jesse Scott."

"It better not be," Sam warns.

"It's not," I say, and Jordan deflates.

"I saw in *Celebrity Examiner* that you and Jesse were dating, but now he's interested in a Greek shipping heiress," Jordan says. "And now you're heartbroken and possibly pregnant with Jesse's triplets!"

"You'd better not be pregnant with triplets," Sam warns.

"That'd be news to me," I say, laughing.

"So are you dating Jesse?" Jordan asks.

"I'm not sure. We're still figuring things out. Jesse wants to take it slow."

"I understand that," Jordan says.

"You do?" I ask.

"Looking back, I'm glad Sam and I took things slow, even if it drove me crazy at the time. And even though it sucked, I'm glad we spent a year apart in college."

Sam nods. "Being single just made us realize we need to be together."

They stare at each other, very much in love. I hope to feel that kind of love one day.

"So you wanted to talk?" Jordan asks.

I reach into my back pocket, pull out the wrinkled letter from *Wannabe Rocker*, and pass it to Sam. He looks at the envelope for a long moment before pulling out the letter and unfolding it.

"This is amazing!" Sam shows the letter to Jordan, and then they dance around the living room like they've won every football game ever. My brother pulls me into a big hug.

"When do you leave?" he asks.

"I can't go," I say quietly.

"Why not?" Jordan asks.

"I thought I could save enough money, but it's just not happening."

"Pffft, money," Jordan says, grabbing up the letter and scanning it again. My brother glares at her. With her former NFL player father, Jordan grew up with all the money in the world, and she's never understood what it's like to eat the free lunch at school or buy your clothes at Walmart.

"I'll give you the money," Jordan says, and Sam places a hand over hers. Their eyes meet and go to war.

"How much do you have?" Sam asks me.

"About eight hundred dollars. I can buy two plane tickets for that—I need to take a guardian. But I won't have enough money left for food or a hotel. They're just too expensive in New York. They're even expensive in New Jersey. I check online every day, and there's nothing cheap."

"Did you talk to Mom and Dad?" Sam asks.

I slowly nod my head. "Dad thinks he can get me a couple

hundred, but I hate to do that to him. I would drive instead of flying, but Mom says her car won't make it, and we can't afford to buy another carburetor and go to New York too. I wanted to see if I could borrow your truck, maybe."

Sam clutches Jordan's hand and stares at her again. "So you have to take a guardian?"

"That's what the rules say, since I'm not eighteen."

"I know somebody who lives in Hoboken, New Jersey. A guy I played ball with in college."

I glance up at him. "You do?"

"Let me give him a call and see if he has room for us. Maybe we can stay a few days. And we'll take my truck. Then all we'd need to do is round up money for gas and food. That'd probably run us five hundred dollars or so?" He looks at Jordan to confirm his estimate, and she nods.

"I've got money saved you can use," she says quietly.

"That's your money," my brother says.

"It's *our* money," she replies, but Sam raises a hand. I guess she takes the hint, because she stays quiet for the first time in her life.

"What about your job?" I ask Sam. "Isn't this your busiest time, with all the college games happening right now?"

"I'll take off."

"I don't want to cause trouble for you."

"This is a once-in-a-lifetime opportunity." My brother pats my back. "We'll find a way."

Seasons of Love

A week after our date at the Spaghetti Factory, Jesse calls and asks for "a huge favor."

"No, I will not have sex with you," I joke.

"No, no. This is serious," he replies, taking a deep breath. "I'm wondering if you'll watch Casper for me while I'm on tour."

I let out a sigh; I'm glad he trusts me, but I'm sad he'll be gone for six weeks. "Of course I'll watch her, but don't you have people who can do that?"

"She likes you, and Grace and my security guards don't like taking care of her 'cause she always scratches and bites them. The little vixen's been known to draw blood."

So the day before he leaves, Jesse shows up at my house with Casper riding in a Ralph Lauren cat carrier, along with a litter box, a scratching post, enough gourmet cat food to feed all cats everywhere, and a specialized water filter for felines.

I help him carry everything to the porch, then he goes back

to his truck and emerges with one of those paper crowns from Burger King. He places it right on top of my head.

"What's the crown for?"

"You're my QueenQueen," he says, referring to my Twitter name. With a mischievous smile, he drops a kiss to my cheek.

Jesse follows me down the hall, peeking through doors along the way. He comes to a halt outside Anna's room. "Is this your room, My?" he asks, tipping his head at a poster of him sitting on a tractor, shirtless.

"Of course it's not."

"Don't worry, Casper. If you get lonely and miss me, just look up at Maya's Jesse Scott shrine."

"Oh hush, that's my sister's room." He follows me to mine, where I flop down on the bed, still wearing my new crown.

After setting up Casper's cat stuff in the corner, Jesse studies the pictures on my dresser, paying particular attention to the one of Dave and me dressed as Mario and the Princess at Halloween, the recently added picture of Jesse and me with the GranTurismo, and a photo of me, Anna, Sam, and Jordan.

Jesse touches the picture taken at Fall Creek Falls last June. Sam had just revealed he could gargle any song on demand, and Jordan cried bullshit. So he sipped some water and then gargled "Respect" by Aretha Franklin, and Anna, Jordan, and I about died laughing because it was so terrible.

Clearing his throat, Jesse pulls sheet music out of his back pocket. "Everything that's happened to you since we met has been weird, huh?"

"Um, being in *People* magazine? *Yeah.*"

"You know my new song? 'Waiting for Christmas'? The one I sang for you at Gibson? It's kind of based on you and me and our first day together, and I've been thinking a lot about our duet on the Belle Carol. It was fun, and I liked how we sounded together."

"Me too!"

He pulls a deep breath. "'Waiting' is actually a duet. Want to collaborate on it? Come record in the studio with me?"

"Me?" I stammer.

"Yes, you. Mark's on board too."

This must be the secret project he mentioned! "Would it, um, go on an album or on the radio or something?"

Jesse shrugs and smiles. "Nah—it would just be for fun. But you'd get some experience in the studio. It would probably be the last song I record."

I look down at my lap, my leg shaking like a jackhammer. Nervous and excited about doing something like this. Mostly upset that he's still planning to retire.

"I'd love to record with you, but why me?"

"I like you."

I think back to Jesse's face when he met that little girl at the fair, the one who said she wants to play piano because of him but can't because she can't afford lessons. Doesn't he know that he could help change lives? "But you don't want to help other people, do you?"

"I would if other people were more like you. So are you in?" He hands me the sheet music, and I bring it to my nose, smelling ink and crisp paper.

Of course I am!

"Why not?" I say nonchalantly.

Jesse sits on my bed with me. "So Holly told me you never returned her call about arranging voice lessons?"

I fidget and flex my fingers nervously. "I didn't...I can't afford them, Jess."

"It's on me, okay?"

"Are you sure?" He nods once. "Thank you," I say, and he returns my smile.

"We can record in January or so. After my tour's over."

"Where all are you going again?"

"All over the place. Dallas, Denver, Vegas, Kansas City, Seattle, Detroit, Cincinnati, Philly, Birmingham, Chicago, Orlando, New York. Then I'm heading over to London, Paris, and Berlin."

"That's amazing!" Casper jumps onto the bed and snuggles between us.

"I'm really excited about the Vegas show. I bought plane tickets for my parents to come out there. It's close to the Grand Canyon, and they've always wanted to go, so I figured we could make a day trip out of it. Ride horses and stuff. And we can have

Thanksgiving together too." He grins to himself as he scratches Casper's ears.

"I'm happy for you. So you're still retiring?"

"Yes."

"I wish you'd reconsider. You have such a gift."

He lifts the Burger King crown off my head, sets it on my nightstand, and brushes my hair behind my ears. "I need to fix things with my family first."

"Anybody who puts how they appear to their friends and coworkers before the happiness of their kid doesn't have their priorities straight."

"I know we have a lot to work out," he says. "But I want to try."

He slips his cowboy boots off and pulls me back on the bed with him. I inhale sharply as I rest my head on his shoulder. Other than that time at the Underground, I haven't curled up with him before. I watch his eyelashes flutter and run my fingers over the stubble on his cheek.

He picks up my iPhone and earbuds, taking the right one and handing me the left. He flicks through my playlists, grimacing at all the Queen and Madonna, then settles on some old-school John Mellencamp. He folds an arm behind his head, and we listen to music with our eyes closed.

The longer we lie here, the more my body wants him. My skin is burning up, desperate for his touch.

When he gently caresses my jaw, I grab on to him and hold on tight. He studies my eyes for a few seconds, then stands to shut my bedroom door.

"This okay?" he asks.

I nod. "Dad's at the garage and Mom's at work."

I hope neither will catch me with Jesse. He rejoins me on my bed, straddling my hips, wrapping an arm around my waist, pulling me against him. Not taking his eyes off mine, he slips the earbud back into his ear, so we can keep listening to music. As soon as his lips touch mine, I know the risk of getting caught is worth it. He inhales sharply when my tongue sweeps inside his mouth.

A kiss that starts out slow becomes a rhythm: hard then soft then wild. His mouth moves lower, trailing heat and shivers down my neck. He pushes the hem of my top up to my ribs. Presses his lips to my stomach. I gasp and gasp again when one of his hands cups my breast. My hips buck involuntarily.

He lifts his head. "You all right?"

I'm panting so hard it takes several seconds to get my breathing under control. I rip my earbud out. "Jess…what are we doing here?"

"What's wrong?"

I swallow, and he brushes my hair out of my face, staring into my eyes. He slowly removes his earbud.

"Remember how you got upset on shadow day and left?" I ask. "And then at the movies, you didn't want to hold hands or kiss or anything?"

"I remember," he says quietly. "I also remember how, on our last date, you stopped kissing *me*."

"I'm scared you'll freak out again."

"I've had time to think since then…I've figured stuff out. It won't happen again."

"But what if it does? I'm sick of kissing someone only to find they've lost interest ten minutes later."

"Why do you think I'd do that?" he asks with a hard edge.

I decide to be honest. "You and Nate both hurt me, okay?"

He rocks back onto his knees, his eyebrows pinching together. "I'm nothing like him. I don't ask girls out very often, you know. I thought you understood I'm serious about this. About you."

I lean against the stiff headboard. "You haven't told me that before, so how could I know?"

"Well, I don't think I should have to pay for Nate's mistake."

"What is *that* supposed to mean?"

"I mean that you put yourself out there with him, and it didn't pay off. I've apologized, and you aren't giving me another chance because some idiot guy hurt you. I have no idea how he let you go, Maya Henry."

I cover my face with my pillow. My voice is muffled when I speak. "You can have anybody. Why are you even interested in me?"

His calloused fingers caress my arm. "You're true to yourself. And you get me. You treat me like I'm real."

I move the pillow and look up at him. At this beautiful

freckle-faced guy with the gorgeous voice and even sweeter heart. I bet it took a lot of courage for him to say that stuff to me. He's right. I hated it when he compared me to his ex. It's not fair of me to judge him for what went wrong with Nate. I'll be alone forever if I compare every guy to Nate. Still, the thought of being in a relationship with Jesse makes me feel nervous, like when I perform a solo. I don't know if I'll make it through the song without messing up.

But I want to get onstage.

"What happens with us while you're on tour?" I ask.

"I'll be back in six weeks. It's not forever."

"It's still a long time…I barely heard from you when you were gone for ten days. I don't want to be the girl who sits by the phone waiting. I need to know if you're going to call me." My heart's pounding. I can't believe I'm putting myself out there like this.

"I can do that," Jesse says and gently pecks my cheek. "We'll text and Skype, and when I get back, we'll figure out the rest."

"I want that," I say bravely. "I want to figure us out. I want to know what we are."

He grins. "I know what I want."

"Oh yeah?"

Jesse twines his fingers between mine and presses my hands above my head. I shiver as his body covers mine.

"I want another kiss."

"You're so demanding," I say, smiling, giving him exactly what he asked for.

♪♫♩

A few days later before first period, Dave dashes up with his phone. "You have to see this!" He pushes play on a *TMZ* video.

The voice-over says, "We got Jesse Scott at Miami airport." The clip shows him making his way through the terminal, reporters circling him like buzzards. The paparazzi ask question after question about the tour and his future plans, but Jesse keeps his mouth shut. Cameras flash in his face. *Click, click, click, click.* A reporter yells, "Why isn't Maya Henry on tour with you?"

No answer from Jesse.

"Are you dating Maya?"

No response.

"What does she think of you being seen with Natalia Naylor?"

"Can you give us *anything* on Maya?"

Jesse stops. The press circles him, and he smiles wickedly at the camera. "If you're watching this, My, I miss you. You're my mean, sexy punk girl."

And when the video flicks off, Dave and I do a little dance in the hallway, chattering about how cute he is, and hope blooms inside me.

That night, I tweet Jesse a picture of me and Dave frowning with a caption that says "We miss you!" and, like, fifty thousand people favorite it. Since I started hanging out with Jesse, I've gained over a hundred thousand followers. I know they aren't following me for me—they just want to see Jesse and me tweet jabs back and forth at each other, but still. It's pretty cool.

A week into Jesse's tour, Mom hands me a postcard from Orlando featuring a muscular man in a Speedo. Laughing, I flip it over and read:

Dear M

Wish you were with me. As you can probably tell from this postcard, I'm having a blast. Aren't you jealous? :) Please tell Casper I love her, and tell Anna and Dave I said hi. Talk to you tonight.

J

Shaking my head, I smile and go hang the postcard on my bedroom mirror.

I change clothes and ride my old bicycle over to the Baptist church, where I'm meeting Holly. She's nice enough to drive to Franklin two days a week to give me voice lessons in the church's music room. I had to cut back on the number of hours I work down at Caldwell's. Taking the voice lessons is worth the time. Holly says I'm getting better and better, and even though she's preparing me to sing a duet with Jesse, I'm getting the experience I need for my auditions in New York too.

With two weeks left, I've saved one thousand dollars. Sam's friend said we could stay with him for a few nights, but my brother said we need to buy him a nice dinner to say thanks. Sam's truck isn't new by any means—it's a 2002 Dodge. It needs a tune-up and oil change before the trip. Sometimes I can't believe this is really happening. I'm so close to my goal.

I still haven't told Jesse I'm going to New York. I want to show him—want to show everybody—that I can do this on my own. And I know I can. Just me, my voice, and my guitar.

But I still have a problem: Casper.

I can't leave her with my little sister, because she would tell the entire world that she's caring for Jesse Scott's cat, and *Access Hollywood* would probably show up at our house. I can't leave her with Jordan, because she's allergic.

So one week before the trip, I head over to see Dr. Salter, and the office assistant with Marge Simpson hair tells me to go on in. I knock on the door and find him poring over a pile of paperwork. He invites me to sit, so I plop down on the ratty couch.

"I need to ask a favor."

"Go ahead," Dr. Salter says, taking a seat across from me.

"Jesse asked me to watch his cat while he's on tour."

"Did he?" Dr. Salter asks, leaning back and crossing his arms. "He must really trust you."

I lift a shoulder in a shrug. "Cats can take care of themselves. It's no big deal."

"Did he tell you where Casper came from?" I shake my head, so Dr. Salter goes on. "When Jesse was about sixteen or so, he was on tour. One night after a show in New Orleans, he walked out the back door of the Superdome and heard Casper crying."

"Aww."

"She couldn't have been more than four weeks old. Jesse took her to his hotel and bottle-fed her, and she's been with him ever since. I think the cat makes him feel good about himself. Everyone coddles him, so it's good he has someone to take care of."

I fidget in my seat, adjusting my bracelets.

"I think he feels the same way about you," Dr. Salter says.

I close my eyes for a moment. The last thing I want is for Jesse to take care of me. I want us to take care of each other.

"Um, anyway, I've had something unexpected come up, and I was wondering if I could leave Casper with you for a week."

"Sure." He narrows his eyes. "But what's going on?"

"I sent an audition tape to *Wannabe Rocker*. And I got into the semifinals in New York City!"

A smile stretches across his face. "Excellent. Congratulations, Maya. What did Jesse say?"

"You can't tell him! I want to surprise him."

"Okay, I won't."

"I'm going to be out of school for a week, but I'll make it up. If I get past the semifinals, I'll need more—"

He waves a hand at me. "We can work the details out as we need to. What made you decide to do this?"

"Jesse told me that I have to take chances to reach my dreams."

♪♫♩

I am in a serious turducken coma.

This was the best Thanksgiving ever. My family went to Jordan's parents' house for dinner, where, I kid you not, they had three huge turkeys and a turducken! After gorging on pecan pie and green bean casserole, I'm now back at home, lounging on the couch, watching *Miracle on 34th Street* with my parents, Anna, and Casper.

My cell rings at about 10:00 p.m. Jesse.

"I gotta take this," I tell Casper, moving her off my lap. "He's probably worried about you."

I step out onto the front porch to answer. The chilly air makes me shiver, but I like being outside when we talk on the phone. It makes me feel closer to him—the same stars hang in the sky, even if he's in Vegas and I'm in Tennessee.

"Jess?"

"Happy Thanksgiving, My." His voice cracks. "How's Casper?"

"She's fine—she's watching *Miracle on 34th Street.* What's wrong?"

I hear him let out a bunch of air. "I really thought they were going to come, and they didn't."

I slowly sit down on the concrete porch and rest my head against my knees. I just let him talk.

"Dad said they weren't comfortable with coming to Vegas." His voice catches, and he breathes hard again. "They said they wanted to come to my concert, but they called and said they couldn't 'cause it was in Vegas and they didn't understand why I'd agreed to sing in such a sinful town."

"But, Jess, you're touring all over the place. In nonsinful towns like Orlando. I mean, Disney is so not about sin."

"That's what you think," he replies, laughing softly.

"Regardless of however you sinned in Disney World, which I don't want to know about, your parents could have come to any of your other concerts, Jess."

"Yeah."

"They shouldn't have abandoned you on Thanksgiving."

"Yeah."

"And I don't think it's fair that you're willing to compromise and stop performing the music you love, and they can't even meet you halfway."

He goes quiet. Shit, did I overstep?

"I miss you, My," he says softly.

Maybe I could get a plane ticket with the money I've saved; forget about the road trip to New York. "I can fly out. We could have Thanksgiving together tomorrow. Just tell me where you'll be."

"It's okay. I'm heading to Chicago tomorrow, and my schedule there is too busy. But thanks—it means a lot."

All I want is for him to feel happy. I would be heartbroken if my holiday was ruined. "I hope you got a real dinner. Turkey and dressing and the works."

"Mark took me out for Tofurky."

"Oh good God," I mutter, which makes him laugh. "That's a crime."

"I knew you'd make me feel better, Maya Henry."

I wrap an arm around my waist, trying to warm up. "Family's not always blood. I have Dave, and you've got Mr. Logan."

"But still."

"I know," I say quietly. I can't imagine how complicated this is for him.

He pauses. "So how're voice lessons with Holly going? She told me you're getting better and better."

Jesse and I chat for a long time, for so long it's like he forgets about his jerkface parents. He's cracking up on the other end of the line, asking me to put Casper on the phone so the cat can say if I'm not giving her enough attention or making her do lame-ass tricks.

When I get off the phone, tears well in my eyes. I can't believe he made such an effort for his parents, and they didn't show. My mom pokes her head out the screen door.

"It's freezing out here, baby girl," she says, rubbing her arms at the chill. I stand up, and she wraps me in a hug.

"I love you," I tell her. It's understood in our family, but we rarely say it out loud. Mom pulls back and stares.

"I love you too. What's going on?" she asks, so I tell her about Jesse and his parents, and how I feel so bad for him.

After a few minutes of listening to me talk about Jesse, Mom takes a deep breath. "Baby, I've been wanting to talk to you about New York… I'm sorry your dad and I can't help more with your trip, but I asked my boss if I could have some time off to go with you and Sam. My boss said I could, and I'd like to come, as long as it's okay with you."

"Of course!" I say and give her another huge hug. I am so lucky. I used to think trust means "never let you down," but really, it's about love. Family can't always help fix a difficult situation, and everybody makes mistakes. We shouldn't expect perfect. But we can hope that the people we love love us enough to try to make it right.

Jesse's parents haven't tried to make things right. I wish he could see that. He can't give up music for them. He just can't. And when he gets home from tour, I will make sure he knows that.

On the Road Again

The order of business: drop Casper off at Dr. Salter's house, obtain doughnuts and coffee from Donut Palace, hit the road, stop at a hotel in Virginia, and arrive in Hoboken by Sunday evening so we can get a good night's sleep before tryouts start on Monday at 8:00 a.m. sharp.

The odds I'll make it through the semifinals aren't good—the show will narrow five hundred contestants down to thirty. Sometimes people get kicked off before they've even had a chance to sing ten seconds. I'm gonna give it my all though. I will prove to myself, if not others, that I have talent.

Sam isn't too thrilled Mom decided to come, because we have to squeeze into his truck, and when you're as big as my brother, you want room to spread out. It doesn't matter how small I am. With me sitting in the middle of the bench, he keeps elbowing me, and I keep elbowing him, and Mom keeps telling us not to fight.

"Let's go through your songs," Mom suggests. "What are you gonna sing for your first audition?"

"'Another One Bites the Dust.' Doing Queen songs worked on my audition tape, so I figure it might work again."

"And what will you sing after that?" Mom asks.

"You mean if I even make it past the first round? You know they make tons of cuts the first day."

"You need to have another song prepared."

"I do, I do." I take a deep breath. I'm happy Mom is so encouraging, but I'm still only one of five hundred. "I'm thinking 'When Doves Cry' by Prince, though I've also been working on a P!nk song so I can show I can sing more than just eighties music. Jesse's voice coach has taught me a lot."

At the mention of Jesse, my brother lets out a long sigh. He knows how happy Jesse makes me, but he has to sigh because that's what annoying older brothers do.

For the next half hour, I practice "When Doves Cry" and "Who Knew" over and over, my mom talking about the strengths of each as a potential second song. My poor brother is wincing, because I'm singing in his ear while he's trying to drive.

"We should've flown to New York," Sam grumbles. "I feel like I've been driving for years."

"Sam, we haven't even made it to Knoxville yet," I say.

"I'm so excited!" Mom exclaims, waving her hands.

"I know! I can't wait to perform in Radio City," I say. It's going to be way different from playing at those tiny metal clubs in Nashville. I've never felt such a high, but getting past the semis won't be easy.

At about noon, we stop at a rest stop in Bristol, Tennessee, and Mom calls Dad to check in. Sam digs around in the coolers and pulls bread, roast beef, cheese, mustard, and mayo out so we can make sandwiches. He lays the spread out on a picnic table, and he dives in. He makes himself a double roast beef sandwich with three pieces of bread. Brothers sure do eat a lot.

Mom makes me a normal-sized sandwich, but I'm too nervous to eat it. Plus Sam forgot to buy pickles, and who can eat a sandwich without them?

"So what do you think will happen during the first day of semis?" Sam asks me as I strum my guitar.

I give him a look. "Uh, were you not paying any attention when I made you watch all those YouTube clips?"

"They change the rules, like, every season. It's impossible to keep up with it all."

Mom pulls the envelope from *Wannabe Rocker* out of my bag and reads the paperwork. "Apparently, the first thing that happens on Monday is the four judges are announced. Then everyone gets to perform."

"If a judge doesn't like you," I say, "he can push a button, and the lights will go off on one third of the stage. If a second judge doesn't like you, the lights go out on the other side of the stage.

And if a third judge decides you suck, he pushes a button, and the entire stage goes dark."

"So to move forward, at least two judges have to like you?" Sam asks.

"Right."

"Who were the judges last year?"

"Um," I pause. "Last year it was Jewel, Steven Tyler from Aerosmith, Slash from Guns, and, uh, Sheryl Crow."

"Is that who it is this year?" Sam asks.

"It usually changes," I reply. "I heard a rumor that Jon Bon Jovi might be one, but I don't know. They haven't announced the judges yet. Jesse mentioned his manager wanted him to judge, but he's not," I say.

We stay overnight at a Motel 6 in Virginia. Mom and I share a double bed, and Sam sprawls out on the other. In the morning, we binge eat at the continental breakfast so we won't have to buy a big lunch. It takes us about two hours to reach the Washington, DC, suburbs, and as we get closer and closer to the city, I can't stop staring out the window, because cars keep getting fancier and fancier.

"Holy crap," I blurt. "That's a Jaguar XK! And that's a freaking Mercedes AMG!"

Sam keeps elbowing me when I lean across him to get a better look.

On the New Jersey turnpike, nobody signals when changing

lanes, and it seems everyone drives twenty miles over the speed limit. This is my kind of road. Sam loves it as much as I do, grinning as he speeds to keep up with traffic.

"Slow down, Sam!" Mom cries, covering her eyes, and I pat her knee.

Then I see it.

The city.

I smile at the bridges in the distance and the twinkling lights and the skyscrapers. We find our exit, and Sam says, "I need more cash. There's another toll."

"I don't understand why we have to pay to drive on the interstate," I say, rooting through my bag for more money. "I wish I'd known we'd have to pay all these tolls. I would've taken out a loan." Driving north is a lot more complicated than in the south, where we have wide-open roads and fields for miles and miles.

After sitting in traffic for the length of six songs—including "Bohemian Rhapsody," which is, like, the longest song ever—we finally make it to Sam's friend's apartment in Hoboken, and not a moment too soon. I really thought my brother was about to throw my iPhone out the window if he had to hear one more Queen song. We circle the block a few times to find street parking, then climb a set of brick steps to a building that's taller than most in Franklin. Inside, we take a staircase to the fourth floor, where we meet Sam's friend Robert, and they immediately disappear out to a bar where they can catch up and my brother can recover from what he calls *the road trip from Hades*.

Mom collapses onto the couch and dozes. Not wanting to wake her, I take my phone into the bathroom and shut the door behind me as I sit down on the bathtub rim and push Jesse's name to call him. He doesn't have a show tonight, so he should be relaxing at the Four Seasons in Philly.

He picks up after one ring. "Hi, you."

I love it when he says that.

Even though I have to get up early tomorrow morning, I talk to Jesse until late in the night. I started biting my fingernails the minute I rolled into New Jersey, but just hearing his calm, cool, country voice draws the nerves right out of me.

♪♫♩

It's 6:15 a.m., and I'm making myself a cup of coffee in Robert's kitchen.

I'm wearing my itty-bitty black dress and some sparkly bangles. Mom pulled my hair up into a high ponytail. Total camp. I also put on my purple cowboy boots. They don't really go with my outfit, and kids would laugh me out of school if I wore this back at Hundred Oaks, but they're comfortable, and I hope they'll be good luck.

I die laughing when I see how my brother's dressed to support me: Sam is wearing a rainbow headband, a purple tracksuit, and high-tops. Given how stressed I am, he knows I need a laugh.

After we've eaten and pulled on our winter coats, we trudge up the slush-covered sidewalk to catch the train to Manhattan, carrying my electric Fender, sheet music, and my application. It takes us several minutes to figure out how to buy tickets and how much money to put on them. Then another minute to learn how to use the turnstiles. I'm trying to stay pumped for today's audition, but I feel totally off my game here. We stand beside the tracks, waiting for the train to arrive. I stare down the dark tunnel.

"What if it doesn't come?" I cry.

"It will," Mom says soothingly.

"When? I can't be late!"

Sam squeezes my shoulder.

Two minutes later, it comes, and I feel silly for freaking out.

On the train, I'm shivering like crazy, but not because it's freezing outside. My brother throws an arm around me, and I lean my head back, close my eyes, and breathe in as much air as I can. The speeding train rocks back and forth on the tracks.

"You okay?" he whispers.

"So, so scared."

He squeezes my shoulder. "Relax. Any time you feel nervous, just pretend you're singing with Jesse on the Belle Carol, okay?"

I adjust my bangles and chew on my nails all the way to Herald Square, where we get off the train. Here, people walk super fast. Some people are sprinting through the subway station like they're trying to get the last hot dog at the barbeque, but a few are going slow, taking their time. Everyone is dressed differently—glamour, goths, jeans and T-shirts, suits and ties, skaters. I bet it's easy to fit in here, which is cool.

It takes a while to get out of the station, because there are so many signs to make sense of and people to squeeze past, but finally Mom, Sam, and I step out into the bright sunlight. The noise hits me first. Cars honking, music blaring, people talking, buses rumbling by. And the smell—I shouldn't even try to describe it, but it's a mix of chestnuts and car exhaust and fried foods. It's weird, and I love it. I twirl around in a circle, smiling up at the soaring buildings.

Sam hails a cab and loads my guitar into the trunk. The three of us crowd into the backseat.

"Where to?" the cabbie asks. He's wearing a beaded vest, like something out of the sixties.

"Radio City Music Hall," Mom replies.

The cab pulls out into traffic, narrowly missing being hit by another cab. Our cabbie honks his horn. "What're you doin' at Radio City?" the driver asks. "It's too early for a show."

"I'm trying out for *Wannabe Rocker*," I say.

"Huh. Never heard of it."

The three of us exchange looks. Everybody I know in Tennessee watches it.

I put my palm against the window as we drive uptown. I've

never seen so many billboards and flashing lights in my life. The cab meter's little red numbers tick up, up, up, finally stopping at $8.10. The cab pulls over to the curb, and Sam pays the driver, then lifts my guitar out of the trunk.

Radio City signs stretch down the side of the super tall building; I crane my neck all the way back, trying to see the top.

Mom taps my shoulder and points at six stretch limos parked outside. "Could be the judges."

I inhale and exhale and inhale and exhale, then step toward the building, carrying my guitar. I lead Mom and Sam inside the lavish red-and-gold foyer that yanks the breath right out of my chest. It's so much grander than the Grand Ole Opry, which means it is *grand* grand.

Video cameras are everywhere, pointing at people in line and as they head inside the auditorium. Excited murmurs fill the foyer.

I get into line with a bunch of other musicians. Some people are part of a group, while others are solo artists. Some are carrying instruments, and others are probably vocals only. There is a lot of variety on this show.

I try to size everybody up. That super cute twentysomething guy probably sings music by Maroon 5. I bet that rocker chick does Fiona Apple and Alanis. There's a band whose look reminds me of Green Day. The people scoping me out probably have me pegged as an eighties freak in a random pair of cowboy boots, which is true. But they don't know I have other music in my arsenal. So who knows what's up with the rest of these contestants? Especially the man with an accordion. And the beautiful African American girl carrying a violin. I can't wait to see her perform.

We inch forward in line until the lady at the registration table says, "Name?"

"Maya Henry," I reply, and the lady gives me a bib to pin to my dress. The bib, which has a large red *156* on it, says my name and that I'm from Tennessee.

"The number is your seat assignment," she says.

Mom has to help me fasten on the bib, because my hands won't stop shaking and I keep sticking myself with the safety pin.

My family and I walk inside the auditorium, which looks nothing like my school's.

Mom clutches my elbow. "Oh my God."

"Wow," Sam says.

Considering he played college football in huge, fancy stadiums, it means something when he is impressed. I tilt my head back to study the cavernous, circular, orange-and-red theater. Huge *Wannabe Rocker* banners hang around the auditorium.

That's when it hits me.

I'm going to perform onstage in Radio City. I, Maya Henry, made it to the semifinals of a national singing contest!

I pass my guitar to Sam and skip down the aisle. I feel like I could pole-vault or sumo wrestle or lift a car off a person. I want to scream, to make my voice echo in this humongous auditorium.

Mom and I pose in front of the stage, laughing, as Sam snaps pictures with his phone. Cameramen are everywhere.

"Maya Henry," a guy named Liam says, peering at my bib. He has a British accent.

"Liam Watson." I read his bib. "From San Francisco. Never been there. What do you sing?"

Liam's grin belongs on a poster in an orthodontist's office. "Jazz. I'm on piano. You?"

"I do eighties tributes on guitar."

"I can't wait to hear them. Your accent is adorable."

"I have an accent?" I ask.

Liam smiles. "Have we met before?" he asks me, grabbing my hand to kiss the back of it. This jazz boy is adorable, but I'm even more excited to be talking to another musician, and one who doesn't think I'm selling out for doing eighties covers.

"No, we haven't met."

He points at me. "I've seen you somewhere."

Mom puts an arm around me. "You probably saw her on YouTube singing with Jesse Scott."

Liam swallows. "I know that video. The one on the boat, right?"

A girl standing nearby whispers to another as they scan me up and down, looking fearful.

"Fame whore," one says under her breath.

The other sneers. "Why were you singing with a country star if you're an eighties rocker?"

Liam interrupts the haters. "Maya, your performance was great."

My hands, which had stopped shaking when I was talking to Liam, shake even worse than before. I hope people don't expect a Belle Carol encore, which, considering how much Jesse and Holly have to say about my poor mechanics, may not happen. I mean, I want to do well at this audition and would love to make it into the top thirty, but I'll be so embarrassed if I bomb onstage. Then, I was singing with a three-time Grammy winner. Now? Not so much.

Mom and Sam go to find seats in the back of the auditorium, and I grab a bottle of water from a refreshments table. I uncap it and sip, taking deep breaths.

Ten minutes later, an older man in a blue pinstripe suit walks out onstage, smoothing his silver hair. He speaks into the microphone. "If you could take your seats, please." After everyone has finished tripping over each other to sit and the murmuring has died down, the man continues. "As the executive producer for *Wannabe Rocker*, on behalf of NBC and Rêve Records, I'd like to welcome you to the season twelve semifinals."

Everyone stars cheering and clapping, and my heart pounds.

"My name is Phil Tyson," the producer says. "Let me give you a rundown of today's schedule. Our judges are going to listen to each singer perform." Mr. Tyson pauses as applause breaks out again. "But this year, we have a new twist."

The girl to my right leans over. "There's always a twist!"

"This year, if the judges turn out all three lights on your first-round performance, you're out. You don't get feedback from the judges. You're to leave the stage immediately. You will get a critique from our judges only if your lights stay on."

Murmurs and gasps fill the auditorium. We don't get any sort of feedback? That sucks and is kind of heartbreaking. I can't imagine coming all the way to New York City to perform and then getting kicked off without even knowing why. But it must make for good television. I fidget, trying to get comfy.

"If you make it through the first round today, you'll get another chance to perform in front of the judges tomorrow. Same rules apply then—if the lights go off, you've been cut. If we still have more than thirty people after that, the judges will listen to you again on Wednesday and Thursday until they've narrowed the number down to thirty contestants. Got it?"

"Got it," we all chorus.

Mr. Tyson claps his hands together. "Ready to meet this year's judges?"

The noise in the auditorium escalates, reminding me of Jesse's concert at the Opry.

"God, I hope one of the judges is Taylor Swift," the guy on my other side says. "She's so hot." He sounds like a real perv; besides, it should be about her music, not her looks.

The first judge to come out is freaking Dave Matthews, and everyone jumps out of their chairs.

"Ahhhhh!" I yell. I'm going to be performing in front of freaking. Dave. Matthews.

He tells us how honored he is to be here. "I hope I get to see some awesome singers today." Then he takes his seat at the judges' table in front of the stage.

The second judge onstage is Joel Madden from Good Charlotte, which makes the girl to my right giddy. She jumps up and down, pumping her fist. Cameramen walk up and down the aisles filming everyone. What a circus this is. I wonder if any of my footage will end up on TV. With so many people auditioning, they'll probably only show the best and weakest when it comes time to air. That's usually how it goes.

Mr. Tyson announces the third judge, Annie Lennox! She sings one of my favorite eighties songs, "Here Comes the Rain Again." I don't think my blood has ever pulsed this hard.

Mr. Tyson says into the mike, "And now for our fourth and final judge this season. The winner of *Wannabe Rocker* season three, Jesse Scott!"

I cover my mouth with both hands while all the other contestants clap and holler for Jesse.

"Oh my God, oh my God, oh my God," I chant. I thought he was in Philly! I thought he was retiring…I thought he blew this gig when he fell off the yacht! Why didn't he tell me? "Oh my God…"

"Please be seated," Mr. Tyson announces, and the other contestants sit down, but I keep on standing, touching my throat.

Jesse scans the audience, and his eyes meet mine. His mouth falls open. Then it slowly forms his famous half-cocked smile.

He grabs a microphone. "Hey, Maya Henry. What're you doin' here? And who's watching my cat?"

Water Runs Dry

It sounds like a swarm of angry bees were released in Radio City Music Hall.

"She should be disqualified!" a guy yells, holding up his iPhone. "Here's the video of her singing with him!"

Another girl calls out, "I saw them in *People* magazine together! It's a setup."

"They talk on Twitter all the time!" another girl yells.

I'm waiting for somebody to lunge at me with a pitchfork.

Jesse leaps off the stage with the finesse of a cowboy dismounting a horse and hustles up the aisle to my row of seats. I stumble past people to reach him, and when I do, he picks me up in a hug and twirls me around. I haven't seen him in more than three weeks, and being in his arms feels like spring becoming summer.

"I missed you so much," he whispers.

"Me too."

He brushes his lips against mine. His soft kiss drowns out the ruckus around us. A cameraman gets right up in our faces. I bury my head in Jesse's white button-down shirt.

"I thought you were in Philly," I say.

"I popped over this morning." He pulls away and sets his hands on my shoulders, smiling. "I can't believe you tried out for the show. This is big-time! I'm so, so proud."

The shouting gets louder and louder—it's like I'm in the ring at a boxing match.

"Why didn't you tell me?" I whisper.

He raises an eyebrow. "Why didn't you tell *me*?"

"I wanted to do this on my own. I didn't want you to think I was taking advantage of you by asking for help." I say the words quietly, and his face falls. "I wanted to surprise you."

"Well, you did. I wasn't allowed to tell anyone I was judging. Only Mark knew."

"I thought you blew it when you fell off that yacht."

Jesse laughs. "These people love drama. Nearly any news is good news."

"But I thought you're retiring," I whisper.

"I made a deal," he whispers back. "Judge the show for one season, and I can get out of my three-year contract with Rêve."

That's when Mr. Logan comes rushing up with the executive producer Mr. Tyson and two men wearing suits and shiny shoes. They must be producers or something.

One of them says, "Jesse, Mark, how could you not tell us about this?"

Mr. Logan smiles and shakes his head at me. "I'm as surprised as you are. I couldn't get her to play around in a recording booth, and now she tries out for a TV show."

The second guy says, "We have a situation here. Perhaps we should talk someplace private?"

So that's how I find myself with Jesse, my mom and brother, Mr. Logan, and the producers in the Roxy Suite. It pimps the socks off Jesse's dressing room at the Opry. It's full of sparkly crystal china and a rainbow of artwork, not to mention flat-screen TVs and leather furniture.

Even though they've only met once—before Jesse took me on our date to the Spaghetti Factory—Mom gives Jesse a hug. I'm glad he doesn't wince or freak out or anything. He acts like a perfect gentleman. Sam gives him a nod, but my brother isn't happy.

"I don't like it when people threaten my sister," he says with a growl. "I was about to kick some asses in that crowd out there."

"Later, dear," Mom says, patting Sam's arm. "Right now, let's hear what the producers have to say."

We take seats on the couches. I wipe my palms on my black dress and sit close to Jesse so our thighs touch. Mr. Logan paces, talking into his cell. "Tell Charles to get on the next plane to New York...I don't care what he says about his golf game, just get him here."

"Who's Charles?" I ask Jesse.

"My attorney. But it's fine—I'll quit so you can perform."

Mr. Tyson and the other two producers exchange freaked-out looks.

With the phone still pressed to his ear, Mr. Logan snaps his fingers and points at Jesse. "You'll do nothing until Charles gets here. You signed a contract."

Jesse crosses his legs, shaking his red cowboy boot, and leans back against the leather sofa like he owns the place. "This is no big deal, right? I mean, I'll treat Maya like I'll treat every other singer."

"I was under the impression Maya is your girlfriend," Mr. Tyson says, folding his arms across his chest.

"We're not in a relationship exactly," I ramble. "I mean, we haven't decided yet—we're planning to talk when Jesse gets home—"

"We're together," Jesse interrupts, squeezing my hand, and I can't stop the smile spreading across my face.

"Every other singer out there will file suit against the network," the younger producer says.

Mr. Tyson holds up a hand. "Tom, let's just take this one step at a time."

"I'll quit," Jesse says. "I'm not letting Maya give up this opportunity."

"What about your deal?" I whisper.

"Jesse, we're excited to have you as a judge this year," Mr. Tyson says. "I want to ensure we start our relationship on the right foot, and—"

The younger producer interrupts. "The show has already

dedicated many resources to ensure Jesse's a judge this season. We've already created the press kits. Our network affiliates will be announcing the judges during today's news broadcasts. It's out on social media already. And we'd have to postpone the semifinals until we could find a replacement judge. We'd expect Jesse to pay for any losses the network would incur."

"Tom," Mr. Tyson says. "Calm down."

"What if I don't judge Maya?" Jesse asks. "Bring in a replacement judge just for her performances."

"That would probably open us up to even more lawsuits," Tom says. "All contestants must be on the same playing field, facing the same judges."

I take a deep breath. "So I'll quit." I'm glad my voice doesn't break.

Mr. Logan snaps and points at me like he did to Jesse. "No more until Charles gets here."

"But the rules on the application say my daughter can't know anyone associated with the show," Mom says, biting her lip.

Mr. Logan throws his hands up in the air. "That's it. No one talks until Charles gets here."

Jesse jiggles his boot on his knee. "Who wants coffee?"

"I told you not to talk." Mr. Logan bops Jesse's cowboy hat with his little black notebook, and Jesse swats at his manager, grinning. He adjusts his hat, acting like this is no big deal.

Mom starts sniffling and wipes her nose with a tissue. Sam

hasn't looked up in several minutes. I feel like I played the lottery and won.

And then all the money got stolen.

♪♫♩

Because the heavens opened and angels sent rays of goodness to Mr. Tyson's heart, I get to perform during the first round of auditions. The producers will decide if I'm allowed to compete after Jesse's attorney arrives. Mr. Tyson doesn't want to hold up auditions any longer—they're already behind schedule thanks to me.

Mr. Tyson says, "Tom, it's obvious neither Jesse nor Maya knew the other was going to be here today. Which shouldn't be a surprise, since we kept Jesse's participation a closely guarded secret."

The younger producer storms out of the Roxy Suite. Mom and Sam grin at that.

Mr. Tyson turns to Jesse. "But I expect you to be completely impartial today, Mr. Scott. Understand?"

Jesse nods, yawns, and pats my back. "Shall we?"

Back in the auditorium, I get heckled like the time I peed my pants in elementary school, but I hold my head high. Mr. Tyson grabs a mike and explains what's happening. "It remains to be seen if Jesse Scott will be a judge this season—"

Cue massive booing.

Mr. Tyson continues, "Or if Maya Henry will be disqualified. Our lawyers will sit with Jesse Scott's attorneys this afternoon to discuss and come to a resolution, but we do not feel this is a reason to postpone today's performances."

Cue massive applause.

"As we honestly believe Jesse and Maya did not know the other would be here today, we will permit her to participate in the first round."

Cue massive booing.

"So let's get started," Mr. Tyson says, clapping his hands.

Jesse comes out from backstage carrying a coffee mug. He tips his cowboy hat at the contestants and takes a seat at the judges' table.

A stagehand explains that we're auditioning in numerical order. I peer down at the 156 on my bib. I have a long time to wait. What if Jesse's lawyer arrives before I get to audition and decides that I can't? I suck in a deep breath and try to relax.

"Number one," the stagehand shouts, and a guy struts onstage, plugs his guitar into an amp, plays a lick, and says he'll be singing "Under the Bridge" by the Red Hot Chili Peppers.

But Jesus, if the Red Hot Chili Peppers heard the way the guitarist messed up that easy progression, they'd probably throw tomatoes and eggs at the stage. After about ten seconds, the lights on one side of the stage go out. I can't tell which judge did it, but I don't blame them. Five seconds later, the lights on the other side shut off, leaving a strip of light down the center. Three seconds after that, the stage goes dark. Number One's dreams of stardom are over. Just like that. He mopes off the stage. It must suck to come all this way and get no feedback as to why the judges turned off the lights.

The guy to my left whispers, "They're harsh. I won't even make it past the first round."

"Don't give up yet," I tell him.

The stagehand calls for number two.

A girl dressed in a plaid skirt and French braids saunters onto the stage and announces she's singing "Don't Speak" by No Doubt. Her performance is not bad, but I'm not getting any soul out of her. Men in the audience, however, stand up and cheer for her. Or for her outfit. I don't know which. Only one light goes out.

"Not bad," Dave Matthews says into his mike. "I'd like to see what else you've got."

"You have talent," Annie Lennox adds.

"I like your vibe," Joel Madden comments.

Jesse sips his coffee before speaking into the microphone. "I turned out the lights. I was bored."

The crowd gasps.

Ten singers later, it becomes apparent that Jesse is the "harsh" judge.

Jesse tells a rocker girl that "if you don't loosen up, your body's gonna freeze. Do some yoga or something."

I almost burst out laughing when he tells one guy that his voice reminds him of Sebastian from *The Little Mermaid*. "You're singing out of your nose, not your stomach."

He tells a boy who looks younger than I am, "Go out and live a little, 'cause there's no emotion in your voice."

I peer at the producers, and they're engrossed and nodding at each other. They love Jesse's drama.

Liam the jazz pianist plays next, and he is awesome. He has this strange Irish rocker, jazzy vibe. No lights turn off during his rendition of "The Way You Look Tonight."

I cheer as Jesse gives his first positive critique of the day: "Big-time."

During the break, I go to the bathroom. Two girls are bawling because they had their lights turned off. I give them tissues and tell them how much I liked their duet. They thank me as they wipe their noses. What will they do after this when they go home? Practice more? Go solo? Find a third member? Whatever they do, I hope they don't lose hope after this one audition.

The most amazing singer so far is a girl—she can't be older than eight or nine—who performs a slow version of "Since You've Been Gone." Everyone hollers and whoops for her, including the judges.

Jesse tells her, "If you made an album today, I'd buy it," and the girl starts crying right there on the stage. I'm happy for the little girl, and for Jesse, because I can tell how much he loved making her life change.

The stagehands are ushering contestants on and off the stage like it's a science, so by the lunch break, we're already up to number 148. All but thirty-two singers get cut! What is that? One in five odds?

I'm up after lunch.

Lunch?

"Oh my God." I scan the spread they've laid out for us in the Rainbow Room. The restaurant is at the very top of the building and has gorgeous views of the Empire State Building and Central Park. I wish Mom and Sam could see this, but lunch is contestants only. I take pictures of the city below until the buffet lines die down.

I grab a plate and head for the pasta station. Jesse's face appears over my shoulder. "That's too heavy. You shouldn't eat that before your performance."

"Well, what do you suggest? A Tofurky?"

Jesse starts laughing and leads me to a table covered in sushi, which is something I've never had before.

"What's in it?" I ask, as Jesse drops a sushi roll onto my plate.

"Raw eel."

"Ugh!" I wrinkle my nose. "I like you, Jess, but not enough to eat that."

"Oooh, try the calamari." Jesse scoops a little fried thing onto my plate. "It's squid."

"Ugh!"

Singers who haven't auditioned yet give me and Jesse dirty looks, but I don't care. After we've loaded up our plates, we sit at a table overlooking Central Park, and I tell him about the road trip as we dig into lunch. As much as Jesse loves sushi, apparently that love does not extend to chopsticks. He eats it with his fingers. The other judges didn't choose to eat with the contestants, so it's pretty cool that Jesse's here, and he doesn't get weird when other people stop by our table to chat. He and that cool Irish singer Liam even seem to hit it off.

"So how long are you in town?" Jesse asks me, wiping his mouth with a napkin.

"'Til I get kicked offstage," I reply nervously. "How long are you here for?"

"We're supposed to wrap up these auditions this week. Then I gotta head back out on tour. I'm in London next."

I cover his hand with mine. "I'll miss you."

A smile blooms on his face. "I'll miss you too. It was a nice surprise to see you here."

A few minutes later, a stagehand announces we need to return to the auditorium. Jesse escorts me back to meet up with Sam and Mom, who grabbed lunch at a pizza place nearby. Sam had been dying for a slice of real New York style since we left Tennessee.

Jesse takes Mom's elbow. "Can I have a moment?"

"Okaayy…" Mom narrows her eyes at me, then follows Jesse backstage. She reappears a few minutes later with a big smile on her face.

"What?" I ask.

"Nothing." She struggles not to laugh. What is going on? "C'mon, we've gotta get you up on the stage."

Only seven singers stand between me and the biggest moment of my life. I wipe my upper lip with the back of my shaking hand as we line up backstage. Of the seven singers, six are immediately bathed in darkness, and only one girl moves on to the next round.

Leaving the stage, she breezes past me and says, "Good luck!"

I breathe in and out, closing my eyes as the stagehand calls my number.

I crack my knuckles and walk onstage with my guitar around my neck. The lights are so bright, I can barely see beyond the stage. Cameras are everywhere. I plug my cord into the amp and check the settings on the distortion. *All set.*

I smile down at the judges, and Jesse grins back at me. I grab the mike with one hand and shout, "One, two, one, two, three, four," and dive into the opening riff of "Another One Bites the Dust."

Instead of using my lucky pick, I take my cue from Queen's guitarist Brian May and use an old penny to strum the strings. Under the bright lights, it feels like the heat from a million tiny suns. I remember to sing from my stomach, recalling everything Jesse and Holly taught me. What's crazy? Contestants in the audience clap and dance. I thought they hated me.

About ten seconds in, part of the stage goes dark, but I keep jamming like I normally would. Another set of lights goes out. My heart chugs along—it might stop.

Please don't let the middle lights go out. Please. I love performing on this stage. It's all I've ever wanted.

When the stagehand in the wings gestures that my time is up, my knees nearly buckle. The other contestants clap and scream. I take a bow. I'm going to the next round!

That is, if the producers let me.

Adrenaline pulses through me as I take off my guitar and wait to see if the judges will make any comments.

"Your performance was fun," Annie Lennox announces. "Great outfit."

I blow a kiss at her because I just can't help myself.

"I think you need more experience," Dave Matthews says. "Your voice isn't there yet, and I don't know if it'll ever be good enough to make it in the business."

Ouch. I nod at him and say thank you anyway.

Joel Madden says, "I agree with Dave, but I did enjoy your tone. And I love the purple boots."

Jesse leans into the mike. "Thanks. Don't I have great taste?" The other contestants groan and murmur. Him being a judge and me being a contestant really isn't fair, is it?

Jesse then turns serious. "Your performance wasn't bad, Maya, but you need to open your mouth more so the sound will be fuller. You also got way into the moment, sped up, and missed some beats."

I thank Jesse and smile at him, even though he basically

clobbered me over the head with a Fender. I unplug my guitar and exit the stage. The judges' critiques are whirling around in my mind like a tornado.

"They didn't turn all the lights off! I sorta sucked, but that was awesome!" I exclaim to anybody who'll listen. "I just played in Radio City! Woooo!"

Mom and Sam come rushing up to congratulate me, and Mom kisses my cheek. Smiling, I pull away to find Mr. Logan standing there with an older man dressed in khakis and a polo, as if he just left the green.

"Good job, Maya," Mr. Logan says, patting my back.

"That was so fun," I reply. "Even if it was my only chance to compete, right? I won't let Jesse get into any sort of trouble 'cause of me."

The smile disappears from Mr. Logan's face. "I'm hoping Charles here will be able to work something out."

I can tell he doesn't believe that. It's either me or Jesse.

And Jesse has a lot to lose. Potential lawsuits, money, his retirement, the "real" life he wants so badly.

Me?

I worked so hard to get here. I worked so hard to get past my fears.

Will I lose who I've become?

Am I about to lose my dreams?

Help!

My high suddenly starts to bleed away.

My adrenaline disappears.

I say, "Excuse me" to Mr. Logan and the lawyers and hightail it to the nearest bathroom. It has a fancy waiting room, so I sit on a sofa and cry and cry and cry until my entire body feels like a wrung-out sponge. I practiced for hours every night, I've killed myself working to make enough money to come here, and it's all over. The producers are sure to disqualify me. And even if they don't disqualify me, there's no way I'll make it through the next round. The judges were harsh.

I need more practice. I need more training. My voice isn't there yet.

But I'm up for that. Regardless of what happens here, I'm gonna work hard on my music until I croak. Performing on that stage proved that music is what I want to do for the rest of my life.

Mom comes in the bathroom and curls up with me.

"Where's Sam?" I ask, blowing my nose.

"Watching the other singers perform and trying not to cry."

"Sam doesn't cry."

"He does when his baby sister's heart is broken." She smiles slightly, her face covered in blotchy red spots. She's been crying too.

Now all there's left to do is wait to hear what the lawyers say. *Please let me stay. Please let me stay*, I chant in my head. Hours later, I hear a loud knock on the sitting room door. "Is Maya in there?" Jesse's sweet voice rings out.

"Yeah," I call. "Come in."

Mom gives me a hug, then stands up as Jesse walks into the women's bathroom. She pats his back as she files past him.

Jesse sits next to me on the couch. "We finished the rest of the auditions. A hundred and fifteen singers are moving on to tomorrow."

"Cool," I say quietly, dabbing my face with Kleenex. "I'm glad you decided to do this. You're helping lots of people."

He adjusts his cowboy hat. "I'm not being that nice to the contestants."

"But you're teaching them how to get better. That's huge." I elbow him. "Even if you weren't the nicest judge, everyone's gonna remember your advice. I know I will."

He squeezes my hand. "Today did feel pretty good, you know?"

Hearing that makes me smile. "So what's going on now?"

"Charles is busy annoying Mr. Tyson and the producers into letting you compete."

"I want to stay so bad, but I don't think that's going to work out."

"You doubt my lawyer's ability to be annoying? That makes you one of a kind." He nudges me, and I chuckle.

"What's the point? I mean, I'm not gonna make it past the next round."

"You deserve a chance just like everybody else in there, and if they don't give it to you, I'll quit. Trust me, they don't wanna piss me off."

I look over at him and smile slightly.

"I'm sure the lawyers will spend hours talking, so can I take you out tonight?"

"Really?" I'm going out with Jesse in New York! "My family too?"

"I've got something planned just for you."

I wipe my eyes one more time. "I need to talk to my mom."

"She already gave me permission," he says with a big, infectious grin.

He guides me out of the bathroom and back into the near-empty auditorium. Sam rushes up and hugs me, and then Mom does the same.

"Jesse has plans for you tonight," Mom whispers in my ear.

"What about you and Sam? Maybe we could all get dinner?"

My brother shakes his head. "You should go with Jesse."

Wow. Whatever Jesse has planned must be big if my brother is letting me out of his sight.

"I'll see you in a bit then," I tell them quietly, and Sam

gives Jesse an earful about how he better take good care of me. Or else.

I pull my warm coat on before we head outside. Jesse snuggles into a light brown suede coat, looking very much a farmer in his ripped jeans, beige hat, and red boots. He puts an elbow out for me, and I link my arm in his. He leads me to a stretch limo.

"Oh my God!" I blurt.

"Wanna drive it?"

"Uh, yeah, kinda."

"Well, maybe later."

A chauffeur opens the back door for us. Taking a deep breath, I climb into the limo and find Holly smiling at me. She's wearing her usual long, flowing, bohemian-style dress.

"Hi, Maya. I can't believe you're here," she says.

"That makes two of us," Jesse says, hip-checking me across the leather bench.

"Where're we going?" I ask as Mr. Logan climbs in the limo.

"It's a surprise," Jesse says.

"Getting me back for the birthday party we crashed?"

"You could say that."

The limo weaves through traffic while we explore the minibar, finding root beer and orange soda. Jesse, the health nut, cracks open a diet root beer.

"Sacrilege," I tell him.

Twenty minutes later, the limo rolls to a stop outside a tall building labeled New York University, Tisch School of the Arts.

I jerk my head to look at Jesse, who has a subtle, but nervous, smile on his face.

"Jess?"

He takes one last sip of root beer before opening the door and stepping out. "For me?"

I take his outstretched hand and don't let go as he leads me up to the building and through a set of glass doors. Holly and Mr. Logan follow, and even though my palm starts to sweat, Jesse doesn't drop my hand. I swallow hard as we go inside.

"You know why we're here?" Jesse asks.

"I've got a guess."

Holly leads us down a long hallway past a few students to a music room filled with instruments. A tall African American man looks up from playing his harp and goes to give Holly a long hug.

"Thanks for seeing me on such short notice," she says, patting his chest. "This is my dear friend Dr. Edgar Davidson—he's dean of Tisch." She introduces Jesse, Mr. Logan, and finally, me. "Maya's got a unique tone to her voice. I wanted you to meet her."

"Let's hear it," Dr. Davidson says in a deep baritone voice.

For some crazy reason, I feel a lot more nervous now than any other time I've performed, including earlier today. I mean, Dr.

Davidson is dean of the NYU music school. This audition could help me prepare for the Vanderbilt tryout. This performance could shape my whole future.

Jesse adjusts his cowboy hat and smiles at me as I sing the P!nk song I'll perform tomorrow for the next round of auditions. I try not to look at Dr. Davidson, because he makes me nervous, but I occasionally peek at him. He taps his chin with two fingers. He seems deep in thought. I finish and clasp my hands together behind my back.

"That was enjoyable," Dr. Davidson says. "Thank you."

"Thank you for letting me sing for you," I reply.

He shakes my hand. "Is this your senior year?"

"Yes, sir."

He smiles. "You should submit an application. We'll consider this your audition for the program."

Jesse throws an arm around me. "Big-time."

I look to Holly, not quite understanding what this means. Did he like my song? Or does he tell everyone to apply? She smiles encouragingly at me.

Mr. Logan claps his hands together once. "I have a business dinner to get to."

Dr. Davidson asks, "Can I take the rest of you to dinner?"

Holly says, "I'd be delighted, but let's not subject Jesse and Maya to our boring gossip."

So after thanking Dr. Davidson again and getting his business card, Mr. Logan takes us back outside to the limo. He pats Jesse's cheek. "I can count on you to behave tonight, right?"

"Of course." Jesse rolls his eyes. "I'm almost nineteen, Mark."

"Yet he still acts like he's twelve," Mr. Logan says to me, chuckling. "Keep an eye on him, Maya. Last time I let him loose in Manhattan, he tried to buy an antique organ from the Met."

Mr. Logan hails himself a cab, and then it's just me and Jesse. Together. In New York City. We slide inside the limo, and Jesse starts rooting around in the minibar again.

"Why'd you do this for me?" I whisper.

He turns away from the snacks to focus on my face. "I wanted to show you that even if *Wannabe Rocker* doesn't work out, you've got lots of options. I know you'd never ask me for help, but I want you to know that you can, okay? I'm here for you. We have to trust each other."

I swallow. "Thanks so much. I don't know about New York though. The people I love aren't here...my family, my friends. You."

A moment of silence passes between us. "We're here now. Ready for the official Jesse Scott New York City tour?"

"Let's go!"

We stand up on the backseat, poking our heads out the sunroof. A cold wind hits my face, but there's no way I'd sit down.

In a very meta moment, we pass a Jesse Scott billboard in which he's belting it out into a microphone. The limo edges by

Times Square, heading north all the way to Central Park, where we get out and walk.

"Where are we going?" I ask.

"One of my favorite places."

I hold my breath as we pass the Plaza Hotel, and then we approach FAO Schwarz, this humongous toy store that's decorated for Christmas. Twin nutcrackers flank the entrance, and animatronic penguins are singing "Let it Snow." It smells of potpourri and hot cider.

I link my arm in Jesse's. "Why's this one of your favorite places?"

"Mark brought me here when I was younger, and he bought me this remote-controlled helicopter, which I loved."

People on the sidewalk take pictures of Jesse, but it's nothing like Nashville where he gets mobbed every two feet. Here, people keep a wide berth as we enter the ginormous toy store.

This place is wild. I gaze up at a life-size replica of a grizzly bear. The toy store back in Franklin could fit in the FAO Schwarz lobby—I would've gone crazy in here as a kid. And being here helps me understand Jesse even better.

"I want that train," Jesse says, peering up at the one chugging around a track on the ceiling.

"I want that elephant." It must be two stories tall.

He looks at the price of the stuffed animal, grimacing. "It's seven thousand dollars. Mark would kill me."

"I was kidding," I say with a smile. "This guy is more my style." I pick up a little penguin. It's twenty dollars.

"That's more like it, Miss Greedy Pants."

"Greedy pants?" I smack his shoulder.

We stop every two feet to look at remote-controlled helicopters and LEGO displays. Jesse plays "Twinkle, Twinkle" on a xylophone, and then we end up in the boxer shorts section. I've never seen so many different kinds of underwear in my life—every superhero, every cartoon, from Barbie to Transformers to *Star Trek*.

"You gotta get these," I say, holding up a pair of Harley-Davidson boxers.

"Sure," he says and adds in a sneaky whisper, "I'll wear them for you later."

After the toy store, we buy pretzels from a cart and just wander around. It's freezing outside, but I don't feel cold—not with Jesse's hand tucked in mine. We gaze into bright, dazzling storefronts and talk about whatever, walking slowly as people pass us on the sidewalk. Before I came to New York, I figured I'd want to see the Statue of Liberty and Central Park, but now that I've seen Jesse's big, bright smile, I only want to explore this new place between him and me.

I may not be fixated on seeing the sights, but Jesse is. He says he's been to New York, like, a hundred times, but he's never been to the Empire State Building before and wants us to see the view together. His limo drives us downtown to Thirty-Fourth Street, then we take a series of different elevators to the top of the

Empire State Building and step out into the frigid night to views of the Brooklyn Bridge and Freedom Tower. The entire city.

For a long moment, I stare at the millions of twinkling lights.

"I love it here," I whisper.

"I do too. I feel like I can be myself here and not worry who's watching...but it's not my home, you know?"

"I get that."

I ask someone to take our picture, and Jesse wraps his arms around me from behind and kisses my neck. It's warm and personal and makes me tingly all over, and when I turn around to hug him, I feel nothing but comfort.

"Can you text me that picture?" he asks.

"Yeah, and I'll make sure you get a print for your mantel."

"I'd like that."

It excites me that he's willing to put our picture up in his living room, because he has no other pictures of family or friends. Jesse's changed so much since I first met him. But I wish he'd realize he can't give up his music just to please his family.

Tonight, I'm telling him what he needs to hear. But what if what I have to say makes him push me away again?

♪♫♩

"This is turning into another Maya Henry's Day Off," Jesse says when we get out of the limo at Wollman Rink in Central Park to go ice skating. I've never gone before.

"Nah. It's a Jesse Scott's Night Off."

"It would be if I could go buy that organ from the Met," Jesse grumbles.

We rent skates and stumble onto the ice. "Jingle Bells" plays over the speakers, and the air smells like cinnamon and Christmas. A lady sails across the ice, spinning and doing fancy jumps. Showoff. Does she think this is the Olympics or something? (Okay, okay, I'd totally do those jumps if I knew how.)

Jesse and I trip and fall around the rink, laughing our asses off, and he pulls me into his arms beneath a towering, sparkling Christmas tree. He tries to twirl me in a circle, but our feet slip every which way. We grab each other to stay upright and share a long kiss.

"This moment is worth coming to New York," I say. Worth every moment I spent working at Caldwell's, worth selling my Suzuki.

Then Jesse announces we're going to this place that makes "big-time bread pudding."

The bread pudding utopia turns out to be a southern-style diner called Mama's. Tons of pictures of mothers are crammed on the walls—and not only famous mamas like Queen Elizabeth, Kate Middleton, and Hillary Rodham Clinton, but regular ole people too.

Jesse hands me a cup of bread pudding while I study photo after photo. "I want to give them a picture of my mom," I say.

Jesse points at the wall with his spoon. "My mom would probably say all these *mamas* are sinners."

"I'm sorry about your parents, Jess. What they did to you on Thanksgiving was awful. What they've been doing to you for forever is awful."

He slowly spoons pudding into his mouth and nods.

I scoot to the other side of the table to sit beside him. "When are you gonna realize your uncle adores you? That Mr. Logan adores you? And Holly? And me?

"I'm sorry, Jess. I know the situation with your parents is complicated. But you can't quit the business because of them. You *love* music. And God gave you a gift. It's time you start owning it."

He drums his fingers on the table, eyes watering. With a sad look on his face, he spoons another bite into his mouth. He must be upset, because no one in their right mind could eat this bread pudding and frown at the same time.

"And if you want to quit to have a life, I think you've already got one. Tonight was great."

A small smile. "I am happy these days."

I decide to change the subject to lighten the mood. "I'm leaving you for Liam the sexy piano player."

"Well, then I'm becoming a roadie for the boarding school babe."

"Wait, what? Who are you talking about?"

"You know, the girl I turned the lights out on? The one with the French braids? I'll be in charge of her little plaid skirts."

"Have fun with that."

Jesse whispers in my ear, "Remember that little black

skirt and corset you wore the day you shadowed me? God, it drove me crazy." He feeds me some pudding and kisses my nose stud.

Then his phone rings. He massages my inner thigh as he speaks. "Hey, Mark… Eating bread pudding… No, I didn't try to buy the organ… I dunno, a bunch of underwear and bread pudding and a stuffed penguin." Jesse suddenly looks up at me, grinning. "This was the best day ever."

When he's off the phone with his manager, he says, "No word from Charles and the producers." He runs a fingertip up and down my arm, making me shiver with pleasure. "Do you want to go to my hotel and relax?"

♪♫♩

Jesse keeps me close as we cross the sidewalk to the Peninsula. I can see why he likes being in New York—people still stare and paparazzi still snap photos of him as bellmen whip open the doors to the hotel, but everybody keeps their distance for the most part.

A bellman gives a slight bow. "Welcome, Mr. Scott."

"Thanks."

In the lobby, I tug off my mittens as I gaze at the chandeliers, the grand staircase, and a twinkling Christmas tree. A man—presumably a manager—rushes out from behind the front desk, shiny black shoes clicking on the marble floor, and accompanies us to the elevator, shielding us from onlookers. The man gives Jesse a key card and shakes his hand. We ride the elevator to the very top floor, and then we're alone in front of a set of double wooden doors. His hotel room.

Jesse opens the door for me, and I hesitate. "My mom and brother are probably online looking at pictures of us entering the hotel right now."

"We don't have to stay here." He slips the key card in his wallet. "I can take you back to your mom."

I touch his arm. "No. I want to be here with you."

"I want to be with you too."

Jesse leads me into an extravagant room that's somehow cozy. There are plush couches and armchairs you can sink into and artwork on the walls, and don't even get me started on the floor-to-ceiling views of Fifth Avenue. I've never seen a grand piano in a hotel room before. This is a long way from the Motel 6 we stayed in on the drive from Tennessee. I turn in a circle, spotting a kitchen and a hallway leading to a bedroom.

"You don't do anything on a small scale, do you?" I ask.

"You know me. Go big or go home." A look of embarrassment crosses his face before he adds, "The TV show pays for the suite."

"Seriously, why does one person need all this space?"

He wraps his arms around my waist. "You mean two people, right?" He gives me a kiss on the cheek that turns my knees wobbly. "Be right back. I'm gonna make sure my guitars and luggage arrived okay," he says and disappears down the hall.

I sink onto a couch and kick off my boots and kneesocks,

digging my toes into the plush rug. That's when it hits me. I'm with my boyfriend in a hotel room without my parents or annoying brother around. We can do whatever we want…we can go further than we did last time when we were making out in my bedroom. I take a deep breath, remembering how warm and solid his body felt against mine. Remembering how jittery and shaky I felt, as if I just stepped off a roller coaster. But I'm not nervous anymore, because I know exactly what I am to him. We both feel the same about each other.

"I need to use the bathroom," I call.

I shut the door behind me, turn on the cold water, and splash my face, then squirt some toothpaste onto my finger and run it over my teeth. Even though I don't know what will happen with *Wannabe Rocker*, today has been the best day of my life. And now I'm alone with Jesse. Now, when I know for sure I want him and he wants me. I stare at myself in the mirror, feeling confident and happy and calm. I like him enough to risk everything, and I don't want to stop falling.

I find Jesse sitting at the grand piano, playing his new song. He doesn't look up when I walk over, lean across the piano, and rest my chin on folded hands.

"C'mere," he says, beckoning me with two fingers. I slide in next to him on the bench and he nudges me. "Let's play 'Heart and Soul.'"

"I have to learn another song, Jess. This one is getting boring."

"Here's something new." His fingers begin tapping out a melody. A ballad. "I'm a swatch of quillllllllt and I want to be sewn into your hearrrrrt."

I elbow him hard in the gut, and with a laugh, he retaliates by giving me a sloppy kiss on the mouth. A kiss that starts out silly becomes focused and intense, and he pushes my hair behind my ears, and his fingertips caress my cheeks as our mouths explore. He breaks away and cradles my neck. "Do you want to go in the other room?"

My face burns in anticipation. "Yeah, definitely."

He holds out a hand to help me up, and we kiss all the way to the bed as the bright lights of New York pour in through the windows. I crawl onto the plush white comforter, but Jesse doesn't give me a chance to get comfortable before beginning to kiss me again. We're both sitting on our knees when he tugs my dress over my head, runs his hands across my black lace bra, and unsnaps it. He mouths my neck and jaw, and I shiver as I unbutton his wrinkled white button-down, running my palms over the warm velvety skin on his lower back, kissing the freckles on his shoulders.

I fall back onto a pillow to admire the view. I love his flat torso, strong chest, and yummy biceps, especially when he settles on top of me. I unbutton his jeans, then bury my hands in his hair, getting a whiff of his citrusy shampoo. His lips trail over my skin, from my collarbone to the sensitive inside of my elbow, to my belly button. I suck in a deep breath when his fingers slip beneath my waistband. I hear the rustle of my underwear landing on the rug.

Goose bumps rise on my skin. I'm excited. Curious, but scared. Nervous that my body won't feel anything, like when I was with Nate.

Jesse kisses my stomach, and I do want to feel his body against mine, but there's also an urge to cover myself, especially when his lips move lower.

"Jess, wait—"

He glances up at me. "Have you done this before?"

I shut my eyes and shake my head. Nate never offered, even though I did it for him. I'm not sure I would've said yes to Nate, because it's such a personal thing, but Jesse is different, and that makes me want to consider it, even if it feels like sharing my deepest darkest secret and asking him to accept it no matter what. Biting my lip, I clutch the duvet, pressing my knees together.

"It's okay," he says, running his warm hands over my thighs. "Just tell me if anything makes you uncomfortable, and we'll switch things up."

Chills and a rushing white heat go to war inside my body as I let go of my fears, trusting that he won't let me fall. When I relax onto the soft pillow and dig my heels into the blankets, I turn into a whole new girl—a woman.

He looks up into my eyes. "By the way, this is what normal guys want in bed."

And the hands that play the most beautiful melodies on guitar gently grip my hips, and I bury my fingers in his hair, and without a word, we make a new song together.

♪♫♩

We lie tangled in the sheets, my head on Jesse's chest, which rises up and down under his heavy breathing. I trace the underside of his elbow and twine my feet with his. The lights of New York fill the dark room with a silvery glow, making this moment feel magical.

"What does the tattoo on your back mean?" I ask.

"It's the Celtic symbol for music."

Music really is his life and soul. "That's perfect."

"You need a tattoo."

"Of what? The Celtic symbol for the Jesse Scott Fan Club?"

He laughs and murmurs into my hair, "You're okay with us being together, right? I kind of made that call today without asking you."

I smile into his chest. I've never said I love you to a guy before, and when I do, I'll be giving him all of me, trusting him to take care of my heart. And I want to try for that with Jesse.

"Definitely," I say. "I can't believe Jesse Scott is my boyfriend. You're so not my type."

"Are you *sure* you don't wanna have sex with me?" He laughs so hard at his own joke he snorts, and I pinch his arm.

"I'll think about it when you get home from tour."

His head lolls back on the pillow. "Great. I was already desperate to get back to Tennessee to you, but now it's gonna feel like my tour will never end."

"You'll survive."

"Maybe we can practice beforehand, you know, on the phone?"

"Oh my God, I will not have phone sex with you!" I say, tickling him, and speaking of phones, his rings.

He grabs it from the nightstand and answers. "Yeah… yeah…okay."

He hangs up and stares at me for a long moment. "They've made some sort of decision. Mark wants us back at Radio City."

♪♫♩

After we locate our clothes and underwear that we flung all over his hotel room, freshen up, and get dressed, Jesse leads me downstairs and outside to his limo. It's nearly eleven o'clock.

"Can we pick up my mom and brother on the way?" I ask, and Jesse makes arrangements with the driver. It turns out Mom and Sam aren't far. Only about five blocks.

We spot them standing on a sidewalk in front of a small coffeehouse, bundled up in their coats and scarves. Jesse has the limo pull over. Mom smiles broadly when she slides across a leather seat and starts pushing buttons just like I did, which makes Jesse laugh.

"I've never been in a limo before!" she says.

"Hi, Sam," Jesse says, and my brother gives him a long, scary look that says *I know what you've been doing with my sister.*

Jesse's Adam's apple shifts as he swallows hard. I hope my brother learns to like my boyfriend, because he's not going anywhere. I grin to myself and my face heats up as I replay our hookup in my mind. Jesse loved how I touched and kissed him *everywhere.*

Mom sits next to me on the bench and takes my hand. "Do you know what the decision is?"

"Not yet," I reply. Jesse squeezes my other hand. "What have you been doing tonight? Did you guys go to dinner or anything?"

With a wide smile, Mom looks over at Sam, who has a sheepish grin on his face. "We were wandering around and ended up in the diamond district, and all these store owners kept asking us to come inside and browse...so we did."

My heart starts thumping wildly. "Did you, um, buy anything?"

Sam shakes his head, continuing to smile. "Not yet. Got some good ideas though. I'll go back tomorrow."

I squeal, excited this is finally happening. My brother and Jordan have been best friends since they played football together in elementary school. Everyone always knew they would end up together—it just took about forever for it to happen, and then they had to date for, like, a million years.

"Do you know how you're going to ask Jordan?" I ask.

"I was thinking about jumping out of a giant cake," Sam replies dryly, and Mom and I scowl at him.

Back at Radio City, before I walk into the Roxy Suite, Mr. Logan pulls me aside. "I'm so, so sorry about all this."

Oh no. That's it. It's all over. I sniffle hard to keep my tears at bay. "I'm sorry too."

Mr. Logan pats my shoulder. Then I go sit on a sofa between Jesse and my mother. Neither can sit still.

Mr. Tyson straightens his tie. "I apologize for keeping you waiting all day, but I believe Charles and our producers have come up with some solutions to our problem."

"You got me out of the contract?" Jesse asks.

Mr. Logan pats his shoulder. "You know we can't do that, son."

"And I won't let you," I whisper in his ear. "You said you felt like something was missing from your life, and I'm not letting you give up something that makes you feel good about yourself. I know you like helping other musicians."

Jesse's mouth edges into a small smile. He demands, "What about Maya?"

His lawyer turns to me. "Maya, how would you feel about participating in next year's contest? Mr. Tyson has assured me you could bypass all auditions up through round two of the semifinals."

Next year? That's forever away, and I am ready to perform *now*. Tears flood my eyes, and I start sniffling. I can't help it. At my reaction, Sam leans over and puts his head between his knees, and my mother covers her eyes. Jesse pulls a handkerchief out of his jeans pocket and passes it to me. I dry my eyes and listen as my boyfriend goes to town.

"That's not good enough," Jesse growls. "What else?"

"NBC will reimburse Maya's travel costs this year and next."

"And?"

"Footage of Maya during this year's first three episodes. Even if she doesn't compete this season, everyone in America will know who she is."

"What *else*?" The edge to his voice sharpens.

"I'm prepared to show a three-second clip of her during the opening credits of the show," Mr. Tyson says with a warm smile.

That would be huge!

"But a whole year?" my mother asks.

"It would be good for her," Mr. Logan says, pointing at me with his little black notebook. "She could work on getting some solo gigs back in Nashville. Get more experience that'll give her a leg up for next year."

"That's true," Jesse says to me. "After you take more lessons, you'll do a lot better in auditions. I'll help you get the training you need."

Sam lifts his head from between his knees. He nods once at Jesse with respect, looking grateful. I feel the same way. After today's auditions, I know I need more practice, but I also know I can become so much more.

I tell everyone I need a moment to talk with Mom and Sam. I lead them out into the grand foyer, where I look around, not quite believing how much confidence I've built in myself. How far I've come. Wondering how much further I can go. There are always second chances.

We huddle like we're on a football field. "I'll come back next year, but only if you come with me," I say.

"I'm in," Sam says.

Mom squeezes my hand. "Me too."

A rush of happiness and love fills me. My family is the best. I lead them back to the Roxy Suite.

"I've got an answer for you." I smile at Jesse. "I'll compete in next year's competition. That is, if I don't have something bigger going on already."

I might've missed a beat, but my performance isn't over.

Bonus Track

Take Me Home, Country Roads

Saturday, February 13—Annual Hundred Oaks Talent Show

I take a deep bow and wave at the audience. Scanning the crowd, I spot Mom, Dad, Sam, Jordan, and Anna. I blow a kiss at them. My family claps and screams my name. Dr. Salter and Mr. Logan are sitting in the front row, keeping an eye on the reporters. Jesse's seat is empty.

The reporters he invited are squatting down in front of the seats, holding cameras and waiting to take pictures of the main attraction, which is definitely not my performance of Guns N' Roses' "November Rain." I do think it was pretty awesome though, and the press took lots of pictures of me. I love getting exposure for my music, and not only as "Jesse Scott's girlfriend."

The first episode of *Wannabe Rocker* aired last week, and while I've received a billion tweets from viewers about how romantic it was when Jesse leaped off the stage and kissed me, I've also received lots of compliments on my audition.

With a final wave at the crowd, I jog offstage. Hannah rushes up to me. "You were great!"

"Thanks! You were too." She performed a Mozart sonata on piano tonight. I love that she took a chance at going solo and played what she wants to play. She's still a part of The Fringe, but I don't think they're getting as many gigs these days. They all seem to be trying their own thing now.

As I'm blotting the sweat off my forehead, I feel fingers poke me in my sides. I whip around. Jesse's standing there in his beige cowboy hat, his cowboy boots with the flames, and torn jeans. He runs his hands over my hips and touches me through the back of my black leather skirt. He always has a hard time keeping his hands off me. I love it. I grip his black T-shirt, lift up on tiptoes, and give him a long, slow kiss.

"You did great," he murmurs in my ear. "Your voice was full, your pitch was perfect, and I could feel the emotion. I wish your skirt had been a little shorter though."

I slap his chest. "You ready for this?"

"I think so." He rubs his palms together. A few of my classmates ask for his autograph. "Sure," he replies. "Right after I do my thing."

"Good luck," I tell him, and he squeezes my hand. He walks onstage, and the audience goes insane when they see him.

"Thanks for coming out tonight," Jesse tells the crowd, pulling a sheet of paper from his jeans pocket. The cheering quiets to where he can speak. "The reason I'm here is 'cause I want to talk to you about music."

Everyone is focused on him.

"My name is Jesse Scott, and I'm sure many of you know that music is my life. For a long time, my music was all mine. I let other people listen to my music, but I never let anyone share it with me. Then I decided to quit.

"But then somebody told me that I have a gift, and I should use that gift to make other people happy… So if Rêve Records will still have me, I've decided I'm gonna take it one day at a time. For now, I'm not going to retire."

The crowd whoops for him, and the press take pictures. *Click, click, click.*

Jesse gazes offstage, finding my eyes. Then he looks down toward his uncle and Mr. Logan. "God's been so good to me. He's given me great friends. A good friend of mine—Maya Henry—told me how she couldn't afford music lessons growing up, and it got me thinking. I want to help as many kids as I can learn music." Jesse pauses to clear his throat. "Maya and I came up with an idea together. I'm starting a music program in Nashville called the Agape Center. It's a place where kids can make appointments for voice, piano, guitar, and drumming lessons. All lessons will be free." The crowd cheers again.

Jesse continues, "I'm gonna work on expanding my program over time, but it'll always be free of cost. We'll be advertising for it soon, so keep a look out. Thanks."

Music begins playing over the loudspeakers. I figured he

would perform "Second Chance," because it seems most appropriate, but of course he had to do "Ain't No City Boy," because I applied to Vanderbilt's music school in Nashville for next year, and Jesse's staying here with me, and "Ain't No City Boy" is about making love on a tractor, after all. Not that I've agreed to do it on a tractor.

At the end of his song, he waves and walks offstage to massive applause. After the curtains shut, he picks me up and twirls me in a circle. "I love you," he murmurs.

"I love you too."

He lowers me to the floor. "Okay, who wants an autograph? I gotta leave soon to get ready for my pool party."

"Who throws a pool party in February?" I ask.

He points at me. "Don't forget, clothing is optional."

♪♫♩

My family takes me to dinner at the Roadhouse to celebrate my talent show performance, but we don't spend a whole lot of time talking about me, because Sam keeps going on and on and on about wedding plans. Mom loves hearing about them, but he discusses the wedding so often the rest of us want to put on earmuffs. Even Jordan wants him to shut up, and she's the one with a glittering diamond on her left hand.

"Carter said his restaurant would cater the dinner for us," Sam says. "And I've already got the cake picked out—Jordan said I could be in charge of the cake. It will have three layers:

one raspberry, one coffee, and one vanilla. And it will have the Detroit Lions logo on it."

Jordan hurls a french fry at his head.

"Do you think Jesse would sing at our wedding?" Jordan asks. "He's so sexy."

Sam throws a peanut at her. "Can we stop talking about how sexy Jesse is already?"

"Seconded," Dad replies.

After dinner, it's time for Jesse's party. It starts right as the clock strikes midnight, just in time for his birthday. Fancy cars and limos are already parked in Jesse's circular drive when Dave, Xander, and I arrive.

I ring the doorbell, and a few moments later, even though it's about forty-five degrees outside, Jesse answers the door wearing only a towel and his beige cowboy hat. He has a mixed drink in one hand and his phone in the other; he's talking to someone. Casper darts out the front door. I barely catch her before she disappears into the night.

"Thanks for calling… Bye." He hangs up.

"Who was that?" I ask.

"My mom. She and my dad can't make it tonight. They have to get up early tomorrow."

"How boring."

"Damn straight," Jesse says with a smile and gives me a kiss, then slurps the pink drink through a straw. "Y'all are just in time for the piñata."

"Oh good God," I say, following him through the house. I peek in the living room to see how he's doing on his decorating. He's up to a whopping five framed pictures now: a print of him, Mark, and Holly backstage at the Grammys; a picture of Dr. Salter and Jesse at a concert; the picture of him and me on top of the Empire State Building; a photo of him challenging Dave to a game of pickup basketball (I took that picture); and my favorite—a photo that a fan sent of me and him singing together on the Belle Carol.

We step onto the patio, where I set Casper down so she can chase bugs. The cat dashes past the executives Jesse invited from Rêve Records, Mr. Logan, and Charles, his lawyer. Holly and her husband are huddled on a lounge chair, shivering next to a large heater.

Dave and Xander strip down to their bathing suits and jump in the guitar-shaped pool, yelling about how cold it is outside.

"You actually got a piñata," I say, staring up at the giant heart hanging from the deck's awning. His birthday is on Valentine's Day, so he's got this whole pink-and-red tropical motif going. I like the white, pink, and red lights he strung in the trees, but the ugly inflatable pink palm trees look like they came from an alien planet.

"I am in charge of decorations for all future parties," I say. "This is heinous."

"Not heinous, *hilarious*. Just wait until you see what's inside the piñata," Jesse replies. "Can I get you a drink?"

I nod at a glass bobbing by on a waiter's tray. "I'll take one of those pink things, thanks."

Jesse leads me to this tiki bar he rented and asks the bartender for a strawberry piña colada daiquiri.

"*Fancy*," I say. "No alcohol though, right? I wouldn't want you falling in the pool."

"Smart-ass." He looks at the bag dangling from my wrist. "Did you get me a present?"

"Happy Birthday." I pass him the gift bag. It's nothing compared to the gift he gave me for my birthday in January: he rented a silver Lamborghini for a night, and I drove it all over Nashville and Franklin. The best part was when I pulled up at Sonic in front of kids from school, then proceeded to order a cherry limeade.

Jesse sets his drink on a table, opens the bag, and holds up the CD I burned. "Aw, did you make me a mix tape?" He reads the playlist on the back. "Queen, James Taylor, Queen, James Taylor, Queen, Jesse Scott? You put one of my songs on a mix tape for *me*?" He laughs. "You're ridiculous."

"Do you love it?" I flirt.

"I do."

I stand on tiptoes to whisper in his ear, "I'll give you the rest of your present later."

His eyebrows shoot straight up to the sky.

"Wanna go swimming?" I ask.

"Sure." He starts to drop his towel.

"You've got something on under there, right?"

"You know me. Go big or go home." He yanks off the towel. He's wearing red swimming trunks.

"You ass."

We take our drinks in the heated pool. Steam rises off the water, wafting into the starry night. Jesse and Dave play a game of basketball in the shallow end while Xander and I sit on the steps and make fun of them for being so bad at sports.

Then Dr. Salter arrives, and Mr. Logan wanders over. My principal says to Jesse, "I'm glad to see everyone disregarded the skinny-dipping instructions on your invitation."

"And why did you send said invitation to the president of Rêve?" Mr. Logan asks. At least he's smiling.

"It said skinny-dipping was optional, not required," Jesse replies.

The party is a blast. Jesse cranks up the stereo system, and nearly everyone, well, everyone except for his uncle and lawyer—*thank God!*—changes into bathing suits and gets into the pool.

Jesse's song "Waiting for Christmas"—the one I just recorded with him—starts playing slow and strong over the speakers. It still surprises me every time I hear it. It sounds so professional and clear. I'm not sure if it'll ever be on the radio, but Jesse wants to use it as part of the advertising campaign for his Agape Center. And I'm excited at the possibility of that. Still, it's weird hearing myself sing a solo.

Everyone at the party cheers for us. It kind of embarrasses me though. I dunk my head underwater and swim toward the deep end. When I come up for air, I shake the water out of my hair.

"Hey, Maya!" Jesse shouts over the music. "Marco!"

He stands up on the steps in the shallow end, giving me that half-cocked smile I love so much, and dives into the water and swims to the deep end. He comes up for a breath, slinging water all over me.

"Polo!"

And under the bright, twinkling stars, I wrap my arms around his neck and we kiss, perfectly in tune.

Jesse's Girl Playlist

Any Man of Mine – Shania Twain

Take My Breath Away – Berlin

I Think We're Alone Now – Tiffany

It's My Life – Bon Jovi

Girls Just Want to Have Fun – Cyndi Lauper

I Wanna Dance with Somebody – Whitney Houston

Total Eclipse of the Heart – Bonnie Tyler

To Make You Feel My Love – Garth Brooks

Don't Dream It's Over – Crowded House

Come Undone – Duran Duran

Carrying Your Love with Me – George Strait

She's Got It All – Kenny Chesney

Express Yourself – Madonna

Acknowledgments

For my high school's career day, my teacher asked me to write down what I wanted to be when I grew up. I loved singing, so I wrote down that I wanted to be a country music singer. Like Maya, I was in my school's show choir, and I loved singing in the church choir on Sundays, but I wasn't all that good.

Somehow, my high school got me a ticket to a Grammy symposium in Nashville, and I spent the day listening to some famous singers—most notably the Dixie Chicks—talk about their careers. It was awesome! And while I didn't end up becoming a country music singer, my experience that day gave me the idea for this book. I'm still surprised that my school got me a ticket to that Grammy event. It always makes me think about how, if you want something, you have to go after it. You have to tell people your goals and tell them what you need. You'll never know what you can accomplish unless you put yourself out there. Whatever your dreams might be, I hope you go after them.

I started writing this book five years ago, and while it was definitely the hardest book I've ever worked on, it's also my favorite. I'm thrilled I stuck with it, and I hope you, my fans, enjoy it as much as I loved writing it.

Many people helped me shape this novel. A humongous thanks to Tiffany Reisz, for being Jesse's biggest fan and for coming up with the name of the book! Tiffany Smith, an awesome librarian/diplomat/pianist, helped me to refocus this novel. Thank you to Chris Crellin for helping me get my guitar facts straight. To my first readers, I couldn't have finished this book without your helpful feedback: Rebecca Sutton, Julie Romeis Sanders, Robin Talley, Sarah Cloots, Tiffany Schmidt, Trish Doller, Alyssa Palmer, Natalie Bahm, Sarah Skilton, Andrea Soule, Ellice Yager, and Michelle Kampmeier. As always, thank you to my agent, Sara Megibow; my editor, Annette Pollert-Morgan; and the entire team at Sourcebooks. And most of all, thanks to my husband Don for reading this book eight hundred times in all its various iterations. You are the best.

To my fans, I love your emails, your tweets, and your letters. Over the years, many of you have asked to hear more of Jordan and Sam's story. I hope you enjoyed seeing them in this book. Thanks to all of you. You rock!

There's no playbook for love.

Don't miss

Catching Jordan

a hail mary and a harem

the count? 21 days until my trip to alabama

I once read that football was invented so people wouldn't notice summer ending. But I couldn't wait for summer vacation to end. I couldn't wait for football. Football, dominator of fall—football, love of my life.

"Blue forty-two! Blue forty-two! Red seventeen!" I yell.

The cue is red seventeen. JJ hikes me the ball. The defense is blitzing. JJ slams into a freshman safety, knocking him to the ground. The rest of my offensive line destroys the defense. Nice. The field's wide open, but my wide receiver isn't where he's supposed to be.

"What the hell, Higgins?" I mutter to myself.

Dancing on my tiptoes, I scan the end zone and find Sam Henry instead and hurl the ball. It flies through the air, a perfect spiral, heading right where I wanted it to go. He catches the ball, spikes it, and does this really stupid dance. Henry looks like a freaking ballerina. With his thin frame and girly blond hair, he actually could be the star of the New York Ballet.

I'm gonna give him hell for his dance.

This is my senior year at Hundred Oaks High, and I'm captain, so I'm allowed to keep my players in line. Even though he's my best friend, Henry has always been a showoff. His antics get us penalties.

Through the speaker in my helmet, I hear Coach Miller say, "Nice throw. This is your year, Woods. You're going to lead us to the state championship. I can feel it…Hit the showers." What the coach actually means? *I know you're not going to blow it in the final seconds of the championship game like you did last year.*

And he's right. I can't.

The University of Alabama called last week—on the first day of school—to tell me a recruiter is coming to watch me play on Friday night. And then a very fancy-looking letter arrived, inviting me to visit campus in September. An official visit. If they like what they see, they'll sign me in February.

I can't screw this season up.

I pull my helmet off and grab a bottle of Gatorade and my playbook. Most of the guys are already goofing off and heading over to watch cheerleading practice across the field, but I ignore them and look up into the stands.

I spot Mom sitting with Carter's dad, a former NFL player. My dad isn't here, of course. Asshole.

Lots of parents come to watch our practices because football is the big thing to do around here. Here being Franklin,

Tennessee, home of the Hundred Oaks Red Raiders, eight-time state champions.

Mom always comes to practice—she's been supporting me ever since Pop Warner youth football days, but sometimes she worries I'll get hurt, even though the worst thing that's ever happened was a concussion. Sophomore year, when JJ took a breather, the coach brought in this idiot to play center, the idiot didn't cover me, and I got slammed hard.

Otherwise, I'm a rock. No knee problems, no broken limbs.

Dad never comes to my practices and rarely comes to games. People think it's because he's busy, because he's Donovan Woods, the starting quarterback for the Tennessee Titans. But the truth is he doesn't want me playing football. Why wouldn't a famous quarterback want his kid to follow in the family footsteps? Well, he does. He loves that my brother, Mike, a junior in college, plays for the University of Tennessee and led his team to a win at the Sugar Bowl last year. So what the hell is Dad's problem with my playing ball?

I'm a girl.

About the Author

Miranda Kenneally grew up in Manchester, Tennessee, a quaint little town where nothing cool ever happened until she left. Now Manchester is the home of Bonnaroo. Growing up, Miranda wanted to become an author, a major league baseball player, a country music singer, or an interpreter for the United Nations. Instead, she became an author who also works for the U.S. Department of State in Washington, DC, planning major events and doing special projects, and once acted as George W. Bush's armrest during a meeting. She enjoys reading and writing young adult literature and loves *Star Trek*, music, sports, Mexican food, Twitter, coffee, and her husband. Visit www.mirandakenneally.com.